A

Douglas Coupland

Generation A

Random House Canada

www.randomhouse.ca

Random House Canada and colophon are trademarks.

Library and Archives Canada Cataloguing in Publication

Coupland, Douglas
    Generation A / Douglas Coupland.

ISBN 978-0-307-35772-4

    I. Title.
PS8555.O8253G37 2009   C813'.54   C2009-901650-8

Design by CS Richardson

Printed in the United States of America

10 9 8 7 6 5 4 3 2 1

To Anne Collins

"Terrorize, threaten and insult your own useless generation. Suddenly you've become a novel idea and you've got people wanting to join in. You've gained credibility from nothing. You're the talk of the town. Develop this as a story you can sell." ,

Malcolm McLaren

"Now you young twerps want a new name for your generation? Probably not, you just want jobs, right? Well, the media do us all such tremendous favors when they call you Generation X, right? Two clicks from the very end of the alphabet. I hereby declare you Generation A, as much at the beginning of a series of astonishing triumphs and failures as Adam and Eve were so long ago."

Kurt Vonnegut
Syracuse University commencement address
May 8, 1994

HARJ

TRINCOMALEE, SRI LANKA

How can we be alive and not wonder about the stories we use to knit together this place we call the world? Without stories, our universe is merely rocks and clouds and lava and blackness. It's a village scraped raw by warm waters leaving not a trace of what existed before.

Imagine a tropical sky, ten miles high and a thousand years off on the horizon. Imagine air that feels like honey on your forehead; imagine air that comes out of your lungs cooler than when it entered.

Imagine hearing a dry hiss outside your office building's window. Imagine walking to the window's louvred shutters and looking out and seeing the entire contents of the world you know flow past you in a surprisingly soothing, quiet sluice of grey mud: palm fronds, donkeys, the local Fanta bottler's Jeep, unlocked bicycles, dead dogs, beer crates, shrimper's skiffs, barbed wire fences, garbage, ginger flowers, oil sheds, Mercedes tour buses, chicken delivery vans.

... corpses
... plywood sheets
... dolphins
... a moped
... a tennis net
... laundry baskets
... a baby
... baseball caps
... more dead dogs
... corrugated zinc

Imagine a space alien is standing with you there in the room as you read these words. What do you say to him? Her? It? *What was once alive is now dead.* Would aliens even know the difference between life and death? Perhaps aliens experience something else just as unexpected as life. And what would that be? What would they say to themselves to plaster over the unexplainable cracks of everyday existence, let alone a tsunami? What myths or lies do they hold true? How do they tell stories?

Now look back out your window—look at what the gods have barfed out of your subconscious and into the world—the warm, muddy river of dead cats, old women cauled in moist saris, aluminum propane canisters, a dead goat, flies that buzz unharmed just above the fray. .

. . . picnic coolers

. . . clumps of grass

. . . a sunburnt Scandinavian pederast

. . . white plastic stacking chairs

. . . drowned soldiers tangled in gun straps

And then what do you do—do you pray? What is prayer but a wish for the events in your life to string together to form a story—something that makes some sense of events you know have meaning.

And so I pray.

ZACK

Cornfields are the scariest things on the entire fucking face of the planet. I don't mean that in a Joe-Pesci-being-clubbed-to-death-with-an-aluminum-baseball-bat kind of way, and I don't mean it in an alien-crop-circles kind of way, and I don't mean it in a butchering-hitchhikers kind of way. I don't even mean it in an alien-autopsy-remains-used-as-fertilizer kind of way. I mean it in a Big-Corn-Archer Daniels Midland/Cargill/Monsanto-genetically-modified-high-fructose-ethanol kind of way. Corn is a fucking nightmare. A thousand years ago it was a stem of grass with one scuzzy little kernel; now it's a bloated, foot-long, buttery carb dildo. And get this: cornstarch molecules are a mile long. Back in the seventies, Big Corn patented some new enzyme that chops those miles into a trillion discrete blips of fructose. A few years later these newly liberated fructose molecules assault the national food chain. *Blammo!* An entire nation becomes morbidly obese. Fact is, the human body isn't built to withstand high-dose assaults of fructose. It enters your body and your body says, *Hmmm . . . do I turn this into shit or do I turn it into blubber? Blubber it is!* Corn turns off the shit switch. The corn industry's response to this? *Who—us? Contributing to the obesity epidemic? No way, man. People simply started to snack more in the eighties. Now be quiet and keep drinking all that New Formula Coke.*

Man, humans are a nightmare fucking species. We deserve everything we do to ourselves.

But *who* the fuck gets stung by a bee in a combine tractor in the middle of a cornfield in Mahaska County, Iowa? Me, fucking *me*.

By the way, welcome to Oskaloosa and all the many features that make Oskaloosa a terrific place to visit. There's something for everyone here, from the historic city square with its bandstand to the George Daily Auditorium, the award-winning Oskaloosa Public Library, William Penn University and three golf courses.

I stole most of that last paragraph from the Internet. What the town's home page forgot to mention was my father's meth distillery ("lab" makes it sound so Cletus-&-Brandeen), which got busted by the DEA a few years back. Dad and the DEA never got along too well.

Six years ago Dad got wasted and in a moment of paranoia stole the Oskaloosa Library's bookmobile, abandoning its carcass in the 14th hole sand trap of the legendary Edmundson Park and Golf Course. Then, in the delusion that he was destroying DEA monitoring equipment, he torched it, in the process losing his eyebrows, his driver's licence, his freedom and his visitation rights to my two half-sisters, who live in Winnebago County.

Once out of the clink, he went right back to business and when his meth distillery was raided, the back of his head was toasted by a canister of boiling toluene. He spent six weeks in the correctional facility's hospital unit until he got into reasonable enough shape to walk around. My uncle Jay, a lawyer and Freon broker from Palo Alto, was able to post bail and had Dad flown out to California for OCD counselling. Dad picked up drug-resistant staph from a set of improperly cleaned in-flight headsets that infected his burn scar; by the time they touched down at SFO, maybe a quarter of his head was eaten up. So then we buried Dad, and Uncle Jay sold half the farm and bought me the world's most kickass corn harvesting combine, Maizie.

Since then, Uncle Jay has sent me a reasonable paycheque

in return for me not making meth (and following Daddy's path), as well as for me doing a slightly more than half-ass job tending the corn (our family legacy), and for me to piss into an Erlenmeyer flask in front of Iowa's creepiest Romanian lab technician (just in case I forgot the former two conditions). The urine was tested on the spot to see if I'd shaken hands with someone who ate a poppyseed bagel since the previous Tuesday; it's not fun being treated like a disgraced Olympian athlete, but Uncle Jay made cleanliness a condition of keeping Maizie. I mean, everyone I know—hell, the whole country—is baked on drugs, clueless as dirt and morbidly obese. Normally I'd have been the perfect candidate for all three, except, 1) I can't do drugs if I want my cheque, 2) I'm not entirely stupid and am at least curious about the world and 3) I believe corn is the devil. Try finding rice and soy grocery products in Mahaska County. Good luck. They might as well add that fact to Oskaloosa's online civic profile: *Oskaloosa's grocers sell a wide array of products into which manufacturers have invisibly inserted a vast family of corn-derived molecules. Should your child decide to go vegetarian or adapt any other questionable dietary lifestyle choice, our grocers and mini-marts will thwart their teen desires at every corner.*

Okay, here's the thing I didn't mention about the raid: the DEA also found a fake-vintage saltine cracker tin containing two dead men's index fingers. Dad had been using them to loan authenticity to a long-running cheque fraud scheme, but there was a third finger the DEA didn't find, which I traded soon after to a DEA server maintenance girl named Carly who was running some scam of her own. In return for the finger, she gave me a killer blowjob and access to the DEA's real-time geosynchronous surveillance satellite cameras. I could have made something long-term with Carly, except she demanded that I cut off my ponytail and donate it to Locks of Love.

Farewell, Carly. Why did I want access to a real-time satellite camera? For my art, of course. Details to come shortly.

So the day I got stung by that goddam bee I was out in Maizie, a harvester so luxurious it could shame a gay cruise liner. I was naked, and why not! The ergonomically sensible operator's cab was fully pressurized and air-conditioned; unibody cab frame, rubber mounts and sound-absorbing material reduced noise levels to near zero. All-round visibility allowed me ample time to throw on some shorts if I saw a visitor arriving on the farm.

I was also listening to some trendy band from Luxembourg or the Vatican or Lichtenstein or the Falkland Islands, one of those places so small that a distinct pie slice of its GDP derives from the sale of postage stamps to collectors and music sales by nanotrendy indie rock bands.

I had my four plasmas on 1) the NFL, 2) some whacked-out Korean game show where people dress in animal costumes to win prizes that look like inflatable vinyl alphabet letters, 3) the DEA real-time satellite view of my farm and 4) a two-way satellite link to an insomniac freak named Charles, who works in the satellite TV media-buying wing of BBDO in Singapore. Charles pays a hundred bucks an hour to watch me work nude in my cab. Did I forget to mention that? Welcome to the new economy. If I can make an extra buck by getting off some Twinkie in another hemisphere, you know what? I'm *in*. Charles, you unzip your trousers. *Zegna* trousers, and I know that about you because I read your secret online profile: lions-and-tigers-and-bears@labelwhore.org.

In any event, the sexy portion of Charles's day seemed to have been completed, and the two of us were talking. Specifically, Charles was trashing the state of Iowa, branding it "The Rectangle State." I quickly disabused him of this notion, pointing out that *Colorado* is technically the rectangle state.

Charles said, "Yes, its overall shape is rectangular, *but* if you look at a county map of Colorado, it looks like a bunch of ripped paper shreds stacked by preschoolers, whereas Iowa is divvied up into 113 neatly aligned rectangles."

"Quit mocking my state's spatial configuration."

"Wake up, CornDog."

Okay, maybe, just *maybe* I was high that day. (Have you ever found a Romanian lab technician who couldn't be bribed?) My personal rule is that I only get high when the weather sets a new record, and, BTW, my name isn't CornDog. It's Zack. And I'm not ADD, I'm just Zack. ADD is a face-saving term my parents slapped on me when they figured out I wasn't Stephen Hawking.

I hear people asking, Where is Zack's mother? Is Zack a plucky orphan? No, Zack has an age-inappropriate future stepfather-in-the-making named Kyle who breeds genetically defective Jack Russell terriers with his mother in a shack in St. George, Utah.

Charles, meanwhile, was relentless: "CornDog, what the hell were they thinking when they were divvying up your state?"

On the DEA real-time satellite cam I was zooming in and out of a map of Iowa, shifting scale and superimposing geo-political borders. Charles was right. Iowa *is* the Rectangle State.

More importantly, I was using the satellite to keep real-time track of that day's masterpiece, a ten-acre cock and balls I was chopping out of the cornstalks to send as a long overdue thank-you note to God for having me be born into the cultural equivalent of one of those machines they use to shake paint in hardware stores. I didn't have to please Uncle Jay with harvesting efficiency that year—the whole crop was contaminated with some kind of gene trace that was killing off not bees (a thing of the past) but moths and wasps. In an uncharacteristic act of citizenhood, the corn industry had decided to scrap the crop. I wasn't too pissed about that—look at the bright side: *subsidies!* So even though the corn was in tassel and at its prettiest, I could clear those stalk fuckers whatever way I wanted.

The fateful moment occurred shortly after Charles told me about a lap dance he'd won in a pre-op tranny nightclub the week before. One of Maizie's windows was rattling a bit, so I went and jiggled it on its hinges. I opened and closed it a few times and, *shazaam!*, that's when I got stung.

SAMANTHA

PALMERSTON NORTH, WANGANUI, NEW ZEALAND

Right.

When I was stung I was standing in a clump of grass beside a blossoming Ramayana shrub while a small flock of Barbary doves whistled over my head. It felt like the old days, when blossoming shrubs and flowers were something we could take for granted. My particular clump of grass was at the corner of Weber Fork Road and Route 52, about as remote as it gets on the island—twenty miles in from the east coast, in the hilly eastern part of Wanganui province.

Thing is, I'd taken a slice of boring white bread from its bakery bag and had slapped it onto a small patch of yellow sandy dirt. I was standing up to photograph the slice of bread using my mobile phone. *Why would you have been doing this?* I hear you wonder. Excellent question. I was making an "Earth sandwich." *What is an Earth sandwich?* Fair enough. It's when you use online maps to locate the exact opposite place on the planet from you, and then hook up with someone close to that place. Then, after you mathematically figure out exact opposite GPS coordinates to within a thumbnail's radius, you put a slice of bread on that spot, then connect via cellphone and simultaneously snap photos: two slices of bread with a planet between them. It's an Internet thing. You make the sandwich, you post it, and maybe someone somewhere will see it, and once they've seen it, you've created art. Bingo.

The person on the other end of the earth was this girl, Simone Ferrero, who was in central Madrid at the corner of

Calle Gutenberg and Calle Poeta Esteban de Villegas, at ten o'clock at night—meaning it was ten o'clock in the morning in New Zealand. All I knew of her was that we had agreed online to make a sandwich together.

The thing is, New Zealanders pretty much have the Earth sandwich game locked up. Most of the planet's land masses are above the equator and are sandwich partners only with oceans. For example, the other side of North America's sandwich is entirely composed of the Indian Ocean. Honolulu makes a sliver of a sandwich with Zimbabwe, but that's all the opportunities there are for Yanks, Mexicans and Canadians.

The thing is that even while I was taking my photo and being stung, my mind was somewhere else. I'd had a strange phone call that morning from my mother. It was my one sleep-in day of the week, but I'd foolishly forgotten to turn off my mobile phone. For the six other days a week I'm up at 5:00 a.m. to be at the gym to train clients for 6:00, and on my one day of rest I picked up the phone and . . .

"Samantha, good morning."

"Mum."

"Did I wake you up? It's 8:30. I thought for sure you'd be awake."

"Mum, what's up? Wait—I thought you were on vacation."

"We are. We're sixty minutes out of Darwin in a darling little cabin room, and at breakfast we had chocolate brioches and milk and—sorry, dear—I'm getting away from my message."

"What's your message?"

"I . . . we . . . your father and I, we have some news for you."

Yoinks. I braced myself for the worst, my brain already screaming for coffee.

"We've had a discussion, and we thought we should tell you something."

Cancer? Bankruptcy? Double yoinks. "What's wrong?"

"Your father and I have decided that we don't believe in anything any more."

"You *what?*"

"What I just said."

"Jesus, Mum, you phoned me up on a Monday morning to tell me you don't believe in anything."

"Yes."

"You mean, like, God? And religion?"

"Both."

I walked to the kitchen to flip the switch on the Braun. My parakeet, Timbo, a happy remnant of a failed relationship, was sitting on a deck chair, squawking the words "the worst toilet in Scotland" over and over and awaiting his morning treat. "Right. So why are you telling me this?"

"Well, I believe you still believe in things."

"What do you mean, *things?*"

"God. Life after death. That sort of thing."

"*That sort of thing?*" My sketchy belief system wasn't something to haggle about at this time of day, and my brain was racing ass over tit trying to figure out the significance of a call like this.

I opened the window and threw Timbo an arrowroot biscuit. "So, Mum, what did you believe in before you stopped believing in things?" In the background the Braun was beginning to hiss, and I was glad that the absent bees hadn't wiped out the planet's coffee crop.

"Not much, really. But we've decided to make it official."

"This is pretty strange, Mum."

"No stranger than that afternoon you announced you were becoming a vegetarian."

"I was thirteen. It was either that or an eating disorder."

"Beliefs are beliefs."

"Crikey *dick*, Mum, but you *don't* believe in anything. You just said so. And I'm going to have to ask you a rude question, but are you on drugs?"

"Sam! No. We're only taking Solon. It's safe."

"Solon? That stuff that makes time pass quicker?"

"No. Solon is a lovely drug and it makes my head feel calm."

"Okay. It's still a drug."

My mother sighed, which was my cue to say something dutiful and reassuring, my role in the family as first-born. So I said, "It was thoughtful of you to call me and tell me properly."

"Thank you, dear. I don't know how your brothers will take it."

"They won't care. They don't think about this kind of stuff."

"You're right."

Thing is, my brothers are two fuckwits, and lately they'd been taxing my good will by hitting me up for loans and asking me to glue them back together after their never-ending streams of failed relationships with the North Island's daggiest women. I poured myself a coffee and cut it with hot tap water. "So how do you think this is going to affect your life?"

"Probably not much. We're not going to proselytize—if people we know still choose to believe in something, we keep our mouths shut."

"That's it?"

"That's it."

"Right."

We hung up and I looked at my laptop clock. Making an Earth sandwich would take my mind off it all. I finished my coffee, showered, dressed and grabbed my asthma inhaler, and soon I was on my way to visit −40.4083°, 176.3204°.

The road eastward out of Palmy was empty.

And my conversation with Mum got me thinking about parents and how they feed your belief systems. I mean, whatever your parents do, good or bad, it allows you to do the same thing with no feelings of guilt. Dad steals cars? Go for it. Mum goes to church every Sunday? You better go too. So, when your parents decide they don't believe in anything, you can't rebel against them, because that'd just be rebelling against nothing. It puts you in a state of moral free float. If you copy them and believe in nothing yourself, then it's the same thing: copying nothing equals zero. You're buggered either way.

I wound around the rolling hills. What *did* I believe in? I'd had five different boyfriends in my twenty-six years, and the boot of each of their vehicles bore a different variation of the Christian fish. Coincidence?

First off, there was the tousle-haired Kevin, the catalogue model, who had an agape fish on his Honda. Kevin always seemed to have a religious reason for avoiding reality, most memorably not picking me up after work so he could shoot hoops with a Christian men's group. Relationship breaker. Then there was Miles, the Deadhead atheist, whose fish had DARWIN embedded in its interior. After him came Hal, whose silver fish was followed by the words "AND CHIPS." After Hal was Ray, who was a total wanker—I don't know what I was thinking when I was with him. Everyone has a Ray somewhere in his or her past. Ray's fish wasn't witty and ironic or anything—it was just a fish. And finally there was Reid, who had a chromed fish skeleton. I thought Reid was going to be the Keeper, but Reid was generic in his willingness to avoid commitment.

Jesus, look at me labelling these guys like this. In all fairness, they'd probably label me a stuck-up gym bunny and claim that it wasn't their duty to provide me with their version of the fish like it was shade on a hot day.

So, yes, I had a few things on my mind when I was photographing my bread slice on a sheep-stinking roadside, not the least of which was jealousy about being in the other hemisphere—the loser's hemisphere—of being the opposite of Madrid, and sadness because the bees had vanished and therefore so many roadside flowers had all but vanished with them: the cudweed, the monkey musk, the brass buttons, the catchfly. I felt a generalized sense of wonder about the size of the planet and my useless little role atop it or under it.

And then my cellphone rang and, as I said, I got stung.

Bingo.

JULIEN

12TH ARRONDISSEMENT, PARIS, FRANCE

I think fate is a corny notion. Everything in this world is cause and effect, process not destiny. A bee sting? How sentimental. How old-fashioned. And then, after we were stung, everyone treated us like a collection of Wonka children. *Pfft*.

I was stung while I was sitting on a bench in Bois de Vincennes beside a pair of aging papist hags who were bickering about identity theft chip-and-PIN credit cards and complaining about how they have to shred their garbage before they throw it out. Yes, the Romanians and the Russians and the Triads must be waiting on tippytoes to pounce on them: *With Madame Duclos's electrical bill, we will bring Caisse d'Epargne to its knees!* Their voices got me so angry—angry at the fabric of time, at whatever it is that makes time seem to drag on forever, that makes life feel so long. All I wanted to do was tell them that their religion is decadent and obsolete. I wanted to tell them that their religion was invented thousands of years ago as a way of explaining to those people lucky enough (or unlucky enough) to live past the age of twenty-one the fact that life is too short. These crones, I wanted to tell them that what I would look for in a religion is an explanation of why life is so *long*. I'm still looking.

Forget religion, I want to *mutate*. I want so badly to mutate. I was sitting in the sun in the Bois de Vincennes, willing my body to mutate into whatever it is human beings are slated to turn into next. Do we get giant drosophila fly eyes? Wings? Elephantine snouts? I dream of the day we mutate into something better than the hyped-up chimps we are, chimps who eat Knorr Swiss cream of cauliflower soup while pretending not to notice that half the planet's at war, fighting over . . . what? Over the right to eat packaged soup without having to emotionally accept our species' darkness. We are one fucked-up claque of monkeys. Groundskeeper Willie called us cheese-eating surrender monkeys: he almost had it right. But it isn't just the French—as a species we are all cheese-eating surrender monkeys.

I am not normally the sort of person who sits on park benches in the 12th arrondissement on a sunny day. In fact, I am the opposite of that sort of person. I didn't even know what time it was when I was rudely and cruelly ejected from the Astrolite gaming centre on rue Claude Decaen. I was having what is called a shit fit. I had this shit fit because I had spent 114 solid days in-game on World of Warcraft, and was at the end of a twenty-four-hour levelling jag, when my avatar vanished. Not even a little pouf of smoke—I, Xxanthroxxusxx, simply ceased to be. I did the usual things. I shut down. I unplugged. I rebooted. I checked the options and preferences. I logged back into the world. And still I was *gone*.

Bleep.

I am willing to agree that I am not the easiest person to be around. That is because I set high standards for myself. If people are unwilling to live up to my standards, I am not willing to accept them, especially Luc, the greasy bastard at the Astrolite's front desk, who expectorates all day into a blue Rubbermaid spittoon.

A *spittoon.*

He considers it a colourful character trait; I see it as the devolution of the species. But even the greasy Luc should know that to have one's "self" vanish from any world for no known reason is *not* something one takes lightly. In fact, one is well entitled to have a shit fit when this happens. Luc should have been more understanding of this, and I, in the midst of my shit fit, should not have criticized Luc's love of anime comics, declaring them bourgeois escapist ecotourism of the brain. Or something like that. I don't remember exactly.

And so I was out on the street, tossed into an outdoor Las Vegas casino of timelessness. It was sunny out—ugh!— morning sun or afternoon sun? Noonish, I supposed. I looked around at the cars and the Starbucks and the shop windows and the middle-aged people looking calm and rich, and I thought, *I hate the world.* I hate the way everything has a surface—hardness; softness—the way everything has a *smell*: chestnut blossoms and roasting chickens.

I hate the way our bodies move through the world, clip-clop, like beef marionettes. I hate how the world has turned into one massive hamburger-making machine, how the world is only about people now—everything else on the planet must bow to our will because there's no longer any other option. Fundamentalists rejoiced when the bees died out; to them it was proof that the planet exists entirely for and was entirely about *people*. How could such thinking not make you want to go out and vomit into the street? And then I thought, *Julien, are you an environmentalist now?* I remembered World of Warcraft and I dragged myself along boulevard Poniatowski, turned down avenue de Général Dodds while avoiding the dog merde and tourists too stupid to realize they're in the 12th arrondissement, and then crossed avenue du Général Laperrine (all these generals; all these wars) and entered Bois de Vincennes, so matronly, so boring, so permanent and a bit too much for my head to absorb just then. My head was a disaster. So I sat down on a bench with two crones afraid of tomorrow. I looked at the trees. What season was it? Summer? Fall? Leaves don't really fall from the trees any more, do they? They just kind of sit on the branch and randomly commit suicide sometime before January. Seasons are passé. Only suckers believe in seasons.

I stared at a dead leaf while the barking of the hags pounded my ears. I made a disgusted sound and said, "God, I hate the real world." That's when I was stung—a feeling like a paper cut concentrated into a single point of skin. At a club, Ralphe once stuck me with a pin and told me I had AIDS—talk about shit fits! Ralphe is an asshole, and the pin was a Coke tab he'd somehow bent into a small jabby thing. But it stung, and so did the bee sting.

I looked at this winged insect on my forearm and swatted it away in panic. The two crones looked down at the bee and then fell to their knees and began to pray.

DIANA

My name is Diana, and yes, I was named after Diana, Princess of Wales, just as my mother was named after Jackie Kennedy. *Plus ça change.* I'm the oldest of the Wonka children (Julien's term), and because of this, at first, I was more like an older sibling than a peer. I remember very clearly how and when I was stung.

It was Sunday afternoon and I'd been on Sunday school baking duty. I was washing out some cake tins that had been soaking in water, and I remember dawdling because the tins smelled so wonderful—almond and sugar and lemon—and then feeling sad because almonds are pretty much a thing of the past. I remember all those photos of California almond groves, the close-up shots of the branches where there'd be maybe one almond per tree. The smell of artificial almond extract in turn got me to brooding about the fact that I was thirty-four and single, with no prospects on the horizon. I dried my hands and decided to go online and perhaps find some nice guy to date on a religious dating bulletin board.

"Bulletin board"—I know, how pre-millennial, but I'm a conservative woman, and while I wasn't achingly desperate to be with someone, it's hard for a woman my age to find something long-term, especially if you're not a putting-out machine like my sister, but she's another story.

This time, instead of looking at M4W, I went to W4M. I wanted to check out the competition:

Hello, my name is Richelle, I'm 23 and I love the Lord passion-ately, I am totally on fire for my King! My relationship with the Lord is central to my life. I am originally from Ontario, but . . .

Hi there! Well, here goes: I'm Michelle, 22, and number one, I'm a Christian. I want Christ to be present in every part of my life. I'm searching for someone who shares this same passion . . .

I'm Sarah, 20. I am seeking a soulmate, someone to live with in Christ and serve Him with. I'm a gentle person and soft-spoken. I try my best to love others as He . . .

My heart sank. How could I compete with these young things? To them, belief is like memorizing the alphabet—they're too young to ever have doubts.

I sat back in my chair, one of those generic black jobs from Staples, and for the first time consciously tried to map out an aloneness strategy for the rest of my life. I had to acknowledge that there's this hole inside me—I've spent my life worrying if people can see this hole. Maybe I should own my hole and be proud of it, even if that sounds disgusting. Maybe I should walk through life slumped over, my face and body reflecting my void.

Fuskshitpisscunt.

Isn't it shocking when it first happens? I have Tourette's—for real. But you get used to it very quickly. Usually, by the fifth volley of "cunts," people can tune me out. I don't notice it much myself any more.

Mind you, I don't walk around saying "fuckshitpiss" all the time. I also blurt out whatever comes into my head as if I'm a living, breathing, inside-out machine. I would argue that we all think such things; I merely say them out loud.

. . . lard-ass

. . . pig-snout nose

. . . fist-fucker

. . . Big Bird

. . . wife beater

With me, what you hear is what you are.

Okay, back to the day of the sting.

I was still slumped in my Staples chair when I heard a dog yelping across the street—Kayla, the Doberman pinscher—one of those yelps that indicate fear and pain blended together. I flew out the front door and onto the sidewalk, hot and wet after a midday storm, to find Kayla's owner, Mitch, pounding on his dog with a two-by-four.

A few neighbours up and down the street were watching but not doing anything to help the poor dog, so I ran up to Mitch and put my face right in his face and said, more or less, "You mean ugly fucker; everyone hates you. Stop hitting your dog, fucker, fuck you and die; I'll kill you any way I can." Poor Kayla was yelping and one of her legs was bleeding, and she was crouched as far away from Mitch as her tether permitted.

Mitch took another token swing in Kayla's direction, but I inserted myself between him and the poor yelping dog. Mitch started brandishing the two-by-four at me, screaming some pretty awful things, but people like him don't frighten me. I could smell peanut butter on his breath, and a small particle of something flew into the corner of my left eye. But still I didn't flinch.

That was when Pastor Brandeis (Erik) drove up with his wife, Eva, in a ramshackle old Ford from the 1990s filled with baby gear, cardboard boxes and that air of poverty you sense when you pass such a car on the highway and think, *Those people will be driving around for the rest of their lives like that, looking for a place they're never going to find, and there will always be a crumpled box of Pampers in the rear window alongside unreadable self-help books and badly folded T-shirts.* Erik and Eva had come to discuss the next weekend's Sunday school session with me.

I will admit that I was in love with Erik, and two weeks earlier, with the touch of a hand and a whisper, had subtly let him know this—but, given the Tourette's, I also said, "Fuck me, please fuck me." My feelings were not reciprocated, and as a result, I was no longer a charity case: I was a distinct liability. On the afternoon of the bee sting he'd only dropped by because he had yet to devise a way to shed me from his flock or find someone else to manage the semi-annual bake sale. He'd brought Eva for protection, which made me angry because, well, I wanted her dead in the worst sort of way. Everyone thinks I'm a doormat, but I want to kill people as much as the next person.

So it was a messy scene. All of the cowardly neighbours decided to come over now that there was no possibility they might need to intervene. Erik asked Mitch the pointedly stupid question, "Why are you hitting your dog?" As if there was some reason that would justify it! Was Kayla the Doberman cheating on Mitch? Did Kayla pawn Mitch's collection of Vietnam-era Zippo lighters and spend the proceeds on lottery tickets and meth? The way Erik asked his question made it sound like maybe there was a chance Kayla deserved what she got. "Erik, how can you ask a stupid question like that? What on earth could a dog do to justify a beating?"

"It's my dog," Mitch said, "and I can do what I like with it."

"She's a living thing, not a lawn mower, and she's a *she*, not an *it*." I was outraged.

Erik said, "Diana, it's an animal."

Mitch looked pleased.

"What's that supposed to mean? He can beat on the dog all he wants with no repercussions?"

"Look, it's not like I approve of beating dogs," Erik said.

Mitch's face fell.

"But the thing is, Diana, dogs don't have souls. In the end, it doesn't really matter what happens to them."

"It doesn't *matter*?"

"This guy's a jerk, but he's not sinning."

Mitch gloated. "See? I'm not a sinner—get your religious ass off my front lawn."

I ignored him. "Erik, you mean you condone what this hillbilly is doing?"

"I don't like it, but it's no sin."

"You're serious?"

"I am." Erik gave me a fuck-off stare.

Eva said, "Come on, Diana. Let's go inside and discuss the bake sale. I'm thinking of making a cobbler."

"If I disagree with you, am I kicked out of the flock?" I glared daggers at Erik.

He offered a shrug. "Well, yes."

Ahh . . . excommunication.

That's when I got stung.

HARJ

When I was young, I had a job helping my oldest brother escort young people—mostly young American tourists—around the island as they tried to "find themselves." Oh, the awful conversations I have had to endure, listening to a Kris or a Max or an Amy or a Craig discuss what it means "to be free inside one's head." I ask you, is it so wrong to want to kill a Craig? The moment these Craigs thought I was out of earshot, they would call my brother Apu and me mini-Apu, and make Kwik-E-Mart jokes. Little did they know that I used my free minutes at the office to watch *The Simpsons* and *Family Guy* online, as well as to investigate some amusing categories I still recommend, such as "time-lapse photography," "Japanese game show," and "owned." So I was onto these Craigs and she-Craigs with ankle tattoos of Tweety Bird and Satan.

I was lucky to have had a stable upbringing—and lucky to have a father who worked in a bank, the HSBC, albeit one of its most remote outposts. The logo on the front door was painted over with brick-coloured paint so as not to anger regional political crazies, and my father's office windows were covered with sheets of plywood that came from the state of Maine; the telltale branding marks on the inside were never overpainted. After returning from school, while waiting for my father to finish work, I would stare at the plywood; I come by my fascination with New England honestly. I would try to imagine the forest it came from: trees so big that the sky was invisible, and rich people like George Clooney riding on horseback across a field of shamrocks, sticking out their tongues to catch snowflakes. These rich people would wear sweaters (I couldn't even imagine what wearing one might feel like), and they would go to their cabins, where servants would feed them turkey dinners.

I think I am one of nature's worker bees, and I spent many a humid afternoon staring at the sky above the Indian Ocean, trying to figure out what direction I would take with my life. I knew that I was done with escorting rich young monsters around the island—a job like that could only escalate in tawdriness, and I would end up like my older brother, deeply engaged in the world of sex tourism—European men, and occasionally women, who would show up interested in the Democratic Socialist Republic of Sri Lanka's "rich and varied culture," who would somehow almost instantly be whisked to the city's handjob district for a holiday of tugs, Kleenex and ugly commands. This was not a world I wanted to enter, but the only other options were plantation work or becoming a JVP or LTTE Marxist militant. What was a young man in Sri Lanka to do?

My father did, however, find me part-time work at his office doing minor janitorial duties. On the afternoon of December 26, 2004, I was at the bank, ostensibly to polish its many brass light fixtures, of which my father was proud. I needed the small pay and truly didn't want to join my family at my cousin's engagement party, eating coconut-and-grouper patties at the beach at Nawarednapuram while making boring chitter-chatter about the fiancé, Arnood—a sulking Hindu swine who collects Christmas tree ornaments on eBay. Arnood is heterosexual, but only by the thinnest of margins. My aunt and uncle were so glad to get rid of my cousin that they'd have married her to a banyan tree, had the tree bothered to ask for her hand.

It turned out that one of the bank's new employees had left wide open an Internet connection at his third-floor desk. I saw it the moment I came up the stairs, and goodbye Brasso, hello Drudgereport! The whole afternoon became a blur of information until I heard raised voices down on the street, and in the distance a sort of rushing noise that I now associate with the ventilation systems at the Centers for Disease Control. I went to the window, opened its louvres and looked outside to see the tsunami's grey flood approach my building, safe only because I was on the third floor and the bottom two storeys were concrete.

Even then I knew to search for my family members' faces within the oozing grey pudding. Even then I knew that the engagement party was a party with death, and even then I knew that I had become the man of the family—except that when I crawled through the salty, stinky debris on the mile-long trek home, all that remained of our house was a slick of red dirt covered with marine litter and a grouper that had drowned in the air. By the time seventy-two hours had passed, I had realized that I had no family left—all of them were gone. It is very strange to no longer have any roots in a country that goes back for tens of thousands of years. I was not allowed to return to my bank job, because my father was no longer there—I had to become everything for myself. I spent a few years subsisting by cleaning up debris and rebuilding structures for NGOs like UNICEF and UNESCO. Unlike many young men my age, I refused to be lured to Dubai, and after the cleanup was complete, I was fortunate to find a job sweeping and cleaning at a call centre for Abercrombie & Fitch in a warehouse building at Bandaranaike Airport. I knew this was only temporary, as my love of American-produced global culture and my knowledge of the inner life of Craigs would one day allow me to become an actual call centre phone staffer, and yes, after some years my wish came true.

I quickly rose through the ranks and was placed in charge of the Abercrombie & Fitch American-Canadian Central Time Zone Call Division. This occurred because I was able to give fellow workers hints not listed on our official standardized greetings sheet—obvious words like "awesome!" or "sweet," and also more subtle phrases such as, "I can tell from your voice that you're totally going to enjoy what you've already bought, and for a limited time only, get two silk-cashmere short-sleeve cable shells for the price of one, *plus* a fleece pashmina wrap at no extra cost. Think about it. You *deserve* it—and think of how *free* you'll feel out in the fall air wearing all these hot items."

I enjoyed helping (I am now quoting an in-house memo) "provide a completely customer-centric operation by consistently enhancing customer service while trying to gain a better understanding of our customers' shopping patterns and preferences."

I was an excellent salesman. But I am supposed to tell the story of when I was stung, so I will perhaps return later to tales of Abercrombie & Fitch.

I quickly became contemptuous of the people on the phone on the other side of the planet, twelve hours away. My territory was the North American Midwest, and the only thing that really kept me on the straight and narrow was the possibility of taking over the highly glamorous, Maine-containing New England Division, located over by the guava bins at the far end of the warehouse. The other good thing about my job was unlimited high-speed Internet access at the end of the day (a twelve-hour day, mind you). For this I would have worked for free.

However, I did not wish to be a passive participant in the Internet. I wanted to add my voice to the babble and so, for fun, I created a prank commerce site on which I sold "celebrity room tones." It was a beautifully designed site (I cloned a Swiss site that sells cutlery) and entirely convincing.

What is a celebrity room tone?

For $4.99 you could visit my site and download one hour of household silence from rooms belonging to a range of celebrities, all of whom promised to donate their royalties to charity. There was Mick Jagger (London; metropolitan), Garth Brooks (rural; some jet noise in the background), Cameron Diaz (Miami; sexy, sunny, flirty) and so forth. For cachet, I threw in household silences from the Tribeca lofts of underworld rock survivor Lou Reed and motherly experimental performance artist Laurie Anderson.

I was quickly flamed by many potential shoppers, hounding me at webmaster@celebrityroomtones.org to ask why their Amex or Visa wouldn't process.

And then came an email from the *New York Times* asking to do a short piece on the site for its weekend Style section. So there I was, sitting in an office chair made from three cannibalized office chairs, dripping with sweat and staring longingly at the guava bins, as a woman named Leslie asked me whether I had a prepared artist's statement and jpegs of myself I could send her. I had told the delightful Leslie that my name was Werner and that I was based out of Kassel, Germany, because it seemed like the kind of place that would be home to over-educated people with nothing better to do than to design commodities like designer silence. I'd affected a German accent and was, in general, very prickly.

"Yes," I said. "I suppose you would want a photo, as your section is dominated by photos."

There was a slight pause before Leslie replied, a pause long enough to let me know that she considered me a pain.

I said, "I plan to launch my new line of room tones in coordination with your article's appearance."

"A new line?"

"Yes, I'm calling them 'Nocturnes: Soundscapes for the Evening,' with an emphasis on nighttime insect noises and a marked deficit of engine and machine noises."

"You're telling me there's a difference between silence in the day and silence at night?"

"Yes. Leslie. Imagine that you are in a completely dark room with your eyes closed. Then you open your eyes. It's just as dark as with your eyes closed, and yet it's a completely different kind of darkness than before, isn't it?"

"It is."

That's the exact moment when I met my bee.

ZACK

When I got stung in Maizie's cab, I had a *whatthefuck?* moment as I stared at the bee on my thigh—and then I began to swell. Charles asked me what was going on, so I moved the pod camera to show him the bee corpse. He thought it was a joke—and why wouldn't he? But then I began to seriously balloon, then hyperventilate, and without him at the other end of the satellite link, I'd be dead and the world would never have known that I was the first person on earth to be stung by a bee in almost five years.

When I fell onto the cab floor I shouted, "Charles, you'd better not be jacking off to this!"—I am a sick fuck to the end—but Charles had already contacted the local hospital, plus the U.S. Department of Agriculture and the Centers for Disease Control. Maybe three minutes later I heard choppers on the horizon, sounding like old-fashioned threshers. A trio of them landed a precautionary hundred yards away from me so as not to tamper with the bee zone. Thirty seconds later, some guy in a white Tyvek moonsuit put his fist through the cab window, reached down, pulled my tongue out of my throat, then jabbed an EpiPen into my unstung thigh. Through all of this, Charles was telling me to hang on a bit longer, and when Moonsuit realized this, he punched the camera and the Zack show was over.

Moments later I was able to breathe again and was already apologizing for the inconvenience—which was when the Moonsuit sprayed something in my face and stuck me into a white Tyvek body bag with a clear oval plastic face shield.

Then he and his associate loaded me onto a red plastic sled and inserted the sled into the middle of the three choppers. As we lifted off, I looked down on the field and saw my cornstalk cock and balls, and Day-Glo pink tapes that were being uncoiled to divvy my field up into quadrants. Another platoon of choppers was landing near my house, well away from the structure itself as well as the line of poplars (the most likely spot for a bees' nest). I was feeling woozy now. I was remembering summer flowers of my youth: hawkweed, harebells, thimbleweed, wild bergamot and blue vervain. A sense of loss overcame me, followed by a wash of hope—the bees had returned, hadn't they! I said a prayer to my personal saint, Saint Todd, patron of rigged slot machines, red tides, kinked garden hoses and uninscribed tombstones, and then I passed out.

When I woke up, I was in what was obviously a hospital room, except that it was a *private* room. Uncle Jay would never spring for a private room, so something else had to be going on here. When I got up, I tried to open the glass door in the corner, but there was no handle. On the other side of the door were three receding glass anterooms with three separate glass doors through which I could see a hallway. Putting my ear to the seal around the glass door, I could hear ventilation hissing so strongly that it reminded me of a rip in the time/space continuum.

I rapped on the glass and called out, "Hello!" but I might as well have been on the moon as assume anyone on the outside could hear me. I went back to my bed and looked for a phone or cell unit. *Nada.*

There was no TV, no computer, no thermostat, no medical apparatus, no light switches, no bed controls, no fridge, no books—it was like being in the future and the past at the same time. "Where the fuck *am* I?"

Silence.

"Who the fuck's out there?"

Silence.

It's a cliché, but I tell you, in real life, when you wake up in a medical facility after being kidnapped by a haz-mat squad and tossed into a helicopter, your first impulse truly is to shout out corny shit like "Where the fuck *am* I? Who the fuck's out there?"

Corny shit. Now *there's* a word picture.

It appeared that whoever was "out there" was temporarily absent. I did a sweep around my room, looking for camouflaged call buttons, speakers, tripwires—you name it—and found none. After maybe a half-hour of this, I noticed something extra spooky about my room: *there were no logos on anything.* There was no little metal plate on the bed showing that it was made in Bumfuck, Wisconsin, by Proud Union Labor—or in Shenzhen by lunch-deprived three-year-olds. There weren't even holes where such a plate had once been screwed in. Somebody had removed it, spackled in the holes, sanded it and then repainted it. That's pretty fucky if you ask me. The mattress? Unpatterned and free of any branding.

I looked at the toilet, a rugged beast with a power flush like those scenes in movies when the terrorist blows out the plane door and everything in the passenger compartment gets sucked into the air. Nothing. I looked at the toilet paper: no logos or daisies were embossed on the paper or printed on the inner cardboard tube, but I have to say, from a connoisseur's standpoint, it was primo shit: three-ply, quilted and bleached, like only the Arabs get these days.

The bathroom fixtures, the toothbrush, the blankets, the furniture—all of it had been stripped of corporate identity. I felt like I was not in a real room but in a room disguised to *look like* a room.

I chugged a few glasses of tap water and my stomach gurgled. I hoped non-brand-name food would shortly arrive.

I sat down on the bed. No technology, no books, nobody to talk to. Being in no mood to jack off, I lay down and tried to recall the bee sting. The stinger itself was gone, and my leg was back to normal; only a small red spot remained.

A bee.

Huh.

I remembered bees. I remembered seeing them in spring among the bloodroot, the yellow goat's beard and the swamp buttercups in my grandparents' back ditch—happy, industrious, slightly furry and oh-so doomed. Then they began to flee their hives, and before there was even time to figure out why, they were all gone. Cellphones? Genetically modified crops? A virus? Chemicals? I remember being upset about it—most kids were. A tornado is awful, but a tornado isn't about you— *you* just happened to be there when it struck. But bees? There wasn't anyone on earth who didn't have that sick, guilty feeling in the gut because we knew it was our fault, not Mother Nature's.

When I was growing up, Mother Nature was this reasonably hot woman who looked a lot like the actress Glenn Close wearing a pale blue nightie. When you weren't looking, she was dancing around the fields and the barns and the yard, patting the squirrels and French kissing butterflies. After the bees left and the plants started failing, it was like she'd returned from a Mossad boot camp with a shaved head, steel-trap abs and commando boots, and man, was she *pissed*. After the bees left, the most you could ask of her was that she not go totally apeshit on your ass. My dad and I used to drive into Des Moines to hook up with his pseudoephedrine dealer, and whenever we saw dead animals on the road, he'd say, "Blank 'em out, Zack, blank 'em out." After I'd seen enough roadkill, it became pretty easy to blank 'em all out. And that's what the world did with the bees: we blanked 'em out. *And now Big Mama's out for revenge.*

Wait—was that motion somewhere out there in the antechamber? I ran to look: false alarm. Should I try to use the bed to ram the door open? Nope. Bolted to the floor. *Fuck.*

My stomach gurgled again. I was *really* getting hungry. A few weeks ago Charles told me he'd bid on a six-ounce bottle of 2008 Yukon fireweed honey at Sotheby's—five hundred dollars—and it ended up going for seventeen thousand *Australian* dollars. [Homer Simpson voice: Mmmmm . . . *honey.*]

Right about then I finally twigged to the fact that my room had to be bugged and monitored for sound and picture. Lying back on my mattress, I simply said, "Warden—some food, please."

I immediately felt deeply sleepy. I passed out and woke up (I'm guessing) an hour later, and there on the table across the room was a plate. *Hmmm.*

On it lay three small rectangular Jell-Oey slabs, pink, white and pale green. I looked at the ceiling: "Can I please get some cracked pepper on this?"

A somewhat mechanical woman's voice replied in cool, crisp tones: "Please eat your lunch, Zack. We have a lot of things we need to do."

"Who are you?"

"*Bon appétit.*"

SAMANTHA

"*¿Una abeja le ha picado?*"

"*¡Si!* Yes, Simone—I mean . . . *what?* Sorry, I . . . *what the . . . ?*"

"*¿Samantha, usted está fingiendo?*"

"No, I'm not fucking with you, I've just been stung."

I'd swatted a bee off my forearm and into the central grooves of a well-established bayonet aloe. The bee was thoroughly dead . . . *murdered*; I felt sick about it, and later on I'd be chided for having done some damage to the bee when I swatted it. Meanwhile, Simone, in downtown Madrid at the corner of Calle Gutenberg and Calle Poeta Esteban de Villegas, was giving me shit: "*¡Llame a policía!*"

"Call the po*lice?* To tell them what—I killed a bee? Like I want to end up in prison."

"*Usted tendrá que hacer algo.*"

"Jesus, I know I have to do *some*thing. But calling the authorities? I don't know."

"*¿Lastimó?*"

"Pain? No. Not really. Pretty much like I remember it from when I was six."

"*Tome una fotografía de ella.*"

"Brilliant idea." I got down on my knees and snapped a jpeg of my bee. The phone was a new Samsung that allowed me to take a 20-meg shot with no blurring or smudginess. I sent the photo to Simone.

"*¡Caramba!*"

"Caramba, indeed."

Here's the thing: unknown to me, Simone was forwarding the photo to everyone on her (it turned out) globally extensive friends list, complete with explicit geocoordinates.

"*¡Hey! No se olvide a la fotografía de la rebanada del pan.*"

The Earth sandwich: Right. I'd forgotten to photograph my bread slice. "Gotcha." I photographed my slice, zapped it to Simone and told her I had to go. I hung up and sat there staring at the bee carcass.

The wind had picked up and I was getting bloody chilly. I looked at the small red bump on my arm where the stinger had gone in. Had this really just happened? The big news the month before had been Sexy Zack with his Samoyed dog eyes being stung in Iowa—imagine having images of yourself driving a corn harvester naked being the most viral video in planetary history—fortunately for him he was hot, but still. Then they'd hidden him away, and the world hadn't seen him since.

But people aren't stupid—well, actually, people *are* stupid—which explains wars. There'd been a slew of copycat stings, and I didn't want people thinking I was another barmy loser looking for fifteen seconds of fame. But wait . . . I *did* get stung, and there hadn't been a bee in New Zealand for six or seven years. Why was I trying to talk myself out of reporting this?

Thing is, when something genuinely cosmic happens to you, your tendency is to believe the experience isn't real. So there I was trying to figure out what dimension of the sting was inauthentic because interesting things don't happen to people like me. They don't.

The sun came out from behind a cloud. I was suddenly sleepy. I closed my eyes and a little while later I was woken up by three biology students from Massey University in Palmy. They were photographing the dead bee in the aloe's crook.

One of the girls asked, "Can I see the sting?"

"Pardon?"

"Your sting."

"Uh. Sure." I showed her. My forearm might as well have been the Shroud of Turin.

And then I heard the choppers.

Okay.

In hindsight, I can see why we were renditioned into sterile environments. And whereas the others were manhandled and drugged, I had a pretty civilized transition. I was standing on the grass with the three rather dim students, displaying my sting, when six choppers morphed from tiny specks on the horizon into hulking brutes threatening to blow us over. They landed around us in a hexagonal formation, each about two hundred yards away. The moment they hit the ground, the blades stopped. The machine's engineering impressed me. Chinese?

Five figures dressed in haz-mat suits emerged from each chopper. Maybe a dozen of them had rifles—yes, rifles, in happy little New Zealand. One of them turned out to be Louise, a fellow of the Royal Entomological Society, head of the New Zealand Project Mellifera Response Team and author of such articles as "Developmental parameters and voltinism of the Rufus pineapple flea, *Hystrichopsylla mannerixi* in suburban Dunedin, New Zealand" and "Five new species and a new tritypic genus *Haliplus* associated with 2009 Norfolk Pine collapse on Christmas Island." Louise's face was framed behind a Plexi-faced haz-mat window. She said, "Young lady, I truly hope this is real. I was hosting a wedding shower when the call came in, and I was actually enjoying myself for once."

I said, "It's a real bee."

"Where is it now?"

I pointed to the aloe and she bent down to look at it. She was silent for a minute or so, and then I noticed that she was crying and seemed embarrassed to be caught in the act. "Curse these damn suits," she said. "The one thing you can't do in them is dry your eyes."

"It's bigger than I remember," I said.

"It is, isn't it?" She tried to pull her breathing together. "Lord, I feel like I've just seen the ivory-billed woodpecker come back from the dead."

In the meantime, I saw that the grad students were being manhandled into a van. Louise got out some gear and gently tweezed the bee into a glass box, then stood up. She looked at me: "We have to go now, Samantha. Come along."

Shit.

She knew my name without having asked me. I had a hunch that Louise knew what I ate for breakfast on this date fifteen years ago, and I wasn't wrong. "You'll be flying with me in that helicopter there, and I'm going to ask you to put on this suit. It doesn't breathe well, so you might sweat. I have to supervise some sample gathering, but we'll be lifting off in a few minutes."

"My car . . . my stuff . . ." I pointed to my car in the distance. Three workers were vacuuming it, the tubes emptying into yellow drums. The midday sun was hot.

"Your car will be taken care of. Don't worry. But do put on your suit. Now."

Shortly after we lifted off and the noise had subsided, she said, "We're headed to Auckland. It'll be a half-hour."

"Will we be there long?"

"No."

There was a silence, and I knew it was pregnant: "So where are we going?"

"Atlanta."

Jesus. "*What?*"

"To the Centers for Disease Control. We don't have the right facilities down here."

"For what?"

"Studies."

"Studying what? Maybe I don't want to—"

Louise looked at me. "Samantha, dear, I have the authority to ask any one of these fine gentlemen around us to gas you and put you on a plastic sled and fix you there with nylon belt restraints. As you can see, I've chosen not to do that since you strike me as the sensible type. For now, just answer my questions. Some of them are direct—rude, even—but today is not a day for niceties."

"Okay."

The thought of flying to the United States in my crap gym sweats with my third-favourite pair of runners wasn't pleasant, but dammit, this was the most interesting thing to happen to me in ages.

From an attaché case, Louise removed a (fully collated and alphabetized printed-out) dossier on me. She flipped through it. The noise from the chopper wasn't bad, but it wasn't good, either. "I have all the basics here: your name, credit data, old emails and all Internet searches from the past two years, your work history, your medical data—and by the way, don't worry, we have lots of asthma inhalers where we're going. What else? A list of known sexual partners—"

"*What the fuck?*"

"Please, just bear with me here. We also have a list of all your fitness centre clients, their medical and occupational histories—"

"Louise, Jesus, why do you even need me here?"

"My dear, because *you* were stung. I didn't get stung. Nobody else in New Zealand got stung. *You* did. Now, tell me everything you've eaten or ingested in the past forty-eight hours."

Right. So I rattled off my sad little semi-anorexic list, throwing caution to the wind. I went into minute detail, right down to how many times I shook the cinnamon shaker over my coffee.

One question really threw me: "Samantha, have you recently picked any scabs and eaten them?"

"Okay, I confess, I did."

"Your own, I take it."

"A small one that was on my elbow." I showed her the almost-healed patch. "Louise, this is getting creepy."

"We have to cover all our bases."

As we approached Auckland Airport from the south, I felt about as pure as an oil spill. The drought had been going on for ages. The city was brown and I felt I embodied the spirit of whatever it was that had made the place die.

I was expecting a luxury jet, but instead our plane for the trip was a U.S. military transport craft with a flat grey fuselage and maybe six windows where there ought to have been forty—the sort of vessel that could contain secrets as well as answers. When our chopper landed, we walked maybe ten steps to a wheeled aluminum gangplank that led into the plane's interior, a huge, hollow echoey mess—like the inside of the van my old friend Gary used to keep for his bungee jumping business: scratched metal panels, cords and snaps and canvas duffel bags. All that was missing was fast-food litter and cum rags. A few rows of thrashed grey leather seats bearing the Alaska Airlines logo were bolted onto the floor.

"You know how the economy is these days," Louise said when she saw my face. "In any event, *you* get the clean room."

She ushered me towards the rear of the plane, where she opened the door to a smallish Plexi-walled room.

It was, if nothing else, clean. White on white on white, with a custom mattress to allow for sleep during turbulence. "How long is the flight?"

"Fourteen hours. You can remove your suit now."

"Louise, do me a favour, can you give me some drugs to make it go more quickly?"

"Drugs?" She closed the door behind us. "Samantha, everything that enters and leaves you for the next month goes into sample jars and will be scanned beneath electron microscopes. No drugs today, especially none from your regular ganja supplier . . ." she rifled through some pages, "Ricky Ngau at the chip stand on Ruahine Street. By the way, their fish isn't fish. It's textured tofu."

"Jesus, why is it so important for you to look at me so closely? My bee sting was random!"

I got a reproachful look. "Your sting may have been random—but what if you were, well, for lack of a better word, chosen."

"Chosen?"

"Selected. Or located. Or sought out."

"I hardly think so."

"We're not taking any chances. Aside from you and Zack, there hasn't been a bee sighting for five years."

"Is Zack still in quarantine?"

"He is."

"In Atlanta?"

"No. In North Carolina—a place called Research Triangle Park. Dreadful name for a city, but there you have it."

"Did you see his . . . *clip?*"

Who hadn't? "More than once." Louise cracked a smile. "He certainly found a perfect way of blending history with comedy and soft porn. *You're* already circulating the planet, too, by the way."

"Seriously?"

"Not as naughty as young Zack, but those students filmed you napping, and then they filmed your bee. You're news."

I wondered what my beliefless parents would make of all this.

The jets began to roar and the plane turned towards the runway. A man came from the front, a very American-looking guy: a no-nonsense, raging, don't-fuck-with-me, play-by-the-rules guy who would tell you that he hated women between the third and fourth beer. Louise introduced him. "Samantha, this is Craig. Craig will be in charge of you the moment we enter U.S. air space."

JULIEN

The Armée de Terre sealed off the 12th arrondissement like a bug beneath a drinking glass. Overreactionary pigs—no subtlety, no finesse.

Papist Hag Number One photographed my bee, cellphoned the authorities, shipped them the image and then returned to her prayers. I picked up the bee corpse, from where it seemed to float atop the pebbles. I put it in my hand and looked at its stinger. It was tiny but undeniably fierce-looking; my eyesight is good. The skin surrounding the sting was pink, and it itched, but I resisted the temptation to scratch. When I looked up, a variety of policemen and -women were approaching me, looking hateful and overloaded with weaponry. They escorted the Hags about fifty metres away and placed them in the care of a trio of cops. An officer cop grabbed my arm, as another demanded to know where the bee was. I pointed to where I'd laid it on the bench; from their reactions one would think they'd found a lithium trigger for a nuclear warhead, not just some stupid supposedly extinct bug. One of the cops made a walkie-talkie confirmation that it was a genuine *Apis mellifera*. Then they asked me what had happened. A crowd was starting to grow curious around us. I probably looked like a busted shoplifter. Fuck everybody. I heard a large motor—a truck like you'd see on the Périphérique, not downtown. It was white; one of those bloated, disgusting things fat Americans drive around their deserts while they wait to die. It pulled up beside us over the lawn of Bois de Vincennes, and a group of (I suppose) scientists got out. I heard helicopters—five SA-330s coming in from the north, over Montreuil. All I wanted was to be back in World of Warcraft, not on this wretched planet with its trees and old crones and cause and effect.

An alpha scientist barked at me to go into the fat American death trailer, which I did only because clubs were being waved in my face. Inside, I was shoved into a small Plexiglas detention room. *Cochons.* I asked one of them if I could use his cellphone. They seemed surprised that I didn't have one and a big to-do was made about that. They told me that if I gave them a number they would dial it, but I would not be allowed to use the phone myself. Fuck all of you. And who was I going to call, anyway? My parents? They'd have to pry my mother away from YouTube, where she sits padlocked to a better era and cries while watching Torvill and Dean skate Bolero at the 1984 Sarajevo Olympics over and over and over. Dad? *Diana Ross sings the theme from* Mahogany, *"Do you know where you're going to?" . . . a black girl from Detroit experiences Rome and history for the first time while seated in the back seat of a shitty yellow taxi with lots of lens flare and bad B-unit camera photography. "I am a poor black American girl! I have been transformed on the quickie ride from Da Vinci Airport! If only the world could see Rome for three-point-five minutes like this, we'd all be living inside some record producer's wet dream of post-capitalist freedom!"*

My father wants to believe that the world is easy to understand. Let him and my mother see me on the news. For the time being, I was sitting on a blue plastic stool inside the plastic room, with two policemen watching me while a scientist orchestrated the arrival of several more fuckpig monster labs on wheels.

The alpha scientist, who told me his name was Serge, asked if I was single or if I still lived with my parents. *Still?* I said it wasn't his business, and he smiled and said, "Ah, with his parents, still." Serge was short and thin and was dressed like a bureaucrat underneath his doctor's whites.

A woman asked where my parents worked. I told them that my mother was employed by a generator company called Asea Brown Boveri and that my father worked in the payroll software division—integrated vertical—at CERN.

"Any siblings?"

"My brother is in marketing at Kellogg's. My sister is at Nokia in Helsinki. Could our family be any more complicit in globalization? I was sent to English immersion starting in kindergarten."

"What do you do?"

"School. The Sorbonne."

"Ahh. *Nous avons un génie ici à notre milieu.* Studying what?"

"None of your fucking business."

Serge looked at the woman. "Céline, aren't we *lucky* to have Sean Penn as our first European bee sting in six years! Look in our refrigeration unit—I think we have some vials filled with the antidote to the Academy Award performance here."

"Very funny."

Serge gave me the let's-play-ball stare. "Look, Julien, you're twenty-two and your frontal lobe is incomplete. Argue all you will, but it's a scientific fact. And part of having a frontal lobe still in development is the sense that you have a right to scorn everything around you, but all you really are is a biological cliché. Your brain has a few more years to go, so for the time being, you're this judgment robot and everything you think and feel is the product of incomplete cortical hookups and hormone-driven whims. So don't try to pull any sort of superiority trip on me, because at the moment, what you consider to be your personality is, to me, an unwanted and boring obstacle in the way of finding out what we need to know."

"Which is what?"

He paused slightly here, one of those pauses you look back on later and say to yourself, *Ah, that's when I should have been more alert.* He said, "We'd like to learn what it is about you that attracts bees. That information might be of astonishing significance to the rest of the planet."

"Oh."

"So act like a fucking man."

Céline said, "Just talk with us. Are you wearing cologne today?"

"Do I look like a club kid?"

"A simple 'no' will do. When did you last shower?"

"Four days ago."

"Okay. Are you taking any prescriptions?"

"No."

"What did you eat today?"

I had to think this over. "What do you mean by 'today'?"

"Excuse me?"

"I think I've been up for twenty-six hours now. I don't think the word 'today' applies to me."

"What were you doing for twenty-six hours?"

"Playing World of Warcraft at this place on rue Claude Decaen."

The woman was perplexed. Serge explained: "It's a massive multi-player quasi-real-time online role-playing game set in a persistent-state parallel world that—"

"Got it." The woman asked instead what I had eaten since I last slept.

"A strawberry yogurt. And half a Toblerone."

"Alcohol? Sweet drinks?"

"No."

The two of them looked at me, then the woman asked, "When was the last time you attended school?"

"Um. About three weeks ago."

"Really?"

"My parents don't know, and I'd prefer if you kept it quiet."

They both looked at me. Serge said, "In a few hours you're going to be rather well known. Your old life is over, Sean Penn. Like it or not, you've got a new life."

Something beeped near the steering wheel. I looked out the windshield to see people in white smocks draping several townhouses with white nylon tarps. The Sean Penn jokes began to pile up.

Has Mr. Penn locked himself in his trailer?
Tell me, is Mr. Penn brooding and lost?
Sean, no smoking on government property!

Inside my degrading plastic box, I felt like a hamster. "My name is Julien," I shouted.

Serge said, "Sean, Sean, Sean . . . watch your temper."

The woman, Céline, said, "Please, Sean, don't hurt us. We're not paparazzi here to take photos of you."

"Actually," Serge said, "we *are* here to photograph you." He held a military-grade Pentax capable of snapping three hundred 2-gig photos per second. "Let's see the stinger."

"Are you going to remove it?"

"In a moment."

Céline held a focus chart while Serge did the zoom. Dozens of police and fire sirens blared away outside our crass, bloated, imperialistic Winnebago. From the racket, it sounded as if they were closing down the entire Bois de Vincennes. I mentioned this to my comedy duo. "The park?" said Serge. "They've shut down the entire *arrondissement*. All traffic north of the Seine and inside the Périphérique has been frozen. Every tree, every shrub, every bouquet of flowers and every building is being tarped and/or inspected. They're determined to find the hive."

"Will they?"

"I hope so."

"What kind of scientist are you?"

He bristled for one billionth of a second before replying, "Typical young person—so self-involved he waits for a half-hour before he even asks. Tell me, Sean, have you been told you're special your entire life? Is everything you do wonderful?"

I said, "This is fucked."

"Ahh. Struck a *nerve*."

"Serge, stop bugging him." Céline caught my eye. "Serge is an expert on . . . proteins."

"Oh?" I didn't know much about proteins. "I saw a diagram of a hemoglobin molecule once, all folded and full of twists and surprises. If I ever design video games, it'd be a good map for a system of caves."

Serge said, "Spoken like a man who still lives with his parents."

There were two holes in the Plexiglas room, with gloves built into them, like something from a Chechen nuclear waste treatment facility. Serge reached in and, with Cirque du Soleil precision, opened a set of mini-doors, took my hand and tweezed out the stinger. He put it in a pillbox. "Now it's time to take some blood."

"Blood?"

"Yup, blood."

Blood freaks me out. It's one of the many reasons I reject the real world. "How much?"

"A bucket," said Serge. "Just like Carrie."

"Shush, Serge!" Céline looked at me. "A litre."

"Hey! I'm pretty skinny. A litre to me is a big deal."

"We have to take it now to establish benchmarks," Céline said.

I looked away while they stuck their needle in, but I made the mistake of looking at the plastic bag when it was nearly full. The deep maroon colour was so . . . *liquidy* looking. I jerked and the needle popped out of my arm and blood sprayed all over my little room.

"Right," said Serge, pissed. He twisted some sort of valve, and the next thing I remembered was waking up, far, far away.

DIANA

When I was stung on that cool Ontario afternoon, my response was the same as it would have been before bees became extinct: I shouted, "Fuckity fucking *fuck*, ow, holy *shit* that hurts, motherfucker!" I slapped my arm and the bee fell to the ground. Mitch, Erik and his wife were staring at me as if I were bleeding from my eyes. "You fucking fuckheads, stop staring!" Even Kayla the battered dog appeared taken aback by my language. "Don't pretend to be so sanctimonious, you cheesy, hypocritical fucks."

Erik looked at Mitch. "She has Tourette's."

Then I realized what had happened to me. I reached down and picked up the insect. "Oh, dear Lord, it's a *bee*." The other three inched towards me. Mitch dropped his two-by-four and said, "It's mine. It's my bee. We're on my property."

"No, it's not. It was in the air," Erik said. "In this country, you own mineral rights to the soil beneath your property, but you don't own air rights."

"The moment that thing landed on Sister Garbagemouth here," Mitch said, "it ceased being airborne and it is hence part of my property."

Erik said, "*Only* if you own Diana's body, too. But slavery's currently illegal. So it's Diana's bee."

Erik's wife looked at it closely. "I'd forgotten how small they are. To think I used to be frightened of them. And look, it's been collecting pollen. See—its little pollen saddlebags are full."

It dawned on me that I should leave before Mitch's greed got the best of him, so I beelined (yes! A pun! I know, puns aren't funny, but I love them! Possibly connected to my Tourette's) to my place, where I shut the kitchen door behind me and locked it, leaving Mitch, Erik and his wife gaping. I swept away some cinnamon and sugar left over from the morning's toast, and placed the bee on top of a white sheet of paper on the kitchen table.

We all wanted the bees to come back, but in our hearts, none of us believed we deserved them—and then here I go and kill one. My temples were thumping furiously. I felt guilty that this living thing was now dead because it chose to sting me. I knew I had to phone the authorities.

I began to pray, then remembered that I'd not only been stung but had also just been excommunicated.

I let my hands drop and considered the act of praying. Does praying make my body emit waves like a cellphone? Am I always emitting waves, even when I'm doing dishes? Does deliberate praying merely increase the power of those waves? What is the physical mechanism whereby prayers are "heard"?

I wanted to pray but couldn't bring myself to do so. Between animal violence, excommunication and being stung by the first bee in Canada for God knows how many years—and losing faith in the process of prayer—I'd had quite the half-hour. And it wasn't over yet. While I was staring at the bee atop its white paper, Mitch started to pound on the door. "Give me back my bee, you stupid bitch!" The door was jiggling, and I doubted its ability to withstand a full-on Mitch attack, so I gathered up my bee and retreated to the basement storm cellar, locking it from the inside. This wasn't cowardice; this was me being practical—and not wanting my specimen damaged. (In a few weeks I'd watch archived news footage of the RCMP doing a takedown of Mitch on my front lawn, smashing his face into the dandelions and sorrel, pulling his arms back with delicious amounts of force and cuffing his hands behind him. *Ahh . . . excess force.* Sometimes I rather like it.)

Maybe five minutes later there was a knock on the cellar door. Much to my relief, it was the RCMP, clad in haz-mat suits. Overkill? Through the plastic they demanded, "Give us the bee. Give us the bee." I did. It went into a small box, like one for a wedding ring. I got to the top of my basement stairs to find my house being tarped with white polypropylene sheets. Outside the front door, the whole neighbourhood was being shrouded. For the first time in my life, the future felt futuristic.

I think I'm coming across as Miss Cool Customer here, discussing the Mitch/Kayla debacle, my bee sting and all those goons wearing haz-mat suits as if I were doing a homework assignment on the 1962 Congo Crisis. I'm such a total fucking hypocrite.

I haven't mentioned how, during this whole bee sting episode, a quarter of my brain was preoccupied with finding a way to stick a Henckels four-star carving knife into Erik's wife's pearl-clad throat to clear the way for my infatuation with him—but another quarter wanted to drag Erik down to Lake Nipissing and drown him for being a smug prick and for taking Mitch's side against the dog, as well as for excommunicating me from my little Baptist escape inside a converted pet food store on McIntyre Street—a place that still smells, after all these years, of kibble, especially at the back, where we keep the piano. Erik and I bought the piano for a song on craigslist from a family warring over who got the dead mother's Audubon placemats. They were too preoccupied to bargain. As long as we had two hundred bucks and a truck to haul the thing away before sunset, it was ours. We celebrated this deal with gin and tonics at a grill on the edge of town, where people wouldn't recognize us. Neither of us are drinkers. In that first boozy flush, I asked coded questions about *Eva* (notice how I hate using her name) to determine if they were happy or not. "Do you guys talk much during dinner?"

"No, not since she got her promotion as day hostess at that new Beatles theme restaurant. Too much on her mind, I guess."

I believed that what was on Eva's mind was actually Miguel, the Beatles restaurant prep chef, a known rake recently separated from his umpteenth, a shitty little Latin sleaze. I saw him and Eva sharing nachos and refried beans at Mexicali Rosa's one night, and they *weren't* discussing shepherd's pie or thirty-percent-off coupons for seniors.

Then I asked, "Any kids on the way?"

"You'd think there would be, but we're having problems in that area—sorry, I shouldn't really be talking about this."

"I'm Switzerland. Consider me a neutral middle party. All I care about is you and Eva and the flock. I gave up on things of the flesh after Andy."

Andy is my ex, a probably gay guy with major father issues and a set list of twenty sugary guitar songs he plays at social gatherings upon the slightest provocation. He smells of Rogaine and failure. Andy and I were never much of anything, but maybe it makes people more comfortable to think I'd at least had *someone* in my life.

I found myself telling all of this to Sandra from the Emerging Blood-Borne Agents Division of Winnipeg's Level-4 lab, one of only fifteen Level-4 labs in the world: thirty coats of paint on every surface, with an epoxy floor three inches thick. Marburg? Tallahassee-B flu? *Screw that*—they cleared out the entire place for *me*. I was H5N, SARS-Guangxu and holy retribution all snarled up into one friendly little bee sting that left the facility in shock. And Sandra was my admitting nurse. Or scientist. Or . . . who knows what anyone does in these places.

I said, "Listen to me talk and talk. I feel like I've just unloaded twenty clowns from a Volkswagen bug."

Sandra said, "Not to worry. How are you feeling right now?"

I'd been flown the twelve hundred miles to Winnipeg inside a plastic bubble like a child's swimming pool. "I feel fine. It was good to vent about Erik and all that. Thank you for listening."

I must add that Sandra was on speakerphone on the other side of a two-inch-thick Lucite window.

"Anything else unusual happen lately?" she asked. "Anything that stands out? A new perfume? An old box you found in the attic?"

I had a vision of my house being taken apart like it was made of Lego. It was the one thing I owned that I actually cared about, an inheritance from my paternal aunt. It was an early 1960s rancher, and boring as dirt, but I loved it.

"Your house is fine. You'll never know we were there."

I was creeped out—was she reading my mind? But Sandra just looked down at her papers. I asked her, "Sandra, what do you know that I don't?"

"How do you mean?"

"When I got here, I looked at the guy pulling the syringe's plunger when I gave my first blood specimen. He was treating my blood like it was Elvis come back to life and performing at Aloha Stadium. His fingers were practically vibrating. Something big's going on."

"I really can't say."

"I'm just wondering . . . when a blackfly bites you, it goes *deep*. When a bee stings you, it's maybe the top layer of skin and a few nerves—it's pretty superficial. How much damage can one bee sting do?"

Sandra said, "Zack's body nearly exploded from one little sting."

Of course I knew about Zack. Everyone on earth did. "Yeah, but Zack was allergic," I said. "Look, my father was a vet, so I grew up hyper-aware of mad cow and bird flu and all that. I'm aware of invisible cooties that jump species."

"I really can't say anything more."

"Gotcha, you lying cunthead with badly dyed roots." Pardon my Tourette's.

Of the five Wonka children, I was the only one who knew from the start that we weren't just random stings. Though Harj figured it out pretty quickly, too, and then his insights dwarfed my own.

HARJ

A bee! A bee! You can't imagine what a thrill it gave me to see one. I remember as a child seeing them swarm the jacaranda trees in the harbour or flitter amid the plumerias beside the post office under the high noon sun. An early teacher, Mrs. Ames from Connecticut, a bored UNESCO housewife, had taught us in detail about bees, training us to think of them as friends, not enemies—a smart decision, I think. One could say the same thing about worms. Unless we are taught from an early age to like and love them, they are rather disgusting things to cope with when encountered. For that matter, a plate of Bolognese spaghetti might be a terrifying thing to encounter for the first time. I could make a list of other such examples, but I will not.

Nobody in the call centre witnessed my bee stinging me. I looked at it, and it was like seeing a long-lost friend—the happiness it brought me!

I quite forgot young Leslie from the *New York Times* on the other end of the line. She probably interpreted my silence as artistic temperament, but she finally asked, "Werner? Werner, are you there?"

I told her that my name wasn't actually Werner, it was Harj, and that I was sorry I had led her on, and that I was actually working in an Abercrombie & Fitch call centre in Trincomalee, the capital of Sri Lanka.

"Don't dick with me. I'm on deadline."

"I just told you the truth. If you like, give me some words and I will write them on a piece of paper and then photograph them for you, and in the background you can see my hateful boss, Hemesh, as well as the guava bins at the far end of the warehouse."

For whatever reason, she gave me the words EASY-BAKE OVEN. I wrote this and then held them up to the camera. The resulting photograph had Hemesh's morbidly obese posterior neatly positioned to the right. I also sent her a photo of myself making a peace sign, and then said to her, "Do you want to know something far more interesting than this?"

"This would be hard to top, Harj."

I photographed my bee on the desktop and sent the image to her. "This thing just stung me. You heard me say ouch."

"Nice try."

"I am not speaking in jest. Let me zoom in on it." This was a chance to exploit my cellphone's micro-zoom lens, which could turn an area the size of my pinkie fingernail into a 200-meg file. I photographed the bee atop the piece of paper that said EASY-BAKE OVEN and sent the file.

Leslie paused, then said, "You're kidding."

"No, I am not."

"Huh."

Hemesh looked in my direction and, hateful boss that he is, was able to intuit that I was not doing productive work for the Abercrombie & Fitch Corporation. He yelled something at me, and I told young Leslie that I had to go. I said, "Thank you for expressing interest in our winter collection, and please shop again in the future with Abercrombie & Fitch."

Hemesh gave me the evil eye. "Was that a personal call?"

"No. That was a difficult customer from New York City."

"You're on Midwest duty. How did that call get through to you?"

"Ask the IT department. I sit here, I answer the phone and I sell our fine array of merchandise."

"I'm watching you, Harj. I don't care how much slang you teach everybody else. If any co-worker starts to slack, then *pfft*, there goes my bonus bottle of Johnny Walker Red."

"Yes, sir."

And so I returned to work, stowing the treasure that was my bee inside the thin drawer of my desk. With hindsight, I see that this was not a particularly smart idea, but then you must understand the wrath of Hemesh and his unceasing quest to win his weekly bottle of Johnny Walker Red.

It was perhaps an hour later when I sensed that something was wrong. I asked Indhira in the cubicle beside me if she thought something strange was happening—she agreed, and then she determined the cause: no flights were coming into or leaving from our next-door neighbour, Bandaranaike Airport. Then our cellphones ceased to function and our Internet access turned to an error message. Hemesh was predictably angered as he watched the gods of mischief partying all night on a bottle of whisky that ought to have been his. He screamed at us to remain seated until we knew what was happening and rushed out.

I have insubordinate tendencies, and I got up and walked over to the guava bin for a snack. I glanced out the side door and saw perhaps fifty men in white biohazard uniforms, as well as perhaps a dozen Sri Lanka police officers in gas masks encircling the building. Three of the policemen were arguing with Hemesh, who probably decided at that very moment to do something grossly inappropriate such as fetch a package of cigarettes from the elastic map webbing on the inside door of his light chocolate 1984 Mitsubishi Delica L300. Whatever it was Hemesh was arguing about, he was definitely losing. When he stepped outside of the ever-shrinking military ring surrounding our building, they shot him and he fell onto the coral-coloured dirt in a sack-of-potatoes way, dead before he hit the ground.

At this point, I added up all the 2+2s of the past hour, then made a dash for my desk and the drawer that held my bee. I sat on my chair, opened the drawer to take a look at it, then slammed the drawer shut just in time to see scores of rifles pointed my way. Arms raised, I nodded towards the bee; a visitor in white quickly scooped it up. I was then marched out of the building and into the parking lot, where a Russian Mi-24 Hind helicopter was landing.

Here is what happened next: three haz-mat workers grabbed the edges of a translucent condom-shaped body bag. They motioned to the policemen, who poked my kidneys with their rifle muzzles, and I stepped into the bag. Its upper seal was then twisted shut and I was loaded into the helicopter like a poorly-taped-together package. We then roared off the call centre's depressing weed-choked parking lot. From within my condom's translucent tip, I looked down upon the world. I looked at the piggledy mess of city streets, brocaded and still unmapped by Google—as if we in small Asian cities don't notice these things—and I remembered the silted monsters coughed up by the waters in 2004. I remembered all the things I usually don't let myself remember about my dreams: things that weren't supposed to happen but do, places where anything is possible, places where I meet Gwyneth Paltrow and a big Dalmatian dog, and together we explore air-conditioned castles.

I looked down on Trincomalee and felt awkward and small—a chunk of disgraced meat at the end of a phone line, forced by the global economy to discuss colour samples and waffle-knit jerseys with people who wish they were dead. Is this a world a holy man might deem worthy of saving? What if there *was* a new Messiah—would he coldly look at atmospheric CO_2 levels and call it quits before he began? Would he go find some newer, fresher planet to save instead?

Oh Lord, I am tired. I am tired of thinking of the day of the sting over and over, and thinking of what I might have done differently. Up there in the Russian helicopter, I felt dead and then reborn, like I'd taken a drug that would forever change my brain. Before I passed out from a quick jab of a somnipen, delivered by a young epidemiologist named Cynthia, I felt like the fetus at the end of the film *2001*, signifying everything and nothing, rebirth and sterility, good news and bad news, the difference between sanctuary and its opposite.

It was not the way I expected to visit New England, but I will take what I am given. Connecticut! Land of stately homes, bored UNESCO housewives and a middle "C" that remains resolutely silent. When my military transport plane landed there, I felt like phoning Sri Lanka to order a waffle-knit Henley with double-reinforced collar buttons, in cream fabric (if available) and with emu-coloured trim. Or perhaps I could locate one of my company's many customers and ask them if I was correct in guessing that they secretly wished they were dead.

We landed at the New London Naval Submarine Base, on the east bank of a river near a town called Groton. "Don't you worry, Apu. We're almost there." My guide was Dr. Rick, an American military physician who joined my journey in Guam.

The moment I said hello to Dr. Rick, he nicknamed me Apu, and I knew there was no point in fighting it, so for my great adventure I became Apu. I believe Americans can only absorb one foreign-sounding word or name per year. Past examples include Häagen-Dazs, Nadia Comaneci and Al Jazeera. I am too humble to ask these Americans to make "Harj" their official foreign word for the year.

Since Guam, I had not been allowed to have visual contact with the land or ocean, but after much pleading on my part, Dr. Rick decided that some scenery couldn't hurt and had promised me a window view on the journey's final leg.

On the ground in Groton, there was some discussion as to how I would be transferred into a helicopter. In the end, owing to biohazard protocols, I had to be carried like a corpse, with Rick holding my hands and a private holding my feet. They placed me into a Bell 206B3 JetRanger III helicopter.

"Wait! I never even got to touch the ground!"

"Can't let you touch the ground, Apu. It's the rules."

"But I wish to set foot on Connecticut."

"Too late, my friend. You're going to Hyattsville, Maryland."

Maryland? Such a bitter disappointment. I had no pictures in my head of Maryland. No snow-covered trails filled with rosy-cheeked Caucasians. No cocoa. No grandmothers knitting scratchy cable-knit sweaters to compete with those sold by Abercrombie & Fitch. I knew nothing of Maryland.

Rick said it was going to be a choppy ride and buckled me into my seat. I restated that the weather seemed beautiful— perhaps seventy-two degrees Fahrenheit?—and Rick said, "You got it, Apu: seventy-two degrees Fahrenheit, with a chance of a blizzard. You've gotta love this century."

"Snow?"

I'd never seen snow, and my bitterness at not setting foot in Connecticut eased. Although, a chance of snow did seem odd, given the gloriousness of the day.

We lifted off and flew east over the Atlantic Ocean. I asked why this was, and was told it was to minimize any contamination between land-borne germs and me—and thus I missed seeing the great cities of the Eastern Seaboard.

After an hour or so we flew in from the Atlantic over some estuarial flatlands to Hyattsville and then over a maze of concrete and highways and large rectangular boxes arranged in clusters: suburbia! Factory outlet malls! Now *this* was interesting—I imagined teenagers having sex to loud music and parents with no morals having flings inside unnecessarily large vehicles. All of these people below me with a calm, elegant death wish, wearing Abercrombie & Fitch garments.

Ahead of me I saw Washington DC in a raging blizzard. Dr. Rick said, "Sorry 'bout this, Apu," and sprayed me in the face with a narcotizing mist, and when I awoke I was in a clean, attractively furnished room with invisible lighting and no-name furniture and bed linens.

"Rick? Anyone?"

There was no answer, nor did I expect one. I felt quite alone, and how could I not? But since the tsunami, solitude is my natural condition, so I didn't worry too much. A good rest in a nice bed with perfect air was a treat I'd never known, not even as a child. I tried to focus on recent memories but to no avail. Rick's narcotic spray—and the brutalizing effects of travelling from the other side of the planet inside a plastic bag—had eroded my thoughts, making them fuzzy and hard to descramble, sort of like the satellite signals that come into Trincomalee from the feeds out of Perth. (Oh, those Australian accents! With a single vowel from a female Aussie, you could cut glass.)

In any event, my incarceration differed little from those of Zack, Samantha, Julien and Diana. When the music stopped, we all ended up in these strange and clean rooms, alone with our shock and confusion and sense of wonder.

I thought about the bee and what it must have done to me. Had it infused me with a virus or bug or some other form of non-Harj information—information that was going to multiply within me to produce possibly horrific consequences? I did not want this. Instead, I hoped the bee had put something safe and kind and healing into my system, something better than me, something that would grow and make the world a place where idiots like Hemesh are not shot to death in parking lots and where outlet malls are always beautiful and are kept at a temperature just cool enough to require wearing a sweater.

I fell asleep.

ZACK

"What's your name, then?"

"Call me Lisa."

"Hello, Lisa. I'm assuming that right now I'm being watched by a hundred different cameras?"

"You are correct in assuming something like that."

"Then I think I'll make myself more . . . *comfortable.*" I'd noticed I'd been garbed in a pair of white cotton underwear that I thought unusual because it had absolutely no logos or branding or any other indication of where it was from. Regardless, I decided to smoulder for the scrumptious Lisa. Nobody can resist Zack in his smouldering mode.

"Zack, I think you need to know that I am actually a composite personality generated by fifteen different scientists feeding text, data and voice information into the system's central character generator. I'm not actually a woman."

Fuck. How embarrassing. "Very funny."

"We're not very funny people. We're all work and no play."

"Then could you maybe change your voice? I don't want to lie here thinking, even for one second, that there's a possibility of you being hot."

"How does this sound?" Lisa's voice morphed into that of Ronald Reagan.

"Better."

"Well then, Zack, I'd like you to think of me as a friend."

How can you argue with Ronald Reagan? It's like crushing baby chicks with gumboots; no wonder he ruled the planet for eight years. "Thanks."

"No problem."

"The food here blows."

"Yes, it's unfortunate-looking, but take solace in knowing that you're helping science. You're a *hero*, Zack."

"I'm no hero. What happens next?"

"Oh, we'll need more blood, but you're young and healthy."

"What do you mean *more* blood?" I searched my arms and legs, looking for needle evidence.

"Don't worry, Zack. Our new blood-removal techniques are invisible and painless."

"How comforting." I stood up and walked over to the table to poke the green gel rhomboid on my plate. I took a small taste: a broccoli smoothie. "How long am I here for?"

"A few weeks, maybe."

"I'll go nuts."

Ronald Reagan said, "You'll be helping your country, Zack. I know we can all count on you."

"At least get me a TV."

"No TV, Zack, sorry."

"Some games, then. Magazines . . . a Mac . . . maybe even some books."

"I'm afraid we can't let you have any information in your room that might skew your mood."

"Not even logos on the furniture and toilet, I noticed."

Silence.

"So I sit in a room and do nothing for a month?"

"Let's speak again soon, Zack. I enjoyed meeting you."

"Thanks ever so much, Ronald."

"I feel good about you, Zack."

I looked around me and said, "You know what, I'm going to lie back down on the bed here so that you guys can spray your CIA sleepy gas in my face."

I lay down, and for the first time since the sting, I began to think clearly about my recent past. I thought of Charles and his webcam . . . *crap.* Well, I guess the world knows everything about Zack there is to see. To cope with this realization, I chose nature's ultimate ego-preservation tool: I decided not to give a shit.*

But in my Level-4 containment facility beneath the surface of North Carolina, I was going crazy. *To jack off or not to jack off?* Later.

I said to Ronald, "Drain my veins completely, for all I care. Good night. Or good day. Or good whatever-it-is in the real world."

The jellied cubes began to taste better and better as the weeks progressed. And then, one day, I was evicted without ceremony. They asked me to pick out a few garments from among those lying inside a lost-and-found cupboard—a witness relocation cupboard? No idea. I chose some vintage Gulf War camouflage pants and a wife-beater like my favourite avatar in MarineWarp3: The Blessing. *Best. Battle. Game. Ever.* They then took me to a tarmac and a waiting C-141 Starlifter transport plane. It looked like it came from a garage sale picked clean by early birds: it was scuffed, pitted and greasy. Its interior smelled like a Salvation Army thrift shop—all it needed was mismatched cutlery and a spew-stained stuffed animal.

---

* It's worked for me lots of times before, and sometimes not giving a shit keeps things lively. For example, a while back I went through this phase where I totally didn't give a rat's ass about anything, so just to mess things up, I wore eyeliner for a week, and raggedy old clothing. Net result: chick magnet. I'd go to convenience stores and hurl myself at the windows in an attempt to make them shatter . . . there's even some security-cam footage of it somewhere in flickr world. Net result: chick magnet plus cool reputation. There's a lot to be said for not giving two flying fucks, Mr. Darwin.

During the flight I asked what was supposed to happen now: was I free? Was I to be a long-term lab rat? Could I lead a normal life? None of the military types were willing to give me any answers.

We landed at Oskaloosa Municipal Airport, and the temperature was around the freezing mark, even though the month before we'd had record heat. Nobody met me at the airport—I thought my cheap bastard Uncle Jay could have at least called me a cab. When I got to the bottom of an aluminum gangplank, the plane's door slammed and within a minute it was airborne, leaving me marooned at the haunted airstrip. When I was little, the place was practically choking with planes all day, and I remember my father stealing a pair of Ray-Bans from the dashboard of a BASF Crop Protection van. These days, there's grass busting through cracks in the tarmac, and as I walked towards the road I saw a coyote skedaddle across the runway's south end.

I caught a ride home with a Mexican who made me sing along to mariachi songs. The bed of his truck was filled with bags of onions. In my tragic Spanish, I tried to make conversation, but the most I could understand was that onions are cheap to grow and require little pollination. He then sold me a bag of magic mushrooms for ten bucks. Good old fungi: take *that*, you delinquent fucking *bees*.

Of course, no one in the system had told me that, while I was locked up, my cheeky little getting-stung video had become a global number one hit. My humble cornfield was the most Google-mapped location of all time. My cock and balls drawing in the corn had become a popular tattoo. I was humbled: creativity, you are nectar.

Maybe a quarter-mile away from the farm, I saw the first souvenir stand: a mobile home with some folding card tables out front, manned by an astonishingly fat woman wrapped in a blue shipping blanket and cuddling a pug. She was so odd-looking that I didn't register the T-shirts at first: enlarged screen snaps of me naked. *What the . . . ?*

There was another stand, then another, and then a small improvised community of people who'd been camping in tents like the farm was Live Aid 1985. There were also tail-gate-partying tourists along the roadside who reminded me of the crowds who used to go to the old space shuttle launches in Florida. Nobody was paying any attention to my Mexican's truck or to me.

At the lane that leads to my place, a pair of armed guards stood before a long, man-high helix of razor wire. I hopped out of the truck and walked up to them, but before a word came out of my mouth, the crowd spotted me—I felt like Kurt Cobain, returned from the dead. The guards panicked and were unable to quickly open the razor wire gate, and so I, Zack, got my first taste of fame. I liked it.

A woman old enough to be my mother asked me to sign an envelope for her. My first autograph! So I did, and then she asked if I could lick the envelope shut. A weird request, but I did, and she ran away happy, but others were visibly pissed off. I asked a comely young lady what I'd done wrong, and she said, "She wanted your DNA, bozo—and so do I!" My mind was blossoming with ideas on how to provide her with a sample when the guards finally cut the razor wire and yanked me inside—but *only* me, no DNA enthusiasts.

The first thing I noticed was that my aging wood barn had been disassembled and the planks stacked like cordwood. Numbers had been spray-painted on their edges, meaning I'm not sure what. It reminded me of the X's spray-painted onto New Orleans Katrina houses.

My house itself was unlocked, and every item inside had been arranged into rows and piles, and numbered with

Sharpies. Many of the items were in plastic zip-lock bags—even an ancient pizza flyer I remembered throwing out the morning of the sting. Fucking hell—to put everything back in place was a task that seemed beyond me. Having said that, my place had never looked so neat and clean.

I sat down on a chair wrapped in a thick, clear plastic condom. I was hungry. Would there be food in the cupboard? I found forty-eight of those meals-in-a-can things senior citizens love. Oh *joy*. I decided that the first thing I'd do as a free citizen would be to go to the bank, take out some money, go find an apple and pay whatever they asked for it. I wanted my teeth to make something go *crunch*.

Drinking a chocolate Boost, I walked into the guest room (in truth, the room in which I kept my barbells and dead elliptical training machine) and saw a pile of U.S. Postal Service bags of mail. Holy fuck! I went to one of them and pulled out a letter at random. It was from a grandmother in Michigan who had written a poem about bees. She'd enclosed a memory stick of the poem set to music. I quickly learned that fan mail was incredibly fun and yet incredibly boring at the same time.

I was halfway through my third Boost and my tenth letter when my cellphone rang. I'd forgotten I even owned one. The ring tone was "Africa" by Toto: Uncle Jay.

"Numbnuts, you were supposed to be home *tomorrow*, not today."

"I don't even know what day today is."

"It's Saturday."

"Who told you I was supposed to be home tomorrow?"

"The woman from the Centers for Disease Control."

Note the absence of a greeting. Uncle Jay is warmth personified.

"I'm fine, Uncle Jay. How are you?"

"Smartass."

I asked, "So what happens now?"

"What do you mean?"

"What am I supposed to do now? Hang out all day with my Wii?" Not farming—that's for sure. A letter from Monsanto Corn had informed me that there were still unrepentant gene traces on the property.

"How about growing something other than corn?"

"Corn still runs the state. You know that's not going to happen."

"You've got a point," Jay said. "It seems to me that you now have the best thing and the worst thing in the world at the very same time."

"What would that be?"

"Too much free time."

"I've just had a month of free time, and I never want any again."

On the table was a stack of Wellbutrin SR Post-it notes. As I stared at them, I realized how much I'd missed logos and brands.

"You're not contagious or anything, are you?"

"Fuck off, Jay."

"Language." Then he said to me, "If I see you on one TV talk show, or if you post anything weird on the Internet, or if I see any fame-whoring, you're cut off. Fame is only going to cause trouble."

"Gotcha."

Being on TV is fun. Producers love me because I don't put on the brakes the way most people do. What I'm thinking and feeling is what I say. Producers also love quietly stealing my food litter from trash bins: DNA trophies.

Q)

Do you think the bee was attacking you?

A)

I don't think bees attack people.

Q)

Were you into insects as a child?

A)

Sure. In second grade Justin di Marco said I was chicken shit and wouldn't eat a dead fire ant. Screw him, so I ate a *live* one.

Q)

What did it taste like?

A)

Crunchy. Salty. I mean, there's not much difference between eating lobster and eating a bug. One's just bigger is all. I think of flying insects as sky lobster.

Q)

You run a farm by yourself. That's a lot of work.

A)

Yes and no. In general, I'm too lazy to hold down the Shift key when I type, but when it comes to my plants, I think of them as art.

Q)

Like the big hoo-hoo you cut out of your cornfield?

A)

Exactly.

Q)

Are you superstitious? Getting stung must have made you a little bit so.

A)

My Uncle Jay's the superstitious one. He honestly believes he got glaucoma because he snorted drugs in the dual-gender handicapped bathroom at Olive Garden.

Q)

He sounds like a character.

A)

He is. When I was a kid, he took me to SeaWorld in San Diego, and he got a four-week suspended sentence for trying to throw pennies into the blowholes of dolphins. Now he's found God and he's not as much fun.

Q)

Did they ever find the beehive belonging to the bee that stung you?

A)

No.

Q)

There was a girl in New Zealand who was stung last week.

A)

Apis mellifera?

Q)

Yes.

A)

Cool. Where is she now?

Q)

In quarantine, the same way you were. It's all online—her and her bee.

A)

Did they find the hive down there?

Q)

No.

A)

Anyone else get stung?

Q)

Three others. One in Europe, one in Canada and one in Sri Lanka.

A)

Huh.

Q)

I wonder if the group of you shares anything in common.

A)

Something genetic?

Q)

 Or viral or . . . who knows.

After the taping, I went online and saw the other Wonka kids for the first time. It was like that dream where you find rooms in your house you never knew existed.

SAMANTHA

The enforced neutrality of our rooms was a bit excessive. The five of us were baffled not so much by the absence of clutter or things that might contain germs as by the absence of any kind of information. Of course, the food was bloody appalling—nursing home food that had been blenderized and formed into gelled cubes. Lisa told me I was the first person to ever use this particular room, and I said I wasn't surprised. It turns out they'd had the rooms ready for years in case somebody got stung, and I later found out they'd given up hope of ever finding anyone. These neutrality chambers had sat in blackness for five years.

Okay.

A moment of pride here: of all of us, I was the only one who didn't mind speaking to Lisa, the feminine voice they'd worked so hard to perfect. But then, I'm one of those people who have no problem with the default ring tone on their mobile. I went two years with Rick Astley's "Never Gonna Give You Up," until friends finally did an intervention at the gym's fifth birthday party.

Zack chose to work with "Ronald Reagan," which is very Zack; at one point I think he almost convinced Ronald to speak in a Scooby-Doo accent. Julien chose the voice of a French pop star named Johnny Hallyday. Diana chose Courteney Cox Arquette and Harj chose Morgan Freeman, which was probably the best pick. Harj understands hierarchy.

Our daily routine was to wake up, answer some questions, meditate, donate a bit of blood, go back to sleep and . . . it was *soooooooooo* boring, like a Qantas L.A. to Sydney flight that never lands. When I wasn't bored, I felt like a little California condor chick being fed by a hand puppet shaped like a mama bird—central to the scene, yet clueless.

But you know, there are limits. After a few days I mutinied and demanded to speak with a human voice I actually recognized—if you've ever phoned a large corporation and been stuck in voice-mail hell, you know the sensation. And so they piped in Louise. "Samantha, this isn't good science."

"Louise, I'm going crazy."

"Don't go crazy. It'll last a bit longer, and then you're free."

"How much longer?"

"I can't say."

"You're no better than Lisa."

"Samantha, the point is that we really have to be as neutral as possible."

"Why?"

"Because science is about being neutral, and our results are too valuable to screw up."

"Then give me something to make time go more quickly. That new stuff, Solon. My mother takes it."

There was a pause. "Solon? Sorry, Sam, I can't give you Solon."

"Why can't I see you, at least? I haven't seen a human being in a week. How come?" (I don't know if anyone mentioned it, but staff never used the corridors outside the rooms. This added a stagy apocalyptic feel to the experience, as though everyone but me had been taken away by a Stephen King plague.)

"Samantha, just take my word for it that what we're doing is based on sound science and your time here is finite."

"Right. As opposed to infinite? *Lisa* tells me my family is fine and all."

"No need for a tone, Samantha. Just hang in there, okay?"

"Fat lot of good you are."

"Goodbye, Samantha."

I tried to calm myself by playing Earth sandwich in my head. The opposite of Atlanta would be about a thousand miles west of Perth, in the Indian Ocean. It wasn't a fun month. But it passed. I did calisthenics, yoga, weight training (with light fixtures) and was systematically sprayed with a narcotizing mist every time they needed my body for whatever scary shit they were doing with me. I lost the five final remaining pounds of flab left on my frame and at least had that as a plus.

I thought about my beliefless parents floating about the Southeast Asian archipelago, eating chocolate brioches while discussing the absence of God as though he were a lost hiker found dead at the bottom of a cliff.

And I did more sit-ups.

And I did more crunches.

And I did more . . . you get the point.

They dropped me off in Los Angeles in time to catch the once-a-week L.A.–Auckland commercial flight. Seeing as the security budget for me was zilch, the combined U.S. and New Zealand governments found me a wig and a slutty dress to conceal my identity for the flight. My discharging officer termed the costume "lifestyle-inappropriate," asked me for my autograph and then dropped me off curbside at the LAX decontamination shuttle.

After the weeks of boredom in my cell, I felt like I'd trashed my school uniform and was now ditching school. The fun thing about dressing like a slut is that people *treat* you like a slut. Feminism be damned; a man came up to me at LAX and gave me an unsolicited shoulder massage. And from my brief experience at the Terminal 6 bar, I learned that a woman need never pay for her own drinks if she plays her cards right. Cripes, listen to me—but I was so effing tired of being the goody two-shoes! My two brothers spent their lives getting away with blue murder, but if I got caught with something as minor as the smell of cigarette smoke on my sweater, I was grounded and had to hear my parents' heavily freighted, judgmental sighs for at least a week.

I was given an A seat and thus had a Pacific panorama for the entire flight. At one point the captain asked everybody to pull down their shades so that people could see their video screens properly. "In any event, there's nothing out there to see." I glanced out and saw the ocean forever, some wispy clouds and a sun too bright to focus on—like a snapshot of life after death—a very boring life after death.

Remember, I'd had a month to mull over my mother's phone call, and hadn't yet drawn a final conclusion. It was hard not to stop overthinking the matter of my own beliefs.

As we flew over the northeast coast of the North Island, there were scrub fires all over; the smoke was sulphur yellow and so thick and tarry it seemed that it, too, might catch fire. It also made it unsafe to land, and we were rerouted to Palmerston North. Hallelujah! That meant a mere twelve-minute cab ride home, and I wouldn't have to wait in Auckland for a shuttle flight. The landing was quick, and my customs and immigration processing non-existent. To be on the weekly flight from L.A., you had to be somebody; nobodies don't take twelve-hour flights these days.

I shared one of the city's ten cabs with a gay dental researcher named Finbar, who took one look at my wig and said, "What the hell died on top of your head? Take that thing off now, or I'm going solo and you're hitchhiking."

I did, and my scalp felt like lungs breathing for the first time in half a day.

Finbar said, "Much better."

It turned out we lived close to each other, and he soon added 2 + 2. "You're Sam, the B-girl! Crap, won't the gang be flubbered when I tell them I shared a cab with *you*." Finbar demanded that we go to my place first. He said much of the neighbourhood had been under a white outdoor tennis court bubble for weeks, and had only recently been reopened for the people who lived there. "Your neighbours aren't going to be too thrilled to see *you* come home."

"But I didn't even get stung there. I got stung out in the middle of nowhere."

"Hardly the middle of nowhere now. Bee-52 has been a massive local tourist draw since it happened. It's like the Klondike out there."

"Bee-52?"

"Where Weber Fork Road meets Route 52. It's the holiest place in the country. Where have *you* been?"

"Incarcerated in a clean facility a hundred feet beneath the surface of suburban Atlanta."

"*Hotlanta!*"

"Why do people always say Hotlanta when you say Atlanta?"

"The place is hot, is why."

We were nearing my apartment. Finbar asked, "Is the drought still going on there?"

"Year seven. Third year with not even a drop of rain."

"Poor fuckers."

"Did they find the hive?"

"No."

———

Finbar was right—my neighbours had been forced out of their houses for two weeks, and once they were allowed back home they were besieged by dumbos come to stare at the flat I'd been renting, wondering if it exuded some sort of cosmic bee-attracting chemical. Nonsense, of course, especially as my flat was no longer there. It was just a concrete pad surrounded by gawkers. I got the driver to drop me off at the end of my family's driveway and said goodbye to Finbar there.

I had no luggage on me, and it struck me that it was strange to have no luggage after such a long trip—as if I'd just been dragged out of a Mercedes' boot by South American kidnappers.

And I was dressed like a cheeky slut.

The key by my parents' door wasn't where it usually is, in the totara shrub's middle crotch, so I rang the doorbell, heard nothing, rang again, then heard my father bellow something rude. I opened the mail slot and called to him. The door soon flew open and my father was radiant. "Sammy! You're home!"

A reunion is always nice, so please insert some generic welcome-home family greetings here. The temperature only changed when I asked why ringing the doorbell had ticked off my dad so much.

"Oh, the zoo we've had around here, Sammy," he said. "And those scientists going through the house and yard like we were concealing strangled bodies. That bee has caused more bloody trouble. You must know that they've dismantled your flat. I think they've got all your bits and things in a warehouse in Cloverlea."

My mother chimed in, "But it's a lovely warehouse, too, very posh."

"Aren't I lucky, then!"

Thanks to Finbar, the whole country soon knew I was back. That first hour home with my parents was the only hour I had with them. The press and the gawkers showed up and the camera flashes began, and it was soon obvious that I couldn't stay with my parents. People seemed to think that Zack and the rest of us possessed some magic X factor that could fix them and answer all their questions. Bloody annoying.

So, then, what do you do? Go find a mini storage locker, lock yourself inside and store yourself forever? Fame without the money to insulate you from it is one of the most wretched human conditions possible. I was stuck.

I figured it this way: the one option I could see was to simply wait for the ruckus to die down. If people found out how boring I really am, they'd drop the woo-woo line of magical thinking.

I was unwillingly famous, broke and without a hideout. The only person I could think of who might be able to help me was my scientist friend, Louise. And though I'd never met him, the thought entered my head that I should be staying with Zack.

JULIEN

Until I discovered World of Warcraft last year, I spent my days mostly in my room, reading a series of translated Japanese illustrated novels called The Voyage of the Battleship *Yamato*. I watched animated versions on DVD—it had been renamed *Star Blazers* in foreign markets, and all the sex and subtle fascism in the Japanese version deleted by non-Japanese distributors. Apparently there are new uncensored bootlegs out there. Somebody *please* post them! I *must* see them! I want them to live on forever as disembodied electrons floating through the world's airwaves and hard drives—and there, they will join the newscast footage of me being carried out of a Winnebago in a thick blue plastic bag and into an idling biohazard truck.

Back to The Voyage of the Battleship *Yamato* . . .

The animated version's *"fromage* factor" was high. It was made in 1973—an animation industry low-water mark— but it seems more authentic than today's tacky computer-generated spectacles. You can tell that the people who made it loved what they were doing, even if they were doing it with a minimum of taste and style.

The story is of a small multinational crew journeying through space in a hollowed-out asteroid in search of the planet Iscandar in the year 2199. An alien race known as the Gamilonians are raining radioactive bombs on Earth, rendering the planet's surface uninhabitable. Humanity lives in refuges built deep underground, but the radioactivity is slowly infiltrating the underground cities too.

Are you still reading? I know, but bear with me.

Earth's space fleet is hopelessly outclassed by the Gamilon-ians', and all seems lost until a mysterious space probe is retrieved on Mars. Blueprints for a faster-than-light engine are discovered, and Queen Starsha of the planet Iscandar in the Large Magellanic Cloud sends a message saying that she has a device, the Cosmo-Cleaner D (a.k.a. Cosmo DNA), that can cleanse Earth of its radiation damage.

Hang on just a bit longer . . .

The inhabitants of Earth secretly convert the ruin of a WWII Japanese battleship, the *Yamato*, into a massive space-ship. Using Queen Starsha's blueprints, they equip their new ship with a warp drive and a new, incredibly powerful weapon called a wave motion gun that fires from the bow. A tiny but intrepid crew of 114 leaves in the *Yamato* to travel to the Large Magellanic Cloud to retrieve the radiation-cleansing device. Along the way, they discover the plight of their blue-skinned adversaries: Gamilon, sister planet to Iscandar, is dying, and its leader, Lord Desslar, is trying to irradiate Earth so that his people can move there, at the expense of the barbarian humans.

And so on.

I guess that's what all sci-fi is about in the end: societies competing for survival. Variations on George Lucas and his pasteurized mythologies. When I was still pretending to go to the Sorbonne, I took a class called Heroes and the Monomyth. The moment I started attending, I simply stopped caring about grades or anything else. I decided that knowledge comes from real life and from travel and interacting with others. So I decided to spend all of my awake time playing World of Warcraft. How amazing to see all that mythology acting itself out in real time, fuelled by genuine human sentience! Real life can be mythologically sci-fi, too. For example, my father spends five days a week at CERN, on the French side of Geneva, and is technically only a hundred metres away from its

Large Hadron Collider. Soon he'll be moving to offices closer to the Low Energy Antiproton Ring. If that's not sci-fi, what is?

So anyway, on the flight to Sweden—specifically to the town of Solna, outside Stockholm, home of the European Centre for Disease Prevention and Control—I spoke at length about the *Yamato* and World of Warcraft to the three military-tards minding me. None of them showed any interest in either the *Yamato* or World of Warcraft—so that shows you the colourless pit we call society. I would have preferred travelling in the company of the hectoring protein specialists, but they vanished once I was loaded into the transport vehicle.

I actually fell asleep en route to Stockholm. I'd been up for thirty hours by then and couldn't keep my eyes open as the three tards haggled over the remaining egg salad sandwich somewhere over Denmark. When I awoke, I was in my room. Watch out, IKEA: viral laboratories know your gig—stylish, neutral and beautifully constructed.

You've probably heard about the neutral rooms, so I won't go on about mine. My contact voice was that of leather-skinned French pop singer/survivor Johnny Hallyday, whose tonsils had been marinating in Scotch and nicotine for half a century. It seemed kind of funny, but then, enough about me—let's quickly learn more about Johnny Hallyday.

JULIEN PICARD PRESENTS:

**A Shameless and Cheesy
Wikipedia Dump on the
Life of Leathery French Pop Star
Johnny Hallyday**

Johnny Hallyday was born Jean-Philippe Smet in Cité Malesherbes, Paris, France, to a French mother, Huguette, and a Belgian father, Léon Smet. His parents separated not long after his birth, and he was raised by his paternal aunt, Hélène Mar. His pseudonym was borrowed from his cousin's friend Lee Halliday; it turned into Hallyday when it was misprinted on a record label. He was married on April 12, 1965, to Sylvie Vartan, a French singer. They have a son, David Hallyday, who is also a singer, born David Michael Benjamin Smet on August 14, 1966.

In those earlier years, Johnny was seen as a less than caring father. His career had taken control of his life; his focus was on his next song rather than on his family. Although Johnny Hallyday and Sylvie Vartan were France's Golden Couple of their generation, they divorced on November 4, 1980, two days after the election of Ronald Reagan. Hallyday married a model named Babeth Etienne on December 1, 1981, in Los Angeles; the marriage lasted two months and two days.

Hallyday's love affair with French actress Nathalie Baye began in 1982, after they met on a television program. Nathalie gave birth to their daughter, Laura, at the end of 1983. They separated in 1986.

He married Adeline Blondiau in 1990, and they divorced in 1992. In 1996, he married Laetitia Boudou. In 2004, the couple adopted a Vietnamese baby girl they named Jade.

In 2011, Hallyday's left foot was severed at the tendon by a Komodo dragon in a petting zoo in Dallas, Texas. In 2012, he admitted to his extraterrestrial origins and was delivered to a waiting alien spacecraft in a shuttle piloted by English-billionaire-turned-rogue-supervillain Richard Branson.

To be honest, I chose Johnny Hallyday's voice because my mother went to one of his concerts when I was small, and took me with her when the babysitter didn't show up. It was the only time I've ever seen her display simian behaviour in public, along with thirty thousand housewives all dressed like cleaning ladies waiting for the Number 18 bus to Porte de la Chapelle. I mean . . . I was kind of embarrassed, but to see my mother express emotion—that was something rare.

The fact that Johnny's still around seems unreal to me—as if he's accidentally dropped into our world from a parallel time stream. And while I'm actually quite a good singer, the few times I tried singing a Hallyday classic in the Neutral Chamber, Johnny's own voice shut me up: too much branded media information.

Fine.

Like the others, I endured the daily ritual of being asked contorted questions, followed by bloodletting.

If you were to commit suicide by jumping off the Golden Gate Bridge, would you do it facing the Pacific Ocean or the city of San Francisco?

Can you imagine a situation where pain might feel good?

Do meek drivers drive you crazy?

Do you like or dislike religious people?

Do you enjoy talking to attractive strangers more than unattractive strangers?

If you had to destroy one beautiful thing, what would it be?

Is recklessness sexy?

There were thousands of these queries, and they could get repetitive and baffling very quickly . . .

Do ringing telephones frighten you?

Do you shoplift in your head?

If you had Tourette's, what would be the forbidden words you would shout out in public?

Some days I'd come away from the interrogation sessions angry, and some days I'd feel as if I'd just watched a really good movie.

Wait . . .

In the previous paragraph I used the word "days," but we had no idea whether it was day or night. We had no time markers. I learned afterwards that I actually run on a twenty-five-hour cycle, not twenty-four. (It's more common than you think). Zack had no cycle at all, and Diana had the most perfect twenty-four-hour cycle anyone in the research crews had ever encountered.

The cretinous scientists who stole a month of my life at least had the good manners to debrief me at the end of my quarantine. Zack and the others never received this courtesy. Their governments pretty much shipped them home in orange crates, with a bag of potato chips, one juice box and no useful information. So, yes, once again I met with the protein scientists Serge and Céline, who flew to Sweden to debrief me.

We were to meet in the canteen. I arrived early and raided the chafing trays like a Viking, thrilled to see real food again, even if it was canteen food.

I was halfway through my third portion of lasagna when they arrived.

"Ah, look, Céline—it's young Sean Penn once more," Serge announced.

"Serge, please don't start with that," I said.

Céline asked what my month had been like. I told her it had been boring—and yet at the same time not. "It was like being in a dentist's chair. You're not doing anything, but at the same time you *are* doing something. I wish I'd had a carton-load of Solon with me."

The two of them made eyes at each other and went to fetch coffee. They reminded me of people who show up for dinner who've been having a raging fight until the moment they knock on your door.

Céline sat down with a steaming cup and said, "Julien, you must have questions. Please ask, and if we can answer them, we will."

That sounded reasonable. I spoke between bites of food. "Why was my room so boring? Why wasn't I allowed any books or TV or movies? And by the way, the bookcase they used wasn't generic—it was *IKEA*, from their Billy bookcase series, and not only that, in my mind I was mentally taking it apart and putting it back together with an invisible Allen key. So much for brand neutrality!"

"Who put a recognizable brand in the room? Idiots," Serge said to Céline, and then he turned to me. "I'm going to tell you something, and it's going to be weird, so brace yourself."

"Okay."

"There are molecules that the human body produces when one enters various states of mind."

"Like adrenaline."

"Adrenaline is a very coarse molecule—a peasant's molecule." Serge found himself amusing. "The molecules we're talking about are almost-invisible proteins that are nearly impossible to recognize and to isolate. It's why we were always taking so much blood from you. The questions we asked you were designed to put you in specific frames of mind, and from these we tried to decode your body's response in terms of molecule production. Books and movies, or any form of culture, would create molecules that would obscure our findings."

I thought this over. "What does this have to do with bees and me being stung?"

"Our thinking is that the bee sensed something in you that it didn't sense in other people, either the absence or presence of one of these molecules."

Céline added, "We don't think it was a virus or germ that made the bees vanish. We think it was one of these newly discovered molecules called 'eons' that made the bees go crazy."

"Eons?"

"Tiny proteins we didn't know about until recently."

"Wait—so *I'm* the antidote to vanishing bees?"

"You flatter yourself," Serge said. "People your age love thinking they're special."

"Jesus, Serge, why is it you have so much trouble with younger people?"

"Serge is just jealous," Céline replied. "He thinks young people aren't people yet. I take the broader view: nature gives young people . . ." she paused, *"fluid* personalities because society would otherwise never get soldiers to fight its wars. Young people are still capable of being tricked by idiotic ideas."

Serge said, "By the way, you won't want to go back to Paris. You're only one of five known bee stings."

"Where were the others?"

"Zack in the U.S., Samantha in New Zealand . . . and then there was one in Northern Ontario, in Canada, and one in Sri Lanka. That's it. And so you're a bit of a rock star. You'd best lie low for a while."

Céline added, "Bigger than Johnny Hallyday."

"I'm so sick of that guy's voice."

Serge said, "Your grandmother lives in Geneva. You should go stay with her. The Swiss will make less of a big deal about you. And your father's there all month."

"When do I leave?"

DIANA

A few years ago, one of the girls, Elaine, was late for a meeting to discuss the Christmas pageant. There were twelve of us at the church wanting to get on with things, so I joked, "Isn't it funny that the Rapture has finally occurred and the only one who got taken away was Elaine?" Talk about the dog farting. Zero sense of humour, those people.

You make my nipples dry-barf, you infected whores.

Oops.

I mention this because when I was placed in Level-4 bio-isolation, I felt like I was the one who'd been taken away and at the same time like the one left behind. Explain *that*. My neutral chamber was roomy, but the boredom, oh God.

One thing I did in my head for much of my time there was compose online singles ads. I think the voice of Courteney Cox Arquette would have told me to stop if she'd known I was doing this, but I had to do *something* to melt away the hours.

Ad one:

"I am God's stalker. I know where He is, and He is not safe from me. Once I find Him, I'm going to tie him up and make him a home-cooked meal and force Him to sit and eat with me and appreciate the amount of work I've gone to on his behalf. Non-smoker preferred."

Ad two:

"Hi. I'm always sad—should I be trying to conceal this from a potential mate? Also, I hate exercise. The astronaut

Neil Armstrong once said, 'God gave us a finite number of heartbeats, and I'm not about to waste mine running down some street.' I love animals, but not those dogs that have *Star Trek* Ferengi foreheads."

Ad three:
"Hello, potential mate. At the moment I'm a prisoner in a Level-4 disease containment facility, where I'm fed strange cubes of food and denied any form of culture or media for reasons of which I'm still unclear. I'm not a vegetarian, but I'd prefer someone who doesn't have two freezers filled with venison and game that's never going to be eaten. That's just scary."

Foul-mouthed ex–church lady here. I want to make you a bet. I bet I can make you think differently about your own head if you read just this one paragraph. Are you with me? Here's what you do: rub behind your ears and then smell your finger—chances are you won't like the result. Now I want you to take your index finger and massage the gums surrounding your top front teeth, squeezing out some of the guck trapped between your teeth and gums. Now rub your fingers lightly together and smell. Pee-*yoo*. The essence of halitosis.

How do I know this? Aside from being a foul-mouthed ex–church lady, I'm also a dental hygienist. I know, I know— why would a person *choose* to be a dental hygienist? Let me tell you, it's not like I was at a career counsellor's office one day, poring through the pages of *Career Magazine*, saw an ad for dental hygienists and said, "Stop! *That's* the job for *me*." No, it's one of those jobs people fall into: perhaps you're interested in teeth but don't want to commit a huge chunk of your life to getting a DDM. Or maybe you just want something to do until you have kids and drop out of the labour market. Or, like me, you just got kind of lazy and had parents on your back telling you to move on with your life and . . . one day you wake up and discover you've become a dental hygienist.

Because I have Tourette's, I make an awesome hygienist. Nobody gets away with anything on my beat. *Have you been flossing regularly? Don't say you have been, because I can tell you haven't—so tell me why you're not following my orders. By the way, your breath stinks, either because you don't brush or because you're doing a terrible job of it.* Once I show people the guck-beneath-the-gums trick, they almost always begin to brush properly.

I spent my first few hours out of isolation in a Winnipeg coffee shop, waiting out a snowstorm for my contact person, named Denny, to pick me up. I was kind of insulted that I was being treated as if I were a duffle bag filled with low-grade pot; I miss the days when governments had money. Denny was apparently snowbound on the other side of town, and so there I was, shunted into a coffee shop, its floor covered in icy grey boot sludge. The age of the clientele appeared to average between seventy and seventy-five. My first five donuts tasted heavenly; the sixth one made me feel like a pig.

The only reading available was religious tracts somebody had left atop the trash can, but honestly, I was so happy to be reading something, anything, that I even read the 4-point Helvetica Light ingredients list on an empty cruller box a previous diner had kindly left on my table. The tracts were a curious blend of Olde Tyme religion, Mormonism and personal hygiene—sort of like me, minus the Mormon part. I read:

JOSEPH SMITH
Born 1805, Sharon, Vermont
Died 1844, Carthage, Illinois

What did I want my own tombstone to read?

DIANA BEATON
Born 1990, Kapuskasing, Ontario
Died 2077, Becquerel Crater, Mars

I am a child of science fiction. What can I say?

My cellphone rang. It was my would-be escort, who'd now encountered a freshly generated snowbank at a Portage Street intersection and would be an hour longer. *Fucking cunt.*

I walked over to the trash can, saw the business section of the *Winnipeg Free Press* and lunged for it. I had sat down and begun to read about new developments in solar fuel cells when I had a "blink" moment and looked up. Everyone in the restaurant was staring at me. I'd never felt so under the microscope in my life. I broke the silence: "What the fucking fuck are you looking at?" *Awkward!* "I'm just waiting for someone. Relax, yes, it's me."

Afterwards, a few people came up to me and lamely asked for an autograph, and the penny dropped that this was going to be the rest of my life.

Fortunately, a guy named Rick saw what was going on and asked if I needed a ride somewhere. I gladly accepted a lift to the airport; screw the useless Denny. I had my Visa card and money in the bank. If the airport gods were rooting for me, I could be back in my own house by dinnertime.

Well, I must say that the good thing about being in wintry places like Manitoba and Northern Ontario is that airports treat snowstorms like summer breezes. Rick bought me a head scarf and some horn-rimmed reading glasses. People yammer on about how hard it is to fly, but not in this part of the world: uranium and nickel discoveries keep the octane flowing. I checked in electronically and, with one hub in Sudbury, I was soon landing in North Bay. I called a cab and headed for home—only to find that home was now a pile of planks and beams and plywood sheets in stacks, the only vertical item being my chimney.

The cab driver was pressing me to either get out or go somewhere else. I told him to fuck off, and when I stepped out of the car for a closer look at what was once my house, he drove away. There I was, the sun about to set, the weather chilly, with no idea of where to go next. I heard Kayla barking from the house across the street. I'd very much been hoping that the Humane Society had taken the dog away from the evil bastard Mitch.

At this point, I was feeling sorry for myself. My parents were in Nova Scotia, and I didn't feel like going there particularly. *Shit, I hadn't even phoned them yet.* Well, it goes to show how family-oriented I am. I realized I could go to the dental clinic and crash there while figuring out what came next. At the dental office, I typed my password into the keypad—it still worked—and was reassured by the office's familiar minty-antiseptic odour. I phoned my parents in Nova Scotia, but their number was no longer in service. Okay.

I wondered where I was going to sleep. Certainly not on the waiting-room sofas, which would be crawling with people's ass molecules. I sat at Patty the receptionist's desk and ordered a pizza. Beside some files I saw a stack of bright yellow boxes of Solon. What was Patty doing with Solon? I thought only people who were rotting in jail or trapped in factory jobs took the stuff. I read the box:

‘PRODUCT INFORMATION

SOLON CR®

(Dihydride Spliceosomic Protein snRNP-171)

Sustained-Release

Chronosuppressant Tablets

DESCRIPTION: SOLON is a protein with chronosuppressive features. It is a synthetic spliceosomic protein, a complex of specialized RNA and protein subunits that removes introns from a transcribed pre-mRNA (hnRNA) segment.

SOLON's interaction with brain receptors mimics that of the diaminoketone class.

SOLON powder is pale yellow, crystalline and soluble in water and oils, and is resistant to damage by heat, cold or UV light.

Introducing SOLON CR

SOLON CR is indicated for the short-term treatment of psychological unease grounded in obsession with thinking about the near and distant future. By severing the link between the present moment and a patient's perceived future state, researchers have found a pronounced and significant drop in all forms of anxiety. As well, researchers have found that disengagement with "the future" has allowed many patients complaining of persistent loneliness to live active and productive single lives with no fear or anxiety.

The makers of SOLON® (dihydride spliceosomic protein snRNP-171) have been helping millions of people cope with stress in a natural and relaxed manner. Our dedication continues today with SOLON CR, a controlled-release prescription chronosuppressant medication that comes in two layers. The first layer dissolves quickly, to help with short-term anxiety and time-based psychological issues. Then the second layer dissolves slowly, to help you stay calm and coping. If you think you are experiencing chronosuppressive illness, talk with your doctor and discuss whether SOLON CR is right for you.

Important Safety Information

SOLON CR is a treatment option you and your health-care provider can consider along with lifestyle changes. It can be taken for as long as your provider recommends. Until you know how SOLON CR will affect you, you shouldn't drive or operate machinery or make major life decisions under the influence of the drug. Be sure you're able to devote 7 to 8 days to sleep before becoming fully re-engaged with society. Sleepwalking, and eating or driving while not fully awake, with amnesia for the event, have been reported. If you experience any of these behaviours, contact your provider immediately.

In rare cases, chronosuppressive medicines may cause allergic reactions such as swelling of tongue or throat, shortness of breath or more severe results. If you have an allergic reaction while using SOLON CR, contact your doctor immediately. SOLON CR is non-narcotic; however, like most sleep medicines, it has some risk of dependency. Don't take it with alcohol.

SOLON tablets are supplied for oral administration as 100-mg (goldenrod), 150-mg (canary) and 200-mg (sage) film-coated, sustained-release tablets. Each tablet contains the labelled amount of dihydride spliceosomic protein snRNP-171 and the inactive ingredients carnauba wax, cysteine hydrochloride, carboxymethylcellulose, magnesium stearate, microcrystalline cellulose, polyethylene glycol and polysorbate 60, and is printed with edible red ink. In addition, the 100-mg tablet contains FD&C Blue No. 1 Lake, the 150-mg tablet contains FD&C Blue No. 2 Lake and FD&C Red No. 40 Lake, and the 200-mg tablet contains FD&C Red No. 40 Lake.

I opened one of the packets and took a sniff—this proved to be a dumb move.

HARJ

My time in the neutral chamber was like The Night of a Thousand Craigs—relentless Craig-ish questions:

Do you feel free inside your head?
If I told you to repaint the inside of your head, what colour would you choose?
I just stole all of your childhood memories. Does that offend you?

In the end, we didn't make it to Maryland. The impromptu mid-summer blizzard forced us to go to a different Centers for Disease Control facility, beneath a city called Research Triangle Park, in North Carolina.

I am an adjustable fellow, so I forced myself to make my peace with visiting Research Triangle Park. But what sort of place could this be? My neutral chamber's control voice, Morgan Freeman, told me in rich, God-like tones that "RTP is the largest research park in the world. It's located in a triangle defined by Durham, Raleigh and Chapel Hill, and it's often compared to Silicon Valley."

"Really?"

"Yes, *really*. It was created in 1959 and covers 7,000 acres and hosts over 160 R&D facilities."

Imagine the voice of God coming through a speaker system of such good quality that you might find it in the Mercedes showroom in Trincomalee—a voice rich, forgiving and blunder-proof. I said, "Surely RTP must be home to some of the largest R&D facilities in the world," and Morgan

Freeman boomed back, "Yes—including those of IBM, GlaxoSmithKline, Google, Ericsson, Monsanto, Sumitomo, Krater and Wyeth."

"Excuse my inquisitiveness," I said, "but why is there a North Carolina and a South Carolina?"

"How do you mean?"

"Are North Carolina and South Carolina so incredibly different that they merit North/South designations? It seems California might readily be divided into two or more states. But Carolina? What happened? Was there a civil war?"

Morgan Freeman said, "Carolina was a land grant by King Charles the First to a subject, Robert Heath, one of his court favourites. It is said that King George the First liked Carolina so much that he bought it back in 1721 and then, nine years later, split it into two colonies—North Carolina and South Carolina."

I said, "And for that reason alone they are individual states? I think Texas ought to be cleaved into several states. Texas is far too large."

"Perhaps."

"And why are there two Dakotas? Why was your country's map-making and state building left to cartographers of such feeble vision? Could you not have at least named North Dakota something more dramatic, like Avalon or . . . Heathcliff? And what about South Dakota? What is its true sense of identity?"

"Why does this concern you?"

"I am just a poor man from a poor country, with no family or friends, but America is the home of my employer, the Abercrombie & Fitch Corporation of New Albany, Ohio."

"It is time for a nap, Harj."

"My name here in your land is Apu . . ." Too late. I was sprayed with narcotizing mist and passed out, again, still angry that Morgan Freeman refused to call me by my new name. I always had the subtle impression that there was a group of people outside my room, laughing at me. It reminded me of when I was a child, when an electric eel attached itself to my right calf while I was swimming in Arugam Bay. My father and brother, in unison, yanked the eel from my flesh while I yelped in pain. Much laughter was had by my family, and a local policeman amused us all by Tasering the lamprey to death.

My family. I have not talked about them. Unlike most of my fellow Sri Lankans, I do not believe in ghosts, and I don't think the dead stay with us. I think they are simply gone. If they should somehow exist somewhere, they're sitting in bleacher seats with pennants and megaphones, saying, "For God's sake, forget about us! Move onward! We're all dead, but you're alive!"

My family's bodies were never found, but I like to think they ended up beneath some coconuts or a banyan that used them as rich, nourishing food and a means of growing strong roots. Or maybe they just ended up as fish food or mud. I find myself not minding when I consider this. I asked Morgan Freeman about American burial practices. He would only tell me so much. I would also ask him questions about the hundreds of questions he was asking *me*.

Morgan, why are you always trying to get me angry?

I am not trying to make you angry. Anger just happens to be your response to some of my questions.

Morgan, why do you always take blood samples at the end of our daily questioning?

I want to make sure you are in good health.

What does this have to do with me being stung?

Maybe nothing. That is what we are trying to find out.

I didn't get some kind of disease, did I?

No.

Are those other people who got stung going through this right now, too?

Yes.

How many of us are there altogether?

Five.

Do we have anything in common?

We don't know yet.

Do emotions create chemicals in the blood that might attract a bee to sting us?

I'm afraid I can't answer that question.

So the answer is yes.

I wish it was that easy, Harj. We don't know. Maybe.

Why am I not allowed to read anything or watch TV?

We don't want your emotions to be contaminated by any outside source.

What about you? You're an outside source.

I am a composite personality generated by a computer system that, at this moment, has seventeen technicians working on it. I am within the confines of neutrality established at the University of Illinois, Urbana 2007 Conference on Interrogation Safety Boundary Polarity.

Are you sentient? Do you have a personality?

I can express only as much personality as is supplied by the technicians working with me. As of this year, I require a minimum of ten scientists working in parallel to generate what you call a personality.

So you're not planning to take over the world?

No.

Have you ever thought about it?

Power is for the living. I am a tool.

When do I get out of here?

Soon.

Soon turned out to be about three weeks later. I woke up one morning and was told by Morgan Freeman that my time in neutrality was over. I was offered the chance to go back to Trincomalee or to go anywhere I wanted in the U.S. I would be supplied with a six-month visa and ten thousand dollars. Given the general difficulty in flying these days, I didn't want to lose my one chance to see the U.S., other than from a helicopter or encumbered by a plastic bag. It was tempting to visit New England—Maine!—and perhaps see an aging sea captain eating breaded fish sticks with a pack of golden Labrador dogs, but my practical side surfaced. If I was going to stay for six months, I would need work to do—and so I asked to be dropped off in New Albany, Ohio, home of the Abercrombie & Fitch Corporation. This was apparently no problem. On waking up, I found a visa on my bedside table. I looked at it: HARJ IRUMPIRAI VETHARANAYAN. I looked in the mirror and wondered if I could pass as Mexican. Not really. I wondered if I looked like a terrorist. Not really. Holding my visa was odd: I'd never had "papers" before. I felt so real and so official, but, then, isn't that how a dog feels when it gets a new collar? A mixed blessing.

My triple glass doors opened in unison. Morgan told me to go to the elevator and push the UP button. I did. I heard a *ding*, the door opened, and I entered.

Six hours later I stood on the cold, windy arrivals curb of the Columbus, Ohio, airport. I don't think I have ever felt so lonely, not even after my family vanished. I did not realize I would so very much miss the voice of Morgan Freeman booming from nowhere and making all of my decisions for me. I was alone on a long slab of empty, silent concrete. *So, this is the land that supplies the rest of the world with Craigs.*

I must say, being alone beneath a big grey sky certainly didn't make me feel free or at one with the world—I have never understood what these Craigs mean about feeling "at one." Maybe they just need jobs. Perhaps all of the antibiotics they took as children damaged the portion of their brains that dictates the sensation of at-oneness.

The day was cold and clear, but I was not totally freezing. The military transport plane had contained a jumbled lost and found section at the back. I rummaged through it and found a bright blue parka and two good thick sweaters. Seeing the sweaters was strange for me, because I knew the garments in ridiculous detail and yet I'd never seen one in real life. The first sweater I would describe as wasabi-coloured lambswool tweed. A half-zipper with lime trim probably added three to four dollars to the garment's cost. The second sweater was an oyster-tint Italian cashmere button-front cardigan popular in 2008.

I was wearing both of my new sweaters beneath my parka. The wind was making a gull-like skreeing sound. Where was I to go from here? There were no taxis. I had no car. If only Morgan Freeman's voice would boom down from the hazy sky, I could feel I was in a land chosen by God. I became angry with myself for having decided to see America instead of returning to Sri Lanka, where, if nothing else, I knew some people and they knew me.

I pulled myself out of this mood and went back into the airport, where I was given suspicious looks by an older janitor fellow washing the floors. I had the impression that he and I were the only people in the building.

"Excuse me, sir, but could you please tell me how I might call a taxi?"

"Taxi—where do you think we are—Manhattan?"

"Columbus, Ohio, is a large metropolis. Surely there must be some taxicabs here."

"With the gas surcharges lately, I doubt it. Where are you going?"

"The world headquarters of the Abercrombie & Fitch Corporation."

"Hmm. They'll get a kick out of your outfit."

Was this gentleman mocking me?

He said, "I'm off in half an hour. I'll drop you there."

"Thank you, thank you, kind sir."

The Internet tells me that New Albany, Ohio, is a village in two counties, Franklin and Licking, a little bit northeast of the state capital of Columbus. It has a population of 18,741 and is 95% white, 1.5% African-American, 0.3% Native American, 3% Asian, 0.2% other races. You can see why someone like me might feel out of place in New Albany. As a mud-coloured person, I decided that my only way to remain unmolested or unjailed was to maintain a comical, non-threatening "Apu" personality at all times. I do not think of this as a compromise, because I think I am basically a lovable shop clerk by nature.

My new friend, Dan the janitor, drove me through an elegant sprawl of stately homes, unnamed mighty trees, lush golf courses and forests. So exotic—so exactly what I had dreamed of back in Sri Lanka.

As we neared "Fitch Path," my heart faltered: what if the fabulous world headquarters of Abercrombie & Fitch did not live up to expectations? Dan offered an editorial opinion: "Pretty fucking green place they have here, Apu."

I said, "Yes. The company sought to create a campus-like community seemingly distant from the outside world. All utilities, parking and traffic lanes are blended into existing natural surroundings to create a gracious work environment."

"You don't say? Whoops—here's the main entrance— here's where you get off."

"Many, many thank-yous. I shall remember this act of generosity always."

Dan sped away as my hand reached for the front door's bronze handle. I entered the lobby, and what I found there shocked me: a canoe hung from the ceiling and beneath it a reception desk at which sat two radiant American youths with perfect teeth and torn jeans. The names on their ID tags? Craig and Craig.

They were friendly and polite. When I told them my name was Apu, they smiled and said, "No way!" I said, "Yes, indeed way," and they said words along the lines of "Dude, that is so incredibly epic!" One of them buzzed a friend, saying, "Dude, you just have to come out here!"

Another Craig came out immediately, his specific name being Dylan, and he asked, "Seriously, your name is really Apu?"

"I joke you not."

"Wow."

Then the three of them leaned against the front desk with casual American elegance and asked what I was up to.

I said, "I have been working in a company call centre in Sri Lanka for many years now, and it has always been my dream to visit the headquarters of our esteemed company."

The first Craig said, "Seriously? I mean, it's nice here, dude, but it's not a destination."

The second Craig asked me what it was like to work in a call centre.

"In Sri Lanka," I said, "I enjoyed providing a completely customer-centric operation by consistently enhancing customer service as I tried to gain a better understanding of our customers' shopping patterns and preferences across Abercrombie & Fitch's multiple shopping channels. I think that, in the end, it is important to always increase overall brand loyalty."

My three new friends were silent. Dylan's cellphone rang. He answered it and said, "Andrea, you have to get out here now."

Andrea—a female Craig—arrived within seconds. "Andrea, this is Apu."

"Seriously?"

"Yes, seriously," I replied.

"Wow."

Craig One said, "He worked in a call centre in Sri Lanka for years."

Andrea looked at me closely, as though deciding what size shirt I should wear.

I said, "I do not see why that is so fascinating. We had a terrific centre with high-quality software suites that seamlessly linked all aspects of the transaction lifecycle, such as order management, fulfillment, reverse logistics and supply chain collaboration."

Andrea said, "Apu, you come with me and Dylan right now. *You*, my friend, are getting a makeover."

"A makeover?" Never in my wildest dreams had I ever imagined getting a *makeover*.

"Hey," said Andrea suddenly. "You're one of those guys who got stung by a bee."

"Well, I suppose I am." This was the first time anybody outside the military had identified me.

ZACK

Ever slept with groupies? They're grrrrrrreat, and if you work it right they'll also do your laundry and cook you omelettes. As a bonus, by allowing them to do this, you're actually helping them raise their self-esteem. In fact, you're actually giving more than you're taking. It's win-win, and I learned all of this in my first few golden weeks back on the farm. Zack was a happy camper.

Uncle Jay's threat to cut off the money tap came to nothing. If you're hot, people pay you shitloads to do TV and webcasts—he'd forgotten that. Also, one of my groupies, Rachel, had a capitalist edge and set up a killer commerce site selling Zack merchandise. Specifically, she would extract blood, mix it with vodka (a bit of alcohol helps, for some reason) and then quickly dip half an index card into the liquid. Once the cards dried, I autographed them. Two grand a pop; easiest money I ever made.

Aside from my harem, another feature of those first golden weeks was visiting scientists who weren't expecting to find a Playboy Mansion lifestyle deep within the armpit of Mahaska County. We'd be talking earnestly about my pre-sting diet, my pesticide usage or my ancestry, and a girl would come walking in wearing a thong and my old varsity jacket. The reactions on the scientists' little faces were priceless.

The thing I like about scientists is that they don't judge you, or if they do, never to your face. I talked about my father's meth hut, my mother's love of meeting a new uncle every week, my own exuberant drug use, and they just made notes and asked me to continue.

Wait. I don't want people to think I am entirely decadent. Believe it or not, I, Zack, was once actually in love with Rebecca Holland, whose daddy was a gene tracker for Cargill. At least, I'm guessing it was love. The thing with Rebecca was that she liked getting hammered, while I liked getting shit-faced. It was destiny—at least, it was destiny until one day when we were making it in the driver's compartment of her family's John Deere combine. We accidentally rolled it into a drainage culvert and we both had to get stitches all over our lower legs. Don't ask. Rebecca's brother, Leo, was the state's bronze medal Tae Bo champion. He showed up at the hospital and went shogun all over me, and it degenerated into a massive, no-holds-barred, deeply vicious hobo fight that put me into intensive care. After that, the thrill was gone. Becky currently manages a Curves gym, "the gym for women."

In any event, back home I'd begun viewing my waking hours as though I was no longer myself, that I was me but not me—hard to describe. But if someone asked me to pass something, instead of doing it, I'd think, *Right—how would Zack pass the butter?*

(BTW: I really missed Ronald Reagan's voice.)

I also began reading about Sam, Julien, Diana and Harj— obsessively so—collecting whatever images and video clips I could find online. I was curious to see if we had anything in common the scientists had missed, things only I (or we) could determine. I discovered that Sam was a fox, Julien looked like a snotty arcade rat, Diana looked like a dental hygienist, and Harj looked like a mild-mannered 9-11 hijacker with a heart of gold. A childish part of me began to wish the five of us could band together and become a crime-fighting supergroup.

Six weeks after getting home, the need to connect with them had grown intense and undeniable, like being horny—and frustrating, too, because there still exists no White Pages or Yellow Pages for email addresses. And none of the other "stingees" had agents or personal assistants (I, on the other hand, had three personal assistants: Chelsea, Haley and Emily, although none of them could ship a FedEx box or run spreadsheet software).

And then, late one night—three in the morning?—I was making peanut butter sandwiches after several hours of stallion sex. I looked over when my laptop pinged, and it was Sam, emailing me.

Hi Zack. This is Sam(antha) in New Zealand.

I stood in the kitchen as though processing the effects of a new drug. My online commerce expert, Rachel, walked in, naked save for a pair of leather chaps. "Zack, are you high?"

Silence.

"Whatever. Tomorrow we have a big shipment, and I need a bucket more blood, so drink lots of distilled water and the jug of wheat-grass smoothie I put in the fridge."

She turned to leave and her luscious ass had no effect on me. Samantha had contacted me and I was now a new man. I clicked the chat reply button, but Sam's computer had an ISP scrambler. *Fuck. That must be one awesome machine she's using.* So I phoned Uncle Jay, woke him up and asked him to use his law firm's descrambler to locate Sam's ISP. I was promptly rewarded with a string of cartoony swearing—@#$%&!—the way people swear in sanitized cartoons directed at religious markets. So I told him that if he wanted any future slice of any revenue I might make, he'd get off his lily-white butt and do this for me. It worked; in the end, my uncle is all about money.

I sat alone in the kitchen, the fridge passing through hum cycles, the window open, the sound of the few remaining insects generating white noise in the yard and the fields. It was strange keeping the window open with the light on in the middle of night and not having bugs fly in. I always thought it'd be bald eagles and manatees that vanished first. But cicadas? Crickets? Even blackflies: now gone or going, and so quickly.

Finally, Uncle Jay emailed that the site belonged to Finbar Manzies of Palmerston North, New Zealand. He was a dental researcher who specialized in using stem cells to regenerate new teeth in adults.

Huh?

He was also in the top zero-point-three percent of Kiwi income earners, flew regularly around the world and had recently spent NZ$3,450.00 for a series of visits to an area businessman named toby@manssage.sx.nz in a way that would show up on his credit card statements as a donation to UNESCO. I even had Toby's unlisted mobile number. *Uncle Jay, you've earned your ten percent.*

I phoned. Finbar answered, obviously a bit drunk. I could hear people in the background.

I did a fake Australian accent: "Hi. This is Toby from Manssage."

Finbar said nothing.

I said, "Finbar?"

"Who is this?"

"This is Zack calling for Samantha."

I could hear Finbar's brain swirl about. "Where are you calling from?"

"Outside the town of Oskaloosa, in the heart of Mahaska County, Iowa."

He handed the phone over, saying, "It's for you" in a way that must have seemed charged with mystery.

I heard Sam's voice. It was heaven: "Mum? Dad? We're just finishing dinner. Can you call back in an hour?"

I said, "This is Zack."

I could hear the voices in the background recede as she carried the phone into a different room. I waited to hear the sound of a shutting door. I did. Sam said, "Hello."

Awkward.

I said, "Hi."

"Where are you calling from?"

"From outside the town of Oskaloosa, in the heart of Mahaska County, Iowa."

"It's dinnertime here."

"What did you have?"

"Chicken Kiev. Fingerling potatoes. Dandelion salad."

"Dessert?"

"Apple strudel."

"*Apple?*"

"I know. It was fantastic."

"I was going to go out and buy an apple tomorrow. I mean today. I miss them so much. The crunch."

"You should have seen them—five tiny little things, malformed, pecked at by birds, the skins all daggy-looking."

"What's 'daggy' mean?"

"Dags are those little bits of shit that stick to a sheep's arse."

"Arse?"

"Excuse me, *assssss*."

"That's more like it. What are you wearing right now?"

"Zack!"

"Is it wrong to be curious? Turn on your phone's camera."

"No. Besides, I don't know how Finbar's works. What are *you* wearing right now, Zack?"

"Grey track pants and a wife-beater stained with pomegranate juice."

"Oh. Did you know that the French word for pomegranate is *grenade*, and that's where the word 'grenadine' comes from?"

"Grenadine, like they use in making Shirley Temples?"

"Same thing. And that's where the word 'grenade' comes from, too. Do you know why hand grenades are covered in little squares the way they are, like chocolate bars?"

"Better grip?"

"No. It's so that when they explode, the squares fly off and make great shrapnel."

"I think I *like* you, Sam. And you still haven't told me what you're wearing."

"Nothing really—some generic high-street jumper and dress. It's a yuppie dinner."

"Who's Finbar?"

"A new friend. We met on the plane coming back from the States."

"Did they put you in one of those rooms too?"

"Yup."

"Not much fun, was it?"

"I almost went mad. When did you get home?"

"A few weeks ago. You?"

"Yesterday."

"What was that like for you?"

"Well, they dismantled the building I was living in, and my parents' place is crawling with photographers and religious nuts. But at least I don't have to eat any more of that creepy jelly food."

"You had that too?"

"It was awful. They were like beef smoothies."

Finbar's phone beeped.

"The battery's dying, Zack."

"Email me."

Dial tone.

Whoa.

I looked around my kitchen, then I went into the living room and saw my assistants conked out everywhere—my ungodly amount of corn-fed poon—and the annoying sensation of being outside myself and looking down was gone. Instead, it was replaced by a sense of being profoundly incomplete.

SAMANTHA

Lazy as dirt.

But in the end, it was easier to phone Finbar than any of my so-called friends. I was at that point in a single woman's life when the friends vanish. Finbar, on the other hand, had planned three dinners and selected a wide array of skin-care products for me before I'd finished my request for sanctuary.

My father and I snuck past a trio of photographers camped outside my parents' place and arrived at Finbar's house in Hokowitu unseen. Pulling into his carport, I saw that his Toyota had a chromed fish emblem on it. I felt like I was falling into a cyclical dream that wouldn't end. This was fish number six—a cloisonné containing the words "sole amandine."

Finbar opened the door wide. "Come in and make yourself at home. I just got word of some Granny Smiths for sale out by the Awapuni Racecourse. I haven't had an apple pie in two years. You're my good-luck charm." With an air kiss he was gone, and I walked into a lush magazine spread of a house of the sort that made me shudder as I recalled my own shabby things currently dozing inside that posh Cloverlea storage facility. His fridge was full of good food, much of it hand-pollinated—some preserved pears impressed me greatly—and on the counter sat a bowl of smoked almonds. Finbar obviously had black market connections, unlike my parents, who live almost entirely on chicken and potatoes.

Two hours later he returned with five Granny Smiths, three of which were malformed, and all of which were distressed with bird pecks. "We're going to have to downgrade from pie to strudel, but it will be very tasty," he said. He removed a bottle of vodka from the freezer. "Martini time, and it's also time for you to tell me *everything* while I cook up a storm. We've got four guests coming for dinner, and you'll love them all. Pour yourself a drink and let's get enbevulated!"

Righty-o.

So we got sloshed on martinis and made a brilliant strudel that smelled like a rare flower. After it was in the oven, Finbar led me upstairs to a beautiful guest room with an ensuite bathroom and a view of a bamboo grove in the house's courtyard. Now *that* was a room I could have spent four weeks in.

I washed up and took a nap to sleep off my martinis, and was woken up by Finbar saying, "T minus one hour. And I imagine you probably want to talk to Zack, so I called in a few favours and found you his email address."

"You *what?*"

"Guilty. And don't worry about your hair. Sylvie can trim it before dinner."

I looked at myself in the mirror and felt like a haggard and bloated Wookie. "Can she, now?"

He ignored my tone. "Yes, she can. I've got a guest Mac set up in the kitchen. Give Mr. Zack a shout."

I went down to the kitchen, sat in front of the Mac and quickly opened a new KMail account. What should I say to Zack? I was still a tad drunk.

Hi Zack. This is Sam(antha) in New Zealand.

And with those few words I fell into a dream. I closed my eyes and squinted, and I saw geometric dazzle patterns before me, and then I opened my eyes and I remembered an image I once read about in a book, of two navy men who swore they saw a black sun setting on the horizon in Moorea in 1947. And I thought about sunsets, and how the amazing thing about sunsets is that no matter how many you see, it always feels as if that specific sunset was generated for you and you alone.

I saw pictures in my head of the massive crop failures of the past few years, of everybody's collective fear about food and what would happen when the pollination crisis accelerated further.

And then I saw visions of Zack—his high school yearbook photo I'd seen online the day before I was stung. Some other online party photos told me that Zack was someone with a healthy dose of excess energy. And of course, the classic bee sting clip. How odd that I'd been thinking of him so much without realizing it.

The doorbell rang. I snapped out of whatever zone I was in. I hit the Enter key and sent Zack my eight words. I knew he'd read them and realize they were an authentic message from me. For the time being, I wanted to attend a real dinner party, with real adults, to be followed by a real dessert made with real apples.

When the phone battery died, I realized I was going to need Louise's help if I was ever going to meet Zack, whether in the United States or New Zealand or Hawaii or in a box with Green Eggs and Ham. I walked down the hallway and into the dinner area, and all five people there stared at me with salacious smiles.

Finbar said, "Welllllll?"

"Well what?"

"I knew it!"

"Knew what?"

"You're hot for him."

"Am not."

"This is so romantic. What are you going to do about it?"

"I've no clue."

The next morning, severely hungover, I phoned around trying to locate Louise at the offices of the New Zealand Project Mellifera Response Team; their old listed number was out of service—unsurprising. In the middle of calling, I had a mild asthma attack. As I'd left my puffer on the flight from L.A., Finbar loaned me his. As with many people our age, our childhood experiences with swimming pool chemicals and antibiotics had wiped out our breathing systems. I made a mental note to visit the pharmacy later that day.

I wanted to email Zack again, but I wanted to be in a clear-headed state while doing so. As a stop-gap I sent him a quick hangover alert, saying there'd be more to come later. In return, he sent me a mini-movie about himself and his farm, not bothering to delete the voices of the young women operating the camera.

In the end, I sent a blanket email to the Mellifera Response Team and took up Finbar's kind offer of a trip to Bee-52. It was a lovely day, perfect for a drive, and we didn't see any fires or smoke anywhere along the way.

By way of conversation, I asked Finbar about the Solon I'd found in his kitchen.

"The box was unopened, I hope you noticed."

"You don't seem like the Solon type."

"Describe the 'Solon type' to me."

"Well, lonely—obviously—but freaked out and worried about bills and ecosystems and weather and . . ."

"I don't seem worried or freaked out or lonely?"

"No. You don't."

"Good."

"Then why the Solon?"

"Just in case. It's a safety net. I worry about the world as much as anyone else. And by the way, you check your wig, young lady."

Finbar had made me wear a Jackie-O wig left over from his student drag days. I felt ridiculous, but once we neared Bee-52, I could see that it wasn't a bad idea at all. The precise sting location was surrounded by a square cyclone fence topped with razor wire—maybe a hundred metres by a hundred metres. Stuck in the fence's links were poems and letters and photos and drawings of bees. It reminded me of New York after 9-11, except nobody had died—instead, some form of hope had been reborn. I got choked up as it dawned on me that what was to me an annoyance was a ray of hope for a hope-starved world.

We parked the car and walked among a crowd of a hundred or so hard-cores. I was delighted to see, mounted on two poles within the sting enclosure, a beautiful photo of Madrid, Spain—the other half of my Earth sandwich—the corner of Calle Gutenberg and Calle Poeta Esteban de Villegas, where a group of people in bumblebee costumes were waving at the photographer.

JULIEN

Switzerland was like the worst drug on earth. I might as well have stayed in the neutral chamber, which at least had the benefit of narcotizing mist to help time pass more quickly. The Genevans have these plump, we-still-eat-like-we-did-before-the-pollination-crisis faces. Dark secrets? They must all surely be keeping near-dead sex slaves locked in their basements, with those rubber balls in their mouths, or something else shameful and diseased. My grandmother is completely gaga and doesn't even realize bees are gone, hence her inability to deal with my problem on any level except noticing that there's not much strawberry jam around these days, and that all the juices taste artificial because they *are* artificial. What else? This is where I learned that my father spent his five working weeknights in the Meyrin neighbourhood, getting hosed on schnapps while YouTubing his past (NASA; Velvet Underground; Leona Lewis performing "Somewhere Over the Rainbow" on *The X Factor*). He had also been taking Solon.

To get even a little bit of star recognition for being the Only Guy in Europe Stung by a Bee, I had to walk around downtown and really linger in front of the Mövenpick window, pretending to read the menu. Even then, the squeals came from the non-Swiss.

Worst of all, World of Warcraft continued to completely, unacknowledge me, even when I tried different aliases and used my grandmother's credit data. It's like it had a Julien detector bot and the moment it got a whiff of me, it shut me down. Perhaps it detected my typing style or my syntax. Who masterminded my obliteration? I, the once-proud Xxanthroxxusxx!

My father is not as dumb or as detached as I make him out to be, though I think he expected more (and better) incarceration stories than he got. "You sat in a room with the voice of Johnny Hallyday asking you questions? That's it?"

"They knocked me out during the flight to Sweden."

"How long will you stay in Geneva?"

"I want to go back to Paris tomorrow. Dad, it's so boring here, it's like a stroke that never ends."

"Julien, I think you should go back to the Sorbonne. I spoke with the registrar two weeks ago. The university has given you a leave of absence, which was kind considering you apparently haven't attended classes in months."

Caught.

"Would you care to tell me why?"

"I got sucked into the Warcraft world and couldn't leave."

"The next semester starts in three weeks—*that's* when you're going to Paris."

My grandmother was watching TV in the background; it showed images of Sam's return to New Zealand. She was dressed more provocatively than I might have expected.

I had no laptop in Geneva, and no hand unit. I wanted to use my father's machine, but he was intently visiting Martian space mission discussion sites, specifically a site touting one-way "colonizing" flights. I asked him, "They can't be serious— sending an astronaut to Mars, knowing that he'll never come back? That's a suicide mission."

"No, it's colonization."

"No, it's a suicide mission."

"They'll wait there for the next colonist to arrive so they can get a civilization going."

"You believe that?"

"I do."

So I went out for a walk on Geneva's clean streets, which made me feel like the planet still had money. I saw a woman in heels and an apron out hand-pollinating a flowering grapevine; a military jet flew over us; I couldn't remember what season it was. A trio of meth-heads slithered past a newsstand and stopped to look at me like I was a billboard advertising something too expensive to buy. In the old days they'd have been heroin addicts, but poppies require bees.

My life was no longer my own. I was outside myself looking in, and it was intolerable. I had to connect with Zack and Sam and Diana and Harj. That was clear to me.

The next morning my father said he didn't want to give the impression that he didn't believe in the future just because he wanted to send colonists on one-way missions to Mars. "Julien, I haven't given up hope for Earth."

My father decided to prove this by taking me on a field trip to his workplace, CERN. I'm not a media whore like Zack, but I hoped to get a *bit* of attention there—but all I got were highly intelligent people staring at me as though X-raying my DNA, wondering if I contained magical bee-attracting particles. I'd gone from never having met a scientist in my life to meeting nothing but scientists. Fortunately (or unfortunately), my visit went horribly wrong (or right), and the net result was my being shipped to Canada.

Here's what happened: we were at the Compact Muon

Solenoid facility, where my father had two friends who worked in a big, ugly underground chamber that looked like the jumbo insides of an air conditioner and went on for twenty-five kilometres. One might wonder what a Compact Muon Solenoid is. I did. It's a 12,500-ton digital camera with 100 million pixels that takes 3-D pictures of Large Hadron Collider collisions 40 million times per second. Want more?

There were twenty people with me in the group—a few scientists, my father and a polytechnic school group from Marseilles. The adults were arguing about whether we were technically in France or Switzerland, while the students were discussing Higgs Boson particles and their stamp collections and staring at me like I was a rare animal. I needed to find a pissoir in the worst way, so I ducked down a steel rampway and into a promising-looking hallway in pursuit of relief. I was wearing a hard hat and a lab coat and fit right in. Suddenly there was an explosion so loud that I was deaf for a few seconds afterwards. The blast blew some signage off the concrete walls beside me, and there was smoke that smelled like no smoke I'd ever smelled before. Alarms were going off everywhere. I ran back the way I'd come to find an automatic security door bolted down in front of me like in a James Bond villain's alpine hideaway. And that was when I realized I'd pissed my pants.

Have you ever pissed your pants in public? It's hard to imagine anything more humiliating. Not only does it look bad, but you also smell of piss. People aren't supposed to smell of piss. It is wrong.

I didn't want anyone to see the blossoming piss on my jeans, so I ran away from the explosion and into a corridor that seemed more janitorial than scientific. At least the air was cool and clean. I walked for a few hundred metres, until I came to a door that led into a classroom of some sort, no windows—it was deep underground—just chairs, a lectern, a screen and a telephone that didn't work. I tried opening the door on the other side of the room, but it was locked down. Fuck. So I tried going back into the janitorial hall; the door was locked behind me.

By this point my pants were getting cold and clammy. The ventilators had been turned off to prevent toxic fumes from spreading within the facility, and I smelled rank.

I heard a smaller boom from somewhere in the building, and then the lights flickered. I think most people might freak in such a situation—it was not unlike being buried alive. I simply lay down on the floor and contemplated the irony of yet again being trapped in a boring room.

I had an ancient PlayStation Portable that I'd found where I'd left it in my father's glove compartment years back, and I played Metal Gear Acid for an hour or so, then had a quick nap, from which I was woken by chilly, wet pants.

The wall phone was dead. I went to the door and began hammering on it and calling out for help. The door was thick, and on the other side my efforts must have sounded about as forceful as a kitten frolicking with a piece of dangled yarn.

I took a sheet from a calendar on the wall to see if I could slip a message beneath the door. No way. I had to laugh at my plight—I was basically back in the neutrality chamber!

How long was I there? Two days. No food or water. I felt like one of those New Orleans senior citizens trapped in their attics by Katrina, waiting for the rescue boat.

God, I was thirsty! Forget hunger; thirst is what obsesses you past hour twelve. When the door was finally blasted open by a crew of Swiss police, I was deliriously happy to see them, but they weren't so happy to see me. They handcuffed me and put a black Tyvek sack over my head and told me to sit on what felt like an electric golf cart. Of course I was shouting out things like, "What the fuck are you morons doing?" but they did not respond. Even my genuinely desperate pleas for water were ignored.

We drove in the electric golf cart for maybe half an hour. When we stopped, some Geneva police, in their grotesque Swiss canton patois, quacked about getting me upstairs. We took an elevator up, and I was taken off the golf cart and seated in a room, dizzy from all the motion.

Then I heard a familiar voice say, "Remove the sack, please," at which point I passed out.

DIANA

You can guess what happened. Out of curiosity I opened that box of Solon. I popped open a blister-packed pill, but I hadn't even put it close to my mouth when, *blooey*, I was lying on the floor, choking on my own tongue. The only reason I'm alive now is because two greasy-haired juvies had broken into the back storeroom, pursuing Oxy. They heard me gagging, dialled 911, put the phone up to my mouth and then fled with their drugs. And good for them! I like it when people accomplish their goals, large or small. Unfortunately, they ate some of their loot and were found strung out in the Lakeshore Drive A&W and are now wearing orange jumpsuits and clearing brush beneath those new power lines the Chinese government just bought up near Hudson Bay.

So then, fuck me ragged, I'd spent a month in a pleasant but boring medical room, only to end up inside another boring medical room within the day. But I much preferred being in a real-world room, and logos made me feel like the universe was back to normal. Some guy walked down the hall in a Tab T-shirt and I felt almost giddy.

I'm told I'm lucky to be alive, but what I remember most about my hospital stay were two visits by the most annoying people in my world: my sister, Amber, and that putz of a pastor, Erik.

Amber came first. "So, are you enjoying your fifteen minutes of fame?" Right out of the gate she had to take me down a peg.

"Well, look at this—it's good old douche bag. Hi Amber,

I'm fine, thanks, and fame is really incredible; you ought to try it some time."

"No need to be a smarty-pants. I'm just glad they got you here in time."

"You should have seen the medic. He was so cute that I ovulated on the spot."

"Ee*yooo*. That didn't sound like Tourette's."

"Sometimes I can be risqué, you know."

"So how *are* you, Diana?"

"I have no fucking idea. Honestly. I got stung, they put me in a very nice cage for a month—"

"Where? Here in town?"

"No. The Canadian Science Centre for Human and Animal Health in Winnipeg. Anyway, I came home but my house wasn't there—so I went to the office because I could still get in."

"You could have phoned me."

"You live two hours away."

We lapsed into silence. Time with Amber is always punctuated by pursed little silences. She sees herself as the family intellectual and listens to NPR. Her favourite topics are things like Cicero, Flaubert, *New Yorker* cartoons involving museums and maybe poets from the Indian subcontinent. Amber is kind of like that mineral kimberlite: there are diamonds inside her, but man, is it a lot of work to find them.

She asked, "Have you called Mama and Papa yet?"

"Their number's disconnected." Amber and I agree about our parents, who joined some wacko cult that scares the pants off us. We just don't like being near them, period.

When she departed, I deeply enjoyed her absence, though I was left to weigh options for my future. No home, no job, nobody close to me . . . and then I heard a knock on the door and saw a bouquet of carnations being carried in by . . . Erik.

My first words were, "How the fuck did you get in here?"

"The woman out front knows you're a part of my flock."

"Like fuck I am."

"Really, Diana, can't you tone down the 'fucks' even a little?"

"No, you sanctimonious, hypocritical weasel dick."

"Oh Diana," he said with a star-fucker's eyes. "You truly *are* a challenge sent to us by God."

"Erik, just stop it."

"Your spark is still alive."

"What do you want from me, Erik?"

"To minister to your soul."

"Ugh. You make me want to take a brain shower. You excommunicated me a month ago. Remember that?"

"We were all a bit hot-tempered that day."

"You just want publicity for your church."

"You make that sound like a bad thing. I was there—so was Eva—when you were stung. We're a part of this, too. If we hadn't called the authorities, your crazy neighbour would have killed you."

"I was quite safe in my storm cellar, thank you." A penny dropped. "You've been milking this whole bee thing all month, haven't you?"

His face confirmed this. Later I googled to find that Erik had been on every news venue possible, from Google News right down to the free sheet they hand out on the North Bay bus system.

"'Milking' makes it sound coarse. But the sting was beneficial for us, yes."

"Jesus, Erik. I've left. It's over. The only reason I joined was to get into your pants, and right now I have no idea why I would have wanted *that*."

"Diana, have you ever heard of the Last Generation?"

"*What?*"

"The Last Generation."

"Don't change the subject."

"I'm not. Your being stung is just one more indicator that the Last Generation is among us and we are it."

"I may indeed think that we're the last generation, but it's not because of your religious mumbo-jumbo."

"But you agree with me."

"Erik, get out of here."

"Your sting was the beginning of sorrows. It is one of the events that will lead to the end of the world."

"Nurse!"

"We are like the generation before Noah built the ark. The people were caught up in the cares of their own lives and were not paying attention to Noah's warning. The same is true now."

"Stop being so high on yourself."

Two orderlies removed Erik, and I asked that there be no more visitors. I was still too weak to do much, but I went online to explore the hubbub surrounding me. Instead, I quickly became more interested in the other four people who got stung. I saw how each of us led lives that were deeply isolated in their own ways. I think the modern world isolates people—that's its job—but there are so many different ways to be lost and there was a unity to the texture of all our lives when the stingers went in. It was a moment when relationships with the planet were in full play: Zack and his satellites; Sam and her Earth sandwich; Julien and his World of Warcraft; me with the air rights above Mitch's property; and Harj and his call with the *New York Times*—a coincidence? I didn't think so. And we all know how this ended, so I'm not trying to sprinkle some pixie dust on it after the fact. We were damaged goods—we *are* damaged goods—but we were damaged in a distinct way that happened to overlap with our mutant protein-making genes. If we were albino, we'd have known from the day we were born, but instead it took bees to point out our difference. Go figure.

HARJ

Oh, to live the life of a Craig—a life of the gods! A heady blender drink of beer, casual American style and questionable morality.

The Craigs and the female Craigs took me to their bosom and made me one of their tribe. The girls, they were in love with me in a way I'd never imagined possible. My intimate knowledge of both apparel and the cleverness of modern retail integration were ambrosia to these lovely, ambitious things, especially young Andrea. We stood in one of the hundreds of tastefully appointed rooms at the A&F headquarters as she introduced me to her co-workers.

"Guys, meet Apu here. Isn't he just the cutest thing!" She turned to me. "You don't look like a terrorist to me at all, Apu. Wait—" Her brows furrowed. "You're *not* in a sleeper cell, are you?"

"No. I do not approve of violence."

"Good. Let's kit you out in some pre-distressed waffle-knit Henley shirts. Apu, we're going to take you from Third World to world class. What's your favourite colour?"

"Shoji."

"Shoji?" A dreamy look came into Andrea's eyes.

"Yes. Sort of an off-white, with hints of the exotic Far East."

I began a medley of banter from the Trincomalee call centre. "Would you like that Italian merino wool cable-knit sweater chunky? For only twenty dollars more, the same sweater is available in cashmere. Perhaps a Prince of Wales vest in Duncan tartan with genuine antler buttons? Buy one now and you'll receive a complimentary three-pack of earth-toned socks made of free-range Chilean fleece."

Someone at the back of the room said, "Apu, tell us about your bee sting."

So I told them about the bee sting, and of my flight to America and my month below ground in the neutrality chamber—and then of my voyage to the fabulous Abercrombie & Fitch corporate campus.

When I was done, Craig Number One came up to me and said, "Apu, my man, *you* are staying at our place from now on. We've got an extra room, and you can stay as long as you want."

New Albany is a magical place filled with massive estate homes built within mighty neighbourhoods with imperial-sounding names like Lambton Park, Clivdon, Fenway and Lansdowne.

"Andrea, the names of these neighbourhoods—they sound so exotic, as if they were high-end alpaca coats selling between the price points of $1,500 and $2,000."

"Apu, you are *so* adorable. I could eat you up right here and now."

I thought, *My, this young lady travels certainly quickly, from zero to frisky, and I've never even met her parents.*

Under a big, warm sun, we drove to an area called Market Square. It boasted a Starbucks, the Chocolate Octopus candy company and the Rusty Bucket Corner Tavern. "That's my hangout," said Andrea. "We have a bunch of famous people who live here in New Albany, too."

"Who might they be?"

"Former race driver and racing team owner Bobby Rahal, as well as Leslie Wexner, the founder of Limited Brands. I'm hungry."

"Oh my."

"Cool, huh?"

"You are very lucky to have such prosperity and access to so much gasoline."

"We kind of run the planet here. It comes with the turf. Let's eat. I'm starving."

We went into a restaurant and Andrea ordered no-fat, no-carb nachos for herself, while I ordered a vegetarian platter. She bought me a beer that was both brewed and bottled in Mexico. I thanked her but kept my mouth shut—why on earth would someone choose a beverage made in Mexico? When it arrived, it sat on the table and I stared at it as though it were from the Dark Ages. People want America, not Mexico. Well, maybe at least the *idea* of America . . . America before the year 2000.

Andrea seemed to know everybody in the restaurant and was talking with people from all sides. Me? I was drunk on the knowledge that a girl as beautiful as Andrea chose to sit with me in a beautiful restaurant. Then my picture appeared on the TV above the bar area. No one there could have imagined that the gentleman in the photo was me, as the gentleman in that photo was standing in Trincomalee and sweating heavily while wearing a wife-beater shirt covered in duck's blood after having helped a neighbour press the bird for a delicious religious feast. Even I did not believe I was me at that point. And I didn't need a beer to get drunk. Life had done that for me. I had (to use a term favoured by the Craigs) "peaked."

My afternoon with Andrea was sadly cut short by her appointments for a bikini wax and a chakra alignment. She dropped me off at the Craigs' place—a miniature White House with columns and a lawn of uniform green, free of any weedy blemishes. I bent down to touch it with my hands—it was soft, like cold fur.

At the front door stood Craig Number One, wearing madras Bermuda shorts (Chesapeake blue with Cherokee red and Sacramento yellow bands) and an XXL acid-washed T-shirt bearing the name of a fictitious football team. *Apu! My man! Good timing! The party's just beginning! Let me show you your new room!*

Do Craigs always put exclamation marks at the end of everything they say? In any event, just at that moment, one of those large American mobile homes—a Winnebago—drove up the crescent-shaped driveway and parked by the front door, and a dozen more Craigs emerged. The party had begun. I was not, however, so hypnotized by the Craigs that I did not recognize that moment as one of temptation. I knew I could either accept or reject the house on the hill and the fun within—life does not throw a person many moments where the fork in the road is so clearly evident. For once, I decided I was going to take the less scrupulous path.

The low road I had chosen was what the Craigs called a "kegger," drinking copious amounts of Czech lager and placing ever more numbers of exclamation marks at the end of everything they shouted at me and at each other.

"Long live Aberzombie & Feltch!! Woohoo!"

"Apu, you're the *best*!!"

"The best at what?"

"Man, you've just gotta love this guy!!"

Another Craig brought in what he called a doobie and lit it. "Monster ganja, Apu!!"

I was horrified: *drugs.* "I am sorry, Craig, but I cannot partake of your doobie—I am a guest in your country and do not wish to be deported. Also, I come from a land of strict drug laws and I have a lifelong fear of becoming bum candy within the Sri Lankan penal system. I'm sure your prisons cannot be much better."

"More for us, then, dude!!"

I looked around for Andrea, who'd promised to come. I very much wished to discuss with her my theories on how to keep the inventories of B- and C-level stores fully charged with as many sizes and styles as possible without engendering undue returns of off-size garments.

That, and I thought she might wish to be carnal with me.

Increasingly large numbers of increasingly drunk he-Craigs and she-Craigs came up to me and made buzzing noises and pretended to sting me. Almost everyone was recording me on some sort of device, and a shadow crept over me, a shadow called . . . *vlog*.

I asked my new friends if the party was being vlogged in real time, and their response told me that a life without vlogging was unthinkable. The Craigs also showed me the cellphone images of me while I was speaking with Leslie from the *New York Times*—as well as the dead bee from that bizarre sting that happened to me in some other life. I had reincarnated while still inside my own body.

My old office: the clutter and its sad cardboard cubicle partitions, the guava bin at the back now a beige clot of pixels on a fuzzy screen. I recalled its smells: incense and the scorch of rubber military plane tires hitting the runway's tarmac; Hemesh's dismal Adidas cologne and the peanut butter and rice cakes I kept in my drawer as lunchtime rewards for when I upsold over ten units of anything priced more than $19.99.

This was when Andrea arrived. I noticed that she was having a heated discussion with a dozen or so people just outside the door who were definitely *not* Craigs. I went over to view these people more closely, and when they saw me, they screamed, then ran towards me in a typhoon of need and desperation.

Andrea was furious. "Bloody hell, who posted tonight's party online?"

Everybody had.

"Get these fucking cud-chewing hicks off of Apu." Andrea orchestrated the removal of non-Craigs from my body. We looked and saw dozens more non-Craigs walking up the driveway like movie zombies. One non-Craig drove an ancient Volvo onto the majestic weedless lawn, branding tire skid marks on its green fur. I climbed up the baronial main staircase. Its carpeting was so deep and lush that I felt I was walking the expensive all-wool gold-card-customers-only version of the front lawn.

I sat on my bed and looked at the chest of drawers that was in my room. I wondered what I could possibly put into it, aside from my stylish new wardrobe. In Sri Lanka, a dog in a doghouse owned more than I did. Could I ever be a Craig? No. A person must be born into Craigdom, with its multiple ski holidays, complex orthodontia, proper nutrition and casual, healthy view of recreational sex.

My mouth twisted unpleasantly—the taste of Czech lager had turned sour. I went to brush my teeth. I opened the mirrored door of my bathroom cupboard to find two shelves heavily stocked with Solon.

Andrea's voice came from behind me. "Don't be shocked, Apu."

I had never actually seen Solon before, though I knew it was that year's new wonder drug. The evil Hemesh once discussed it, calling it a drug for spinsters and convicts. "My old boss said Solon was for people who did not want to think of the future."

Andrea smiled. "Sort of. You live in a constant present. It makes life more intense. You're not needy. You don't stress about things. You can take people or leave them. Solon turns you from a dog into a cat."

"But to not think of the future? All of you smart and rich young people—whose future could be more charming and golden?"

"The future? Not for me. Not for us. I'm happy to think about next year's product lines, but I don't want to think about next year's web headlines and enter a doom spiral." She came close to me, and I could feel the heat from her body radiating through her blouse. She smelled like apricots. "Wouldn't want *that*, would we?"

"*All* of you take Solon?"

"*Absolutely.*"

I hesitate to say this, but at that point she dragged me over to the bed and straddled me. I was feeling . . . *heightened.* This was the first time I had ever—well, you can understand. I had always imagined it would be with the Vietnamese girl who works at the naan stall beside the Vespa repairman in the local farmers' market.

"Andrea, this is so . . ."

"It's the first time for you?"

"I am perhaps not a man of the world . . ."

"Oh, be quiet."

We had started to kiss—*bliss*—when the door swung open. Craig Number One: "Christ, it's *Dawn of the Dead* out there, Apu. Those people want your blood. We have to get you out of here."

"Where will I—?"

"Out the window! Come on, Apu, *schnell!*"

ZACK

The apple was delicious. It snapped cleanly to my bite, was crisp without being hard, and was oh so juicy. I sat in the truck's cab, savouring its tart, pear-like notes. It was a Braeburn variety that had been hand-pollinated in a boutique apple ranch in Southern Oregon. Braeburns had once been an important commercial apple variety. They had originated in New Zealand in the 1950s, and by the last decades of the twentieth century had been planted in all the major apple-growing regions of the world. Braeburns once accounted for forty percent of the apple production of New Zealand. Even in Washington State, the largest apple-producing area in the U.S., where Red Delicious and Golden Delicious had always held sway, Braeburns had been in the top five varieties grown, prior to the pollination crisis.

The parallels between the dildo-ization of corn and the crunchification of apples are hard to miss. Braeburns grew quickly, produced heavily and stored well. Best of all, they shipped without bruising. At a time when consumers were starting to look for something more exotic in their weekly shopping, Braeburn was the right apple at the right time. Unfortunately, when the bees vanished, they were totally fucked.

I finished my Braeburn and stashed the core in the glove compartment and then squandered my generous gasoline credits driving from nowhere to nowhere, watching the listless small clouds in the sky. They reminded me of my appendix floating in a rubbing alcohol–filled mayonnaise jar when I was ten.

I saw a dozen bee-themed mailboxes and fields of grass without flowers, no hawkweed or wild yarrow or blue vervain; my mission became to collect a bouquet for my hard-working harem of raging she-beasts, even though this made me feel hypocritical, as, since I talked with Sam, I'd just stopped being into them. I drove and drove, but all I could find were dandelions, efficient self-pollinators that basically reproduce through floral masturbation. Even flowers have their scuzzy side.

I came home empty-handed, but that was moot, as those girls who remained looked at me with the enthusiasm teenagers feel for summer school. They were clearing out. Rachel had already packed most of her things onto a truck bed and was just loading her rationed gas canister into the truck's strongbox when I got home.

"Rachel?"

"Save it for your Aussie friend, Sam. We're outta here."

"She's Kiwi, not Aussie. Where are you guys going?"

"To find someone who thinks of us as special. That's all *any* girl wants, Zack."

"But all of you *are* special to me—"

Rachel shushed me. "No need to phone it in, Zack."

End of an era.

SAMANTHA

Hello earth!

It was as Finbar and I drove home from our day trip that I had my first big out-of-body event—in one swoop I was up above the car, watching Finbar and myself. I knew that it was me in the passenger seat, yet all the strings had been cut between me and . . . *me*. I was dead, yet alive; alive, yet dead. I thought, *Cripes, is this the afterlife? If so, I've screwed up royally.* Was I a ghost? From my aerial viewpoint, I tried to see if I had arms, and when I couldn't see any, I freaked. I remembered a TV show where the hero is immortal and is stabbed and shot but always survives. But what if he got vaporized in an atomic blast? Technically, he'd still have to be immortal, right? But his problem is that he's now nothing but dust. Do the dusty scraps and bits of rubble from his body magically come together from the jet stream and make him a fresh new hero again? Does he rise from the ashes? Or does his spirit still live, except now he's screwed because he has no body in which to put himself, so he becomes a disembodied entity blanketing the planet, everywhere and nowhere, like ozone.

And then I was back in Finbar's car and the moment was over. Finbar looked at me and asked if I was okay. I gave him a patently fake yes, and he didn't push it. "Home in twenty minutes," said the dashboard, using the voice of Peppermint Patty from the old Charlie Brown cartoons.

When we got back to his place, I ran to the computer and called Zack while linking my camera into the house's wireless system.

"Sam?"

"Zack."

"Hi."

"Hi. Did you buy your apple?"

"You remembered! It was crisp and juicy, thank you. It was a Braeburn."

"Braeburns? My uncle used to grow them. I wrote a Braeburn essay almost every year going through school."

"You did?"

"I did. Braeburns were one of the first 'bi-coloured' apple varieties, a trait that in the 1990s came to be essential for sales success. The first wave of supermarket apple varieties were either bright red Red Delicious or shades of solid yellow or green like Golden Delicious and Granny Smiths. But the Braeburn had modern colouring and a sweet but never sugary flavour that made it first of the new-wave of modern apple varieties."

"I'm impressed." Zack then sent me a link, and I watched Harj at a house party with hundreds of Aberzombie & Felch staffers somewhere in Ohio.

"*What?*"

"That's what I said."

Harj was walking up a staircase, dressed like a Fitch clone—he certainly didn't look like the guy in the photos from the *New York Times*.

"*That's Harj?*"

"It is. They've made him over and christened him Apu."

"How on earth did he end up with them?"

"No idea."

There was a pipping sound on our connection, a sound that the world had gotten used to since the Americans stopped paying their satellite bills to the Chinese—the sound of disconnection. "*Zack call me when—*"

VeeeeeeeeEEEEp!

Dial tone.

Silence.

Bloody hell.

Doorbell.

I opened the door to find Louise from the Project Mellifera Response Team on Finbar's steps.

"Hello, Sam. How are you?"

"I'm doing okay. Do you want to come in?"

"Sure." Louise doffed her coat and looked around. "Nice place."

"It is." I went to the computer. "You're never going to believe who I was just online chatting with."

"Who?"

"Zack."

"Good. That saves me some time searching around. The global Response Team wants to get you and the four others together."

"Why?"

"Research, I imagine. This comes from the top. I'm just following orders."

JULIEN

The black hood was removed from my face, and before me was . . . *Serge?*

"How was your coma, Sean Penn?"

"Shit. How long was I out?"

Serge's expression implied bad news. "It's been three months, Julien."

My face collapsed and he burst out laughing. "Sorry, I couldn't resist. You've been out for five minutes. Drink some orange juice, and when you're done that, we'll get some potato salad and some wurst in you."

A purse-lipped woman gave me a carton and a coffee mug. The orange juice was real. I said, "This is real orange juice. Who's paying for it? My father will freak if he gets the bill. He's an accountant. This is Switzerland."

"Don't worry about it."

"What's going on—am I under arrest?"

"No, you're not under arrest. You're in my care, and we're going on a trip together."

"Where to?"

"Haida Gwaii."

"Haida *what?*"

Serge said, "It's a remote island off the western Canadian coast—near the southern tip of the Alaska panhandle."

Haida Gwaii? Canada? Alaska? Antarctica? He might as well have said we were visiting the moon.

I shrugged. "At least I won't have to go back to the Sorbonne."

Serge handed me a plate of food. I ate it like a dog eating from a bowl. When I'd taken the edge off my hunger, I asked, "So why are we going to this Gwaii place? What's there?"

Serge said, "It's the site of the last known active bee's nest. The others will be there, too. Zack and Sam and Harj and Diana."

"When do we leave?"

"After you eat."

"What about my stuff?"

"You don't have any stuff."

He was right. I owned nothing. The contents of my room had been taken away and had yet to be returned.

I finished the last of my food. "Let's ditch this dump."

Crossing the pole in a military transport plane was a new experience for me. I stayed up in the cockpit for much of the flight, curious to see the soot lines the Russians had drawn— crazy zigzagging patterns of carbon stripes on the remaining ice packs, soaking up heat, accelerating ice breakup to create new shipping routes. The pilot said, "The carbon speeds up iceberg calving by a factor of a thousand."

As I looked down on the world, I had a fleeting sensation of mastery over my universe. I felt like I was helping the SS *Yamato* flee a destroyed planet in pursuit of a new home amidst an overwhelming darkness . . .

The *Yamato* and her crew—aided by an antimatter woman, Teresa of Telezart [known as Trelaina in the dubbed English version]—face the onslaught of the Comet Empire, a civilization from the Andromeda Galaxy that seeks to conquer Earth, led by the Great Prince Zordar.

The Comet Empire has restored to life Earth's greatest enemy, the Gamilonians' leader, Desslar, who is eager for revenge.

After a massive battle that destroys both Earth and Comet Empire forces, the *Yamato* crew defeats Zordar's, but at the cost of the ship and their lives.

Finally, my life was a story. My days would no longer feel like a video game that resets to zero every time I wake up, and then begs for coins.

DIANA

I arrived in Haida Gwaii a few hours after Serge and Julien.
Apparently, Serge had been instrumental in landing us all in
our neutral chambers—which at the time seemed like a
good thing. And he was also pretty hot, and we were on an
island, soooooo . . . *fuck me ragged, Johnny Bravo*. Julien, on the
other hand, made very little impression on me, nor I on him:
Annoying baby dumbfuck.

"Nice to meet you, Diana."

He had a generic European accent and was ill-dressed for
the sheets of rain that greeted our arrival and our subse-
quent piling into an ancient Carter-era pickup truck. "Learn
to coordinate your clothes, dipshit. The bees chose you?"

"Yes, they did."

We drove to the site of the last known active beehive,
which was now a UNESCO World Heritage site. It was in a
mossy region on the north coast, just south of the Sangan
River, where the wet peat soil drowns the roots of ever-
greens. Scientists and wannabe shamans had long ago picked
the site clean of dirt, gravel and rocks.

This strangely lifeless circle rested within a landscape that
was not unlike a six-foot-deep sponge cake. Serge told us that
the bordering forest has the highest density of living organ-
isms per square foot of any place on earth, and that was easy
to believe. Within that forest, from all directions—up, down
and sideways—life squished out like a Play-Doh Fun Factory.
We stood quietly, and I felt I could hear the forest growing. We
heard a raven's *chalk-chalk* cluck.

In any event, nature wasn't as novel an experience for me as it was for Julien, who seemed to have been born inside a video arcade. In the wilderness of our new island home, he flip-flopped from awe to boredom to awe to boredom, finally settling on petulance.

We were staying in the small town of Masset, population 770, in one of many government-built houses left behind when the Canadian military decommissioned a radar facility in the 1980s. Since then, the buildings within their untreed lots had variously stood empty, been made over by hippies, been vandalized, been burned down, been converted into salmon smokeries and, in the case of our house, been given just enough care throughout the years to ensure inhabitability. It could have been a house in my neighbourhood in Northern Ontario; to Julien, it was no better than a crack den. He promptly hogged the best room—"the best," in this case, having a view of a snippet of ocean; my window looked out onto the charcoaled stubs of a similar house that, to judge by the growth of brambles and huckleberry, had burned down before 9-11.

"Oh, Diana," Julien said, "we're going to be living like farm animals."

"Don't whine. We have everything we need." Though the place did resemble a halfway house furnished with two hundred dollars and a dream that died en route to the thrift store. "Julien, try to think of this as an adventure."

We bought fish from the locals while we waited for a supply barge to make the trek from the coast. These locals were all members of the Haida tribe (non-Haida had been given the boot some years earlier), and they tolerated us only because Serge had persuaded them that our presence might, in some way, bring back the bees. In any event, their feelings were made clear when they showed up around sunset that first night and examined everything in our house, like CSI techs looking for evidence. "They're looking for Solon," said Serge. "It's banned here."

"Really? How come?"

"Because once you take Solon, you stop caring about the tribe."

"Really?"

"Really."

After my overwhelming reaction to even the smell of its blister packaging, I was happy that it was banned from the island.

In those first few days, all we did was walk around the village area, trying not to attract too much attention to ourselves. Most of Masset's dozen or so stores were shut down, and along the wide streets, crows and ravens loitered like bored teenagers. The Haida were trying to return to their older way of life, fishing and hunting. At the end of a small street, where a co-op grocery store once stood, were racks of skinned Sitka deer awaiting conversion into pemmican. An introduced species, the Sitka deer roamed the island, multiplied like Norway rats and were a delicious, readily available treat.

After a week, Serge came down to the beach, where Julien and I were skipping stones on an ocean that had turned eerily glassy, as the Aleutian currents rip past the islands like steel wool. "Zack and Sam will be joining us tomorrow," he said.

"Really?"

"Really."

That night we celebrated with deer stew and dandelion wine, got a bit drunk and then, out of boredom, decided to search every nook of our house for clues to who had lived in it before us. At the bottom of the bathroom drawer, we found an ancient calcified toothpaste tube containing Tweety Bird's Berrylicious Looney Tunes toothpaste, with clinically proven fluoride protection.

"And look," said Julien. "It comes in a 'no-mess stand-up tube.'"

We locked eyes.

We looked back at Tweety's preposterous body and head.

We locked eyes once more.

I said, "Let's get right to the point. Tweety Bird: gay or straight?"

"A raging homo, I think. Or at least a eunuch."

"Julien, we haven't even established if Tweety Bird is a boy bird or a girl bird."

"Good point. I used to think boy, but now that you ask directly, I don't know. A female-to-male transsexual, most likely. Is it possible for birds to experience gender dysphoria?"

"This may be the first known incident. What species of bird is Tweety supposed to be, anyway?"

"A canary?"

"A canary, sure—if you're wasted on peyote."

"Tweety does have a hydrocephalic skull. And that voice . . ." Julien tried doing an impression, and it wasn't pretty.

"Tweety Bird is just plain spooky," I said.

We stared at the toothpaste tube some more. Then Julien said, "Gender and sexuality are kind of irrelevant with Tweety Bird, because it's impossible to imagine him/her having sex, anyway."

"Hot wild-assed monkey sex."

"Sex with *toys*."

It was a nice moment. A bonding moment. So we finished the dandelion wine and then Julien began rambling about a Japanese sci-fi cult he's into, the Battlestar Tomato. My eyes glazed over. Then he began telling me about that online world he was addicted to, which accelerated my passing out drunk. I hadn't done that in a long time and it was *fun*.

HARJ

Oh, my bitterness at missing my chance at carnal bliss with Andrea! And oh, my shock at learning that the Craigs were colour-coordinated Solon users. I tumbled out the second-floor window into the remains of a dead magnolia, only to land *plop* on a half-deflated vinyl pool toy promoting beer from Mexico. Through a window, I could see that the house was filled with non-Craigs, while approaching sirens and helicopters told me the situation was about to grow even more perilous to me. So I headed into the wooded area behind the house, and oddly, it reminded me of walking through Gomarankadawela Park in Trincomalee during the annual mongoose festival.

Fortunately, I am fleet of foot, and after a period of hours, I emerged onto Interstate 71—which I knew from Google Maps began in Louisville, Kentucky's famous "Spaghetti Junction" and ended twenty miles south of Cincinnati. Kentucky—a new goal.

It was a lovely walk. Deep in the night, hours went by without a car. I walked down the middle of the passing lane, feeling the newly born grasses poking up from the pavement—tickling against the bottom of my jeans. An occasional startled deer pranced away and I was able to hear one or two crickets, and I felt like I was truly in America and my time with the Craigs was only a dream, such as I would have after eating ill-spiced stews prepared by Hemesh's untalented wife.

What more bad news would come my way as a result of having taken the low road? Where would I go for the long-term? What would I do? To make such decisions, I needed to rest. I stepped over to the side of the road, crawled into a thicket of grass and fell asleep. I was awakened by a strange combination of bright sunlight and a rather strong rain—as well as the sound of a cocking rifle in my ear.

"Okay there, Sleeper Cell, upsy-daisy."

"I am very sorry, sir, you have the wrong person. My name is Harj Vetharanayan, but people generally call me Apu."

"A comedian, huh?" With a deft jolt, he drill-pressed my chest with his rifle butt. His face was melon-like but pink. A fleck of spittle hit my left cheekbone. "Found him, boys!" The rifleman's colleagues joined him. "I'm Chief Clancy Wiggum, and it's a perfect day for a dose of *terror*, huh, Sleeper Cell?"

"Who is this person you keep telling me I am? I am no such person."

"So, Mr. Cell—which was your favourite—the North Tower or the South Tower?"

"Excuse me?"

Chief Wiggum continued to hector me with absurd accusations as the other officers handcuffed me and pushed me into the rear seat of a sheriff's sedan that was in worse shape than a pirate cab driver's vehicle back home—it smelled of cheap cologne and diesel fumes. I did not enjoy being in the back seat at all, but I did become curious as to our destination when we drove past what was clearly the police station and into a once prosperous residential neighbourhood now clad in plywood and NO TRESPASSING signs.

We arrived at a house whose occupants still made an effort to be middle class—a mowed square of lawn out front, dappled with freshly cleaned white plastic lawn furniture of a sort burped out by tsunamis. I felt a wash of homesickness before I was harshly pushed through the front door and down a mildewy hallway.

"Okay, Sleeper Cell, don't make one single fucking move until we tell you to. In."

They locked me in yet another strange bedroom, this one with a barred window that overlooked a rusted-out pair of snowmobiles on the thistled rear lawn. The room's walls were papered with Mother Goose characters, and scented by a basket containing potpourri, a popular seasonal accessory item ordered in December along with yuletide-themed sweaters.

Upon closer inspection, I saw that there was no aspect of the room, aside from the barred windows, that wasn't trying to cheer me up or make me feel childlike—and yet the room did not feel like the room of a child. It felt like the sort of room an adult might wish to inhabit if he wanted to ignore the real world and dream about the children he would never have. It depressed me and spoke of a belief in nonsense and magic.

I shouted through the door, "Gentlemen? Hello? Could I have something to eat or drink? A simple cup of coffee?"

Clumsy footsteps approached my door, and the sheriff's baritone voice boomed, "Coffee? Who am I—Scrooge McFucking Duck? The deposed Prince of Nigeria? Maybe you'd like some goose liver pâté and a chiffon cake while you're at it."

He walked away, sniggering.

I sighed and wondered what it was about me that I was always ending up in odd bedrooms, but never ending up in them in a good way. I removed my shirt and looked at the bruise on my ribcage, the shape and size of a cucumber. This was when I had the odd sensation that I was being picked out of myself—or that my body was doubling like a bacterium, a newer me rising above my body seated on the edge of the bed. I went through the ceiling and roof of the house and was above the fields of Ohio, like a helicopter, but higher and quieter. I kept rising and rising and soon was up where the atmosphere turns into space. I turned and looked at the sun, but instead of being blinded, I felt a moment of awe, a recognition that life on earth was fragile and delicate, and owed everything to the sun. I turned around and looked at the universe and shivered because it was so vast and essentially empty. I thought about Earth, this cosmic pebble circling a D-class star—and even then, this thing we call life inhabits only a tiny skim-coat of this fleck, and even within that thin coat, there isn't that much life at all. I looked back down at the planet and I thought, *What a marvel to be among the fewest of few molecules in the universe allowed to experience this thing called life—stars and nebulas and black holes by the quadrillion, and yet only a few molecules on Earth get to be alive.*

And then I began to fall back down. Not quite falling, but the descent startled me. *Plop*, there I was, back in the Mother Goose bedroom, a prisoner, with the door now being kicked in by a syringe-toting Chief Wiggum and two very stupid-looking goons as might be seen on 1970s police shows found on a satellite station with a seven-digit channel number.

"We're going to need a sample of your sleeper-cell cells," he said, advancing on me.

I resisted but I was coshed on the forehead and woke up with a sore inner arm onto which a Band-Aid had been slapped. My chest was throbbing. I looked on the floor and there was a pizza pocket that had been microwaved but that was now cold, a pitcher of water, an empty but dirty water glass and a half-used, very old-looking bag of orange crystals labelled TANG. I felt like going home, but had no clear idea what home was to me any longer.

So I lay there on the bed, attempting not to panic by concentrating on remembering the names of colour samples from a series of old Martha Stewart brochures Hemesh had forced us all to study. (The contract went instead to some company in Tasmania that became our bitter rival, but that is another story.) In any event, I find that when you think of a colour, the chattering part of your brain turns off and you are calmed. I recommend this technique to anybody in need of peace.

ATLANTIC FOG
BABY BLANKET
BAKERY BOX WHITE
BELL FLOWER
BITUMEN
BLUE ASTER
BLUE CORN
BOX TURTLE
BROOM HANDLE
CAKE BATTER
CAMEO
CASHEW
CHALKBOARD GREEN
CLOUDLESS DAY
CURLEW
DAGUERREOTYPE
DUCK'S BILL
DUCK'S EGG
FADED INK
FOXGLOVE

I was just about to envision "Galapagos" when there was a roar, like the leaf blower of the gods, and several men shouting. My room's door was busted open yet again! It was a team of DEA agents, just like in movies, except that their outfits were old and threadbare, so shoddy, in fact, that I was unsure if my rescuers were genuine DEA agents—but an open door is an open door. I fled, and as I did I saw my hill-people captors being clubbed on the head like Canadian baby seals. It is uncharitable of me to say so, but I was quite happy to witness them in pain.

Near the house was a helicopter. Somebody shouted, "Hop in!" And so I did, all the while thinking about how blasé I'd become about air travel in recent weeks. We soon landed at a private airstrip where a small corporate jet blazoned with the Disney logo awaited us.

"We are going to Disney World?"

"No. *You're* going to Canada. We got this jet cheap from Disney."

I'd read about Disney's huge fire sale the year before, on reuters.com.

I boarded the jet and the doors closed. I was the sole passenger. Through a smooth five-hour flight, I ate a bag of potato chips and drank a bottle of water. We landed in Masset, on Haida Gwaii, at sunset. Zack and Sam arrived at the small airstrip moments after me, on two different planes.

Who could be paying for all of these extravagant flights? Vintage honey brokers?

At first, the five of us were bashful together—as when a friend tells you there's another person you must meet, and of course the new person is as awkward as you are. We were on a bizarre and beautiful island on a quintuple blind date or, as Zack would say, a five-way.

Diana shocked me with her swearing disorder, but it is amazing how easily the brain will cancel out a dozen "fucks" in a row.

I had been worried that Zack and Sam would be Craigs, but they were not and that was a relief—nor did they seem like the sorts of people my brother would escort into Trincomalee's handjob district. One might think Zack could be that type, but in the tropics, men like Zack sit on a beach and remove their shirts and the pleasure dome comes to them; no need to poke through back alleys or bribe a concierge.

Julien was a surprise to me, rather immature for his age. It's not that I am such a beacon of maturity, but he seems to have had no experiences that might temper him as a soul. He lives in his head, and I am unsure of the depth of anything he feels.

And then there was Serge, who is someone with a secret— I suppose that is everybody, really—but in his case a secret he wants to keep only from *us*. I know, he brought us together and saved us from many potentially ugly situations, but there was a moment when I was hanging up my coat when I first arrived at the house, and we made eye contact for not even a second. I could see that he was calculating something, and I knew we weren't in our northern Galapagos simply to bring back the bees.

We tried to suss out if and how well he knew our former handlers—Sandra, Dr. Rick and Louise. His response was arrogant and dismissive: "Them? I suppose. Why on earth should I care?"

Diana whispered to me, "Okay, we get it, Buster. You run the show."

As for our lodgings, even I, with almost no understanding of North American housing, could tell that our house was at least a half-century old, maybe older—it had phone jacks and an antenna and a garage for two cars. It was humble and musty, and the rooms felt like drab tissue boxes. I was told that Haida Gwaii's economy had been free of booms and busts for the entire twentieth century; a chart showing its economic progress would be a flat line. So it wasn't as if there was a better place to stay. And the rain, so cold! And the storms, so violent and so common!

The morning after I arrived, we all walked around the town, garnering suspicious stares from the Haida. Our task was to locate alcohol for Zack. He is a declarative fellow: "The dandelion wine here tastes like rat piss, there's no cough syrup or muscle relaxants anywhere, so a-hunting we will go."

It is always nice to have a minor goal to motivate a pleasant walk. We stopped by the one local store that remained open. It sold only packages of chewing gum and potato flakes.

Zack's temper got the better of him. "Booze, dammit, I want booze!"

A Haida man came into the store. Zack said, "Hi. I'm Zack. I'm one of the bee-sting people. Where can I find some decent fucking booze around here?"

The man was tall and had the widest, flattest nose I'd ever seen. He said, "Booze is no problem."

"Thank Christ. Where do I have to go?"

"Here—later today."

"What is it?"

"Blackberry wine."

"Consider it sold. By the way, I saw a basketball court over the hill. Want to shoot some hoops?"

"Sure."

So we sat on tumbledown bleachers to watch Zack and some new friends shoot hoops. I was shivering, Sam was running laps around the block, Julien was lying down with a coat over his head, and Diana was inspecting the local women's teeth to see who needed a cleaning. They, in turn, wanted to know who was sleeping with whom, and they must have been very bored with the answer. In a Hollywood way, one would expect Zack and Sam to become a glamorous power couple, but that was not to happen.

The sun poked out from behind some clouds and we all stopped to bask for a moment, and then one of the women, toying with Diana's Tourette's, said, "So, then, where are our fucking bees?"

Perhaps one had to be there.

From nowhere a storm erupted, and we raced back to the house, soaked. The storm got worse, and then it got even worse. The power failed and out came the candles. We sat by the fire on a large braided rug, and at sunset the clouds cleared, shooting bolts of beer-coloured light at us from the west. I felt as if we were visiting the past, and yet it wasn't a déjà vu.

Into the silence Serge said, "We have a mission here on this island."

I asked, "What kind of mission?"

"An odd one."

"How odd?"

"Our goal here is for the group of you to make up stories and tell them to each other."

"What?"

"It is as simple as that."

"That's absurd," Julien said.

The five of us tried to absorb the minuscule scope and borderline random quality of this mission.

"What kind of stories?" Sam asked.

"Whatever you like. Fairy tales. Literary fiction. Detective stories. Horror."

"Why stories?" Julien asked.

"Just trust me," Serge replied.

Diana: "How long do they have to be?"

Serge: "As short or as long as you choose."

Sam: "Do we write them down? How many words minimum? This feels like homework."

Serge: "It is not homework, and no, you don't have to write them down if you wish not to."

Zack: "I'm ADD."

Serge: "But you are still creative. You'll do just fine."

I asked, "Why stories?"

Serge replied, "Right now, it's probably for the best that I do not tell you the specific purpose. But then, remind yourselves that you spent many weeks in an underground chamber without words or books or TV or the Internet or even logos on the mattress. Being asked to invent and tell stories is surely not as weird as that."

Diana asked if it had anything directly to do with our not being allowed books or TV or computers in our cells, and Serge said, "Yes, it does."

Julien asked if we were being graded on these stories, and Serge said, "Ah, Sean Penn, always the lazy student. All that is required of you is that you invent your stories on your own."

It's strange to be asked if you have any stories to tell. Did I? I wasn't sure.

Zack asked, "Can I tell the story about the time I spent a lost weekend with a Japan Airlines mechanical crew who were abandoned in Sioux City during the Oktoberfest riots?"

Serge said, "I do not want anecdotes from your life, Zack. I want stories. Stories you *invent*. Stories that have no other goal in life than to be stories."

Sam asked, "How long do we have to do this for?"

Serge replied, "Maybe a week. Maybe a year. It may all be for nothing."

There was a quiet patch where we sat trying to imagine something to tell, trying to engage that portion of our brains or our selves that handles that activity. Hours passed in the room lit by candlelight.

Zack finally said, "I think I have one."

Diana, clearly a little jealous, asked him, "What's it called?"

"It's called . . . 'Superman and the Kryptonite Martinis.'"

Superman and the
Kryptonite Martinis
by Zack Lammle

One sunny afternoon, Superman was at the beach and got tar all over the soles of his feet. He went to his car and removed a Clark Kent shirt from the back seat, and then he popped his gas cap and dipped his shirt in just far enough to soak the tail of the shirt. He pulled it out and began to wipe the tar from his feet, and was promptly nailed by the Carbon Squad patrolling the lot. They gave him a $200 ticket for using gasoline frivolously, and a $150 ticket for destroying a shirt that had a thirty-percent synthetic-fibre content. Meanwhile, a group of fellow beach-goers surrounded the car and began heckling him.

"Ooh, look at me. I'm Superman. I can leap tall buildings and make time go backwards, but nooooo, instead I waste gasoline *and* destroy permanent-press clothing."

"Gee," said another, "I think I'll go fight crime—whoops! My footsies are dirty. Looks like I'll just have to eat shit like everyone else in this world."

Superman asked, "What is *wrong* with you people?" He threw his shirt into the back seat and got in his car and put it in reverse, narrowly missing a quintet of snarling beach bunnies. As he drove away, he rolled down the window to shout, "You make me really happy I left my home planet to come and fight crime for you ungrateful fucks!"

Someone threw a Frisbee at the car; it bounced off the roof and landed in a ditch.

Superman turned on the radio and was listening to a program discussing profound corruption at the heart of UNESCO when he passed a bar whose sign read TASTY COCK-TAILS FOR THOSE WITH A HEAVY LOAD. "Man, I could use a drink right now," he said. Right there in traffic, he did a U-ey and pulled up in front of the bar.

The bartender, who happened to look and sound a lot like Yoda, said, "Ah, Superman. I think for you a terrific drink I have."

Superman said, "Bring it on." The air inside the bar was cool, and he readjusted his cape and looked around. There were a few barflies in the back, but otherwise the place was dead. The jukebox was playing "The Logical Song" by Supertramp; it brought the superhero a flood of memories. As Yoda arrived with his drink, he said, "This song was in my first colour movie ever."

"That be the one with Christopher Reeve?"

"That's the one."

"Ever meet him, did you?"

"Once, at a Golden Globes after-party. We were both kind of wasted. I don't remember much of it."

"Your drink is on me, Mr. Caped Crusader."

"I don't know about that 'caped crusader' stuff any more. Today it's all I can do to not blast this planet to smithereens. But thanks."

Superman looked at his martini, frosty and chilled, dew dripping down the sides. He took a sip—*Ahhhhhhhh*—and then his mouth turned to fire. "You dirty little shit, what the hell is in this thing?"

Yoda, wiser than Superman, said, "The first time you tried wasabi you remember?"

"Yeah. In Osaka, when I was helping Sailor Moon during her Asian fragrance launch."

"And did it not burn at first? Did not your nostrils feel aflame?"

"Why . . . yes, it did."

"So finish your drink you will. And enjoy it you will."

Yoda went to the other side of the bar and Superman sipped a little more of his martini. He yelled to Yoda, "These things kick like a bound and gagged hitchhiker. Very tasty—*mmmmmmmmm*." The burn was like a new spice, and Superman became an instant addict. "Yoda: hustle with the next one."

"Yes, Mr. Caped Crusader."

As Superman awaited his next martini, he wondered why he bothered fighting crime any more. He still had all his superpowers, but people just didn't seem to want him to use them. He'd recently received a condescending letter from the United Nations:

Dear Mr. Superman,

We appreciate your willingness to fight crime, but at the moment what we really need is a superhero who can separate transuranium isotopes in the soil of Northern Germany—or perhaps a superhero who can distill Pacific waters to render them free of plastic particles larger than two hundred microns. We at the UN acknowledge that everyday crime and everyday criminals are on the rise, but please also remember, Mr. Superman, that evil supervillains have all been eradicated with your help. (Note: you left your thank-you plaque and goodie bag at the dinner table after the presentation ceremony. I can ask my assistant, Tara, to forward it to you.)

In any event, we want you to know that we appreciate and support your drive to be as super as you can possibly be, and we look forward to convening in the near future!

Yours, Mbutu Ntonga, Secretary-General, United Nations Temporary Headquarters, Saint Louis, Missouri

Prick.

Superman downed his third martini in one gulp. A barfly near a keno machine clapped at this, and Superman roared, "I *am* a fucking superhero, you know." He turned to Yoda. "What's in these things, anyway?"

"Magic ingredient is kryptonite."

"Kryptonite!?" Superman was about to induce vomiting with his index finger when Yoda said, "Frightened be not! It is only at a strength useful for flavour, not enough that you lose your superpowers."

The martinis *were* tasty. "You're not shitting me? No lost powers? Seasoning only?"

"I shit you not. Mix you another I will."

"Done."

Soon Superman was hanging out every day at the bar, from its noon opening time until two a.m., with a few time outs to go to the Wendy's next door, plus one isolated incident when he chased down a teenager who had jimmied the Hyundai logo from the front grille of his car. Being drunk, he miscalculated his speed, and the offending delinquent was flattened like a taco shell between Superman's body and the wall of the local rental storage facility. But nobody had witnessed the event, so Superman squished the teenager into a diamond and, once back in the bar, tossed the diamond over towards the barflies.

"Nasty little prick."

Yoda said, "Hear you I did not. Mr. Superman, I am sorry to inform you, but you owe several thousands of dollars for the martinis you so much like."

"Bar tab, huh?"

"Yes."

"Forget cash. I know—how about I pay you in *diamonds?*"

"Diamonds I like."

"Good."

Superman picked up the new diamond from the floor and gave it to a smiling Yoda, who promptly made him another kryptonite martini. All was well for several days, until his next bar tab came due. Superman excused himself, went outside and jumped up and flew around the skies for a bit, trying to find someone committing a crime who might deserve the fate of crystallization. Finally he saw some guy holding up a rice warehouse. With just a small amount of vigilance, Superman was able to snag him and crush him, and soon he had Yoda's diamond.

But as the months passed, Superman's superpowers waned. And there came the fateful evening when, upon capturing a burglar in the act of entering somebody's rear window, instead of being able to squish the perp into a diamond, all he created was a blob of stinking bloody mess that got all over his crime-fighting suit.

Shit.

Superman's crimes grew uglier as his superpowers dwindled to mortal levels. Yoda, addicted to Superman's diamonds, refused to accept any other form of payment. Superman tried offering a Patek Phillipe watch he had ripped from the wrist of some guy who was selling weed behind the Office Warehouse. No go.

And so he robbed a Zales in the strip mall off the interstate. Bad decision. He went down on the third bullet; by the sixth, he was dead.

Back at the bar, Yoda trawled the news sites for exposés on Superman's private life: the whores, the spare bedroom filled with emptied and unrecycled cans of Boost and Ensure, the back taxes that went all the way back to the Reagan administration. Yoda sighed, fondled his sack of diamonds and then smiled as he looked up and saw Batman enter the bar.

"Ah, Batman. I think the drink for you I have."

SAMANTHA

So, right, I've never been the brown-noser in school, but I *have* prided myself on getting good grades throughout my life, and Serge was the teacher I wanted to please. Zack telling a good story was like the special-needs kid in the class knowing a Keats sonnet. Bloody annoying.

Serge said, "Your turn, Samantha."

Bloody hell. "Serge, I'm not creative that way."

"If you relax, you might surprise yourself, Samantha. The brain uses stories to organize its perceptions of the world. Every moment of your life it's doing things for you that you can barely imagine."

I went silent from nerves. Serge smiled and said, "Is your PDA working? Go online and look up *The Decameron*."

"Spell that for me."

He did.

I read aloud: "*The Decameron* is a collection of short stories written from 1350 to 1353 by an Italian writer, Giovanni Boccaccio. The collection begins with a description of the Black Death. Then we meet a group of seven young men and women who flee from plague-ridden Florence to a villa in the countryside. To pass the time, each member of the party tells stories about lust, the nobility and the clergy.

"*The Decameron* was made into an Italian movie in 1972. A Japanese version, *Tôkyô Dekameron*, made in 1996, featured lesbian torture chambers."

We sat there digesting this piece of information. Diana dropped a log on the fire, saying, "Well, I guess we'd better update our notions of lust, the nobility and the clergy. Zack is totally on the right track. Let's tell stories about stalking, superheroes and cults."

The room became warmer and more intimate. I felt like a child again.

I said, "If Zack can do this, I can do this. But I want to tell a story with a real king, not a superhero."

Zoë Hears the Truth
by Samantha Tolliver

Once upon a time there was a princess who had no brothers or sisters. Since she was fated to become queen, she spent much of her early life wondering exactly what it is a queen does, aside from displaying excellent table manners and cutting ribbons at the openings of horticultural festivals. Her parents had always told her that when her day came, she'd receive special instruction. In the meantime, she was told to enjoy life.

So Princess Zoë, which was her name, went to the gym. She read ancient scrolls. She played tennis. In order to promote her kingdom's industrial base, she once had lunch with a Japanese-made robot that simulated Elton John. It was an interesting life. Then one day, during a month of heavy rains and floods, her father became sick and a hush fell over the castle. He called Zoë to his bedside and said, "It's time we had a talk."

Zoë's stomach fluttered because she knew this was when she was to receive her special instructions on how to be queen.

"What is it, Father?"

Rain drummed on the ancient lead-glassed windows.

"It's simple, really. You need to know that your mother and I don't believe in anything."

Zoë was shocked. "*What* did you say, Father?"

"Your mother and I don't believe in anything."

"As in . . . religion?"

"Absolutely. No religion for us."

"Politics?"

"Nope."

"The monarchy?"

"Absolutely not."

"Why are you telling me this? How can you just sit there and tell me you don't believe in anything. You're the king! You have a kingdom, and subjects who worship you."

"If it makes them happier to worship me, then let them."

"So wait. You mean you don't even believe in any form of higher being?"

"That is correct. Nothing."

"But you're divinely chosen!"

"So?"

Zoë didn't know how to handle this information. The room began to tilt like a dock on choppy water. "Did you *ever* believe in anything—when you were younger, maybe?" she asked.

"I tried. Quite hard. Really."

Zoë got mad. "Papa, you're a fraud!"

"Grow up just a bit, my little cabbage. Don't you ever wonder how I get through all my days in such a good mood, even when the peasants threaten to revolt or the queen of Spain overstays her welcome?"

"But don't you have to believe in *something*?"

"Princess, you're too old not to have had, how shall I say, certain *experiences*. You've had bad Internet dates. You've had people be creeps to you. You've seen what you've seen; you've felt what you've felt. Ideology is for people who don't trust their own experiences and perceptions of the world."

"I feel like I'm going mad."

"Madness is actually quite rare in individuals. It's groups of people who go mad. Countries, cults . . . religions."

Zoë said, "I wish I smoked. If I smoked, right now would be a very good time for a cigarette."

"I'll have the butler bring us one." Her father leaned over to a speakerphone beside his bed and said, "Please bring me a cigarette." Almost instantly, the butler arrived with a mentholated filter-tipped cigarette resting atop a burgundy pillow. "Try it, Zoë. You'll see what you've been missing all these years."

The butler lit the cigarette for Zoë. She breathed in some smoke, coughed and grew dizzy. "This tastes awful."

"Sometimes what's bad for our bodies is good for the soul. Smoke some more. You'll love it. Soon you'll be unable to stop."

Zoë inhaled again. It wasn't as bad as the first few puffs. "Does anyone else know you don't believe in anything?"

"Just your mother."

"Don't you worry about death?"

"For every living person here on earth, there are millions of dead people before them—and there will be billions of dead people after us all, too. Being alive is just a brief technicality. Why are you so upset?"

"This is a lot to absorb in one blast."

"*Pshaw*. There's nothing to absorb. That's the point. And soon you'll be queen and you'll have to go through your days displaying flawless table manners and cutting ribbons to open horticultural fairs. And you'll have to deal with a few monsters as well."

"Monsters?" This was news to Zoë.

"Yes, monsters. People who believe in things to the exclusion of their senses. Everyone dumps on politicians as monsters, but they're actually very easy to handle because at least they're up front about the system they're using to avoid reality. The real killers are the quiet believers. It's always the sullen twenty-year-old who wears the vest into the market square."

As Zoë sat and finished her cigarette, there was a pleasant quiet moment between father and daughter. The rain pounded on the window like a crazy person trying to get in. She stubbed out her cigarette in an ashtray designed to look like a miniature version of the Magna Carta. She said, "You've heard the news this morning about the floods?"

"I did."

"They say the Royal Cemetery will soon flood."

"Won't *that* be something," said the king.

"Papa, it's where you're going to be buried."

"Just imagine all of those bejewelled skeletons washing away down into the river."

"Papa, we're going to have to find somewhere else to bury you. What are we going to do? Where can we bury you if not in the Royal Cemetery?"

"Surprise me," said the king, and died, making Zoë queen. And as she sat there thinking about her future, she looked at her cigarette butt and had the strangest sensation that the cigarette was looking back at her.

And then she realized that she, too, didn't believe in anything.

Then she wondered if not believing in anything robbed her of the ability to fall in love.

And then she rang for another cigarette, her first act as queen.

JULIEN

Zut! I never would have imagined that I, Julien, would one day enjoy spending an afternoon sitting on a stump watching ravens dropping *moules* onto boulders, or watching a tide come in and eat the sand, or listening to the waves pummel the rocks on the shoreline north of Tow Hill Road, where every rock is the size and shape of an egg. And telling stories? *Holy fucking zut!*

I asked Serge, "Can you tell us why it's so weird and so difficult to invent a story? How difficult can it be? And yet it is very difficult."

Serge said, "Stories come from a part of you that only gets visited rarely—sometimes never at all. I think most people spend so much time trying to convince themselves that their lives are stories that the actual story-creating part of their brains hardens and dies. People forget that there are other ways of ordering the world. But now it's your turn to tell a story."

I was smacked by a wave of jet lag—an old-fashioned condition like dropsy or croup or leprosy. When was the last time you heard of anyone with jet lag?

I needed a minute to collect my thoughts—what story to tell? *Fuck.* I reached for my PDA and looked up "storytelling" for ideas.

Meanwhile, the wine flowed and Harj told us about the Craigs. I bought myself a little more time by telling everybody about the explosion at CERN, and Sam discussed her Earth sandwich. Then Diana told us about her evil neighbour,

Mitch—it was getting late by then—and finally Zack began telling us his theories about corn.

And then Serge said it was really time for me to tell a story. *Nique ta mère!*

"Okay. Here goes nothing . . ."

Coffinshark the Unpleasant
Meets the Stadium of Pain
by Julien Picard

Everyone stared at me.

I said, "I'm being ridiculous here! The title of my story is definitely not 'Coffinshark the Unpleasant Meets the Stadium of Pain!' . . . but I *did* generate millions of story titles using the uncountable numbers of online plot and character generators."

I held up my PDA to display its small brilliant aqua screen.

"All genres, all levels of culture, high, low, Marxist and bourgeois. Here's just one vampire character description out of 2,500 instant vampire descriptions generated online.

"'Character No. 2,428: This sinful male vampire has narrow eyes the colour of charcoal. His thick, straight brown hair is worn in a style that reminds you of a trailing ribbon. He's got a beard and a graceful build. His skin is completely transparent, and the blood flowing beneath it seems to glow. He has a small nose and a boxy chin. He can turn into a jaguar, and he has few vampiric disabilities. His diet consists of blood, but he can also eat normal food. He feeds not through his mouth, but via a long tongue with an eel-like end.'"

Sam said, "It's sort of the death of culture, isn't it? The death of books. The death of the individual hero. The death of the individual, *period.*"

I passed my PDA around and scrolled through the plots and names and places that spewed into my laptop's windows.

Sam said, "Seeing all of these story options is making me feel seasick."

"They're not even *ideas*," Diana said. "They're like those kitschy splatter paintings they sell at carnivals."

Serge said, "You're not off the hook, Julien. You still have to tell your story."

I felt fortified by outrage at the modern world. I said, "Okay, here's my real story. Screw you, plot generators."

Fear of Windows
by Julien Picard

Kimberly Kellogs was a well-nourished, upper-middle-class twelve-year-old girl who lived in a good suburb of a good American city. Her parents were happy that she hadn't yet turned into an insolent, shoplifting, purge-dieting, binge-drinking nightmare like all the other girls in the neighbourhood. They counted their blessings.

One night Kimberly was watching a horror movie with her parents, one about outer space aliens invading the suburbs. The movie was made in a cinéma-vérité style, so that the naturalistic and provocative camerawork made the everyday world seem more charged and real, ready to explode like a black nylon backpack in a crowded train station.

Halfway through the movie, a scene showed a family inside their house; they heard funny noises, so they went from window to window, trying to see what the noise could be. When nothing turned up, they stood in front of the living-room window for a moment, admiring the front garden. Suddenly, a huge mean-motherfucker alien with tentacles and fangs and a massive cranium jumped in front of them and spat blood and venom and human body parts onto the windowpane.

Kimberly began screaming and couldn't stop. In the end, her parents had to give her some Valium they'd been saving for an upcoming holiday flight, and still she spent the rest of the evening in bed with her curtains tightly closed. Through the walls, she could hear her parents fighting over whose idea it had been to let a twelve-year-old girl watch a PG-17 horror movie.

Before he went to bed that night, Kimberly's father came up to see how she was doing and said, "Let's open the curtains and let in some fresh air."

Kimberly freaked out again. It took her father some minutes to make the connection between the curtains, the windows and the monster, and by then Kimberly was so upset that she ended up spending the night in her parents' room, the blinds drawn.

The next morning Kimberly was fine again—until she remembered the monster. She froze, realizing that there were windows everywhere and that the monster could appear at any one of them at any time.

She willed herself out of the house and onto the school bus, and that was okay because it was moving and raised above the ground, until she realized that an alien could be on the bus's roof. At school, she spent the day trying not to look out the classroom windows.

During the last period of the day, science, one of her class-mates, Luke, said, "Kimberly, come over here. There's this cool eye-perception test I want to show you."

"What does that mean?"

"It's to test your eyes to see what you notice more, motion or colour. It's fun."

Kimberly was glad to have something to take her mind off the aliens, so she went to sit beside him.

Luke said, "What you do is stare at this image really intensely."

On the screen was a picture of a boring middle-class living room.

"Let your eyes relax and let your body relax, and then things in the room will move just slightly, or the sofa may change colour just a bit. The image is going to change very slowly. Tell me what changes you notice—colour or shape or motion or whatever."

So Kimberly sat there and let her body relax for the first time since the horror movie. She stared at the picture and thought of how much it matched her own family's living room. She was imagining herself in the room, feeling safe and happy, when all of a sudden the screen cut to a full-size screaming vampire face, fangs bleeding, eyes full of murderous bloodsucking rage.

Kimberly went totally apeshit, and nobody knew what to do. Finally, her teacher and a few of the bigger students were able to drag her to the nurse's office, where she was forced to sign several waiver forms and show proof of her family's fully paid up-to-date medical coverage before she was given a rich and delicious syringe-load of Dilaudid. Still, the only reason Kimberly didn't flip out further was because the nurse's office had no windows and she felt slightly safe there—but she dreaded the fact that she would have to leave the room and walk down windowed hallways and out a door into a car with windows (her mother had been called) and then into a house that had twenty-seven windows as well as one chimney and three ventilation holes for the dryer and the bathroom showers.

The drive home was traumatic. Once inside the house, Kimberly was unable to leave her mother, even for a second.

That night her parents tried reasoning with her, but the harder they tried, the more anxious she became. At two in the morning, they gave her the remaining eight milligrams of Valium and decided to see if everything would be better in the morning. It wasn't. It was much worse—a Valium hangover amplified every misfiring neuron in their daughter's brain. Kimberly, teeth chattering, crept inside the linen closet and shut the door.

"Shit. We have to get her to a doctor," said her father. "Can you get the day off?"

"Can't. Today is our annual End of Season Blowout on Winnebagos. Can you do it?"

"Fine. Come on, pumpkin," Kimberly's dad said. "Get dressed and let's go see if we can make these spooky things go away."

They drove to the clinic with Kimberly crouched in the nook in front of the front passenger seat. Her father hoped to hell he wouldn't get stopped for a seat-belt violation.

At the clinic they saw Dr. Marlboro, who was quick to grasp the problem. "Sedatives won't work," he said. "Nothing will work. A horrific lifelong phobia has been created. The most we can hope for is that the fear will dwindle with time and become manageable. The decay rate for young people traumatized by the wrong movie at the wrong time is usually six weeks—but the aftershocks linger forever."

"What kind of quack are you?" Kimberly's dad said.

"Language, Mr. Kellogs. Goodbye."

Angry, Kimberly's father took his daughter to another doctor whom he'd heard would write anyone a prescription for anything.

Kimberly spent the next month in a velvet fog. Then the prescription ran out, and when her parents went to get her another, they found that the pill doctor had fled to Florida to avoid multiple malpractice charges. All the other doctors in town were off-duty, watching golf marathons on TV, and an unsedated Kimberly returned to her full senses. She was yet again horrified by the world.

While Kimberly had been in her fog, spring had turned into summer. Kimberly's mother had an idea: "Why don't you sleep outside on the lawn? No windows there."

She had a point. That night Kimberly slept in the back garden, midway between the house and the fence.

"Well, Einstein," said her father to her mother. "Glad to see something works. She can't be living on sedatives forever."

With a 360-degree view all around her, sleep came quickly to Kimberly. The next morning, she jerked awake, filled with fear, then realized where she was and relaxed. This went on for a month, during which time she stayed outside, only going inside when it was absolutely necessary. The weather was good, and so was life.

Then one morning she woke up to see two men dressed like politicians coming through the carport. They approached the side door and rang the doorbell. Kimberly's mother answered it and let them in.

As quietly as she could, Kimberly crept up to the house. She snuck from window to window, looking inside, and as she did, she discovered that windows are perfectly fine if you're on the outside looking in.

Finally, she came to the living-room window. She looked in to see her parents kneeling in front of the men, who were opening up their heads like tin can lids. Jellyfish tentacles emerged and wrapped themselves over her parents' skulls. After thirty seconds, the tentacles retreated and went back inside the men's heads and the heads snapped shut. The creatures pulled dog leashes from their pockets, which they attached to Kimberly's parents. They led her parents out the front door, down the driveway and out onto the road, where other aliens were busy rounding up the neighbours.

I wish I could say that Kimberly did a brave thing and fetched the loaded Colt from her father's bedside drawer and tried to rescue her parents.

I wish I could say that she ran after her parents in a vain effort to save them, in the process becoming a house pet, too.

But instead, Kimberly looked at her parents' house, which was now all her own. She went in the front door, threw open all the windows, let fresh air inside and sang, "It's mine, mine, mine now! All of it, mine!"

DIANA

Julien's story resonated for me because when I was young, we had to stay in a cabin out in the country, and the wire mesh windows and forest noises scared the pants off me. And this got me to thinking about my screwed-up parents, who I almost never discuss, and so I dawdled a bit to figure out the gist of my story. A bit more wine was poured, and after we found a bag of stale lemon-flavoured cookies, and after a bathroom break, we reconvened in the candle-lit room.

"Serge . . ."

"Yes, Diana?"

"To echo what you were saying earlier, why is it so hard to invent a story when every moment of our lives we're basically winging it and writing stories on the fly?"

"What do you mean?"

"I mean, even me asking you this question is part of the story of my life—and the lives of everyone here. I could have grabbed a knife and gone psycho on everybody. Or I could have hopped around like a bunny rabbit."

"But you didn't," Serge said.

"So then, why do most of us make such boring choices for the stories of our lives? How hard can it be to change gears and say, *You know what? Instead of inventing and telling stories, I'm going to make my life a more interesting story.*"

"I agree," said Zack. "Why is it that, instead of going off on a cross-country killing spree, we stay home and surf for porn?"

Julien said, "Now you know why I like online war games."

"Okay," I said, "time for me to tell my story."

The Short and Brutal Life
of the
Channel Three News Team
by Ms. Diana Beaton

Chloë was sitting at her kitchen table, looking out at the sunny day, when her front doorbell rang. It was the police, come to tell her that her mother had been arrested for murdering the local Channel Three News team—two anchorpeople, the weather guy and four studio technicians. Her mother, acting alone, had arrived at the TV studio carrying an oversize rattan handbag and pretended to be a sweet old thing interested in meeting the hostess from a cooking show. The moment she was close to the newsroom set, she asked to visit the washroom, slipped away, removed several guns from her handbag and came back firing. She was knocked to the ground by a surviving cameraman and her pelvis fractured. She was in hospital, in stable condition. A video of the event was already circling the planet on the Internet. Chloë watched the ninety-second sequence with police officers flanking her; its violence was so otherworldly that Chloë thought she was in a dream. The police asked if she would go to the hospital with them, and she said, "Of course," and off they drove, cherries flashing.

The main entryway was cordoned off, but the cruiser was allowed to slip past the security guards and story-crazed media. They elevatored up to the top floor, where a quartet of officers guarded her mother's room. Chloë had always expected that one day she would visit her mother in the hospital with a broken hip, just not under the current set of circumstances.

"Mom?"

"Hello, dear."

"What the hell were you thinking?"

"I'm more than happy to tell you."

"Wait—where's Dad?"

"He's not available right now."

"Oh Jesus, he's not going to go out and shoot somebody, too, is he?"

"Aren't you quick to jump to conclusions!"

"Mom, you killed seven people."

"Good."

Chloë tried to compose herself while her mother serenely smiled. "So, why'd you do it?" she finally managed to ask.

"Our New Vision church group had an 'enlightenment fasting' up in the mountains last weekend. It was glorious. And during group prayer, I was lifted up above Earth and when I looked down on this planet, it was black like a charcoal briquette. At that moment I realized that Earth is over, and that New Vision will take me to a new planet."

"You're kidding me."

"No, I'm not kidding you, Chloë. Your father and I want you to join us."

"Mom. This is awful. Wake up—wake *up!*"

Chloë's mother looked at her with the same bland face she used when she thanked polite men for holding a door open for her. "You should be thrilled for me, dear. I believe it was *you* who was a fanatic of that comic strip from the 1970s—what was it—the *Yamato*? You of all people must understand what it feels like to want to leave a destroyed planet and roam the universe trying to fight an overwhelming darkness."

"It was just a *comic*, Mom."

"For 'just a comic' it certainly took hold of your imagination. I think you're jealous of me, dear."

"*What?*"

"You're jealous because right now I'm actually inside that cartoon—on the other side of the mirror—and you aren't. But you *can* be. Join us."

"Mom, just stop it. Why did you kill those people?"

"I killed them because they were famous."

"*What?*"

"The only thing our diseased culture believes in is fame. No other form of eternity exists. Kill the famous and you kill the core of the diseased culture."

"So you killed the Channel Three News team? They're barely famous even here in town."

"If you watch the news right about now, you'll see that New Visioneers around the world have shot and killed many people at all levels of fame. To decide who is 'more famous' than anyone else is to buy into the fame creed. So we have been indiscriminate."

Chloë's sense of dread grew stronger. "Who is Dad going to kill?"

"What time is it?"

Chloë looked at her cellphone's time display. "Almost exactly five o'clock."

"In that case, right about . . ." Chloë's mother looked at the ceiling for a second, whereupon she heard small cracking sounds coming from the hospital entranceway. "Right about now he's just shot the news reporters covering my shootings."

"Oh God, oh God, oh God . . ." Chloë ran to the window: pandemonium. She turned to her mother: "Holy fuck! What is wrong with you?"

"Is your father dead?"

"What?" Chloë looked out the window again and saw her father's body sprawled on a berm covered in Kentucky bluegrass. "Yes. Mother of God. He is!"

"Good. He'll be on the other side to greet me with the rest of us who have fulfilled our mission today."

Chloë staggered out into the hallway, gasping, but police and hospital staff paid her little attention as they braced for the next wave of wounded, dying and the dead. She shouted, "Dear God, I am so sorry!" and was ignored.

On a nursing station's TV screen, newscasts were coming in, showing the faces of murdered celebrities from around the world.

Chloë ran back into the room to find her mother glowing.

"Mom, you're crazy. Your cult is crazy."

"I want all of your generation to come join me and band together to smash all the shop windows of every boutique in the country, to set fire to every catwalk, to shoot rockets into Beverly Hills. It will be beautiful—like modern art—and people will finally stop believing in the false future promised by celebrity."

Chloë wanted to vomit. Gurneys loaded with bodies were shunted quickly past the room's door and her mother went on talking: "In the last days of World War Two, the Japanese emperor told the Japanese to sacrifice themselves, to die like smashed jewels. And so I say to you, Chloë, die like a smashed jewel. Destroy, so that we can rebuild."

Outside it had grown dark—not regular darkness, but a chemical darkness that felt linked to profound evil. The moon was full. Chloë and her mother caught each other staring at it at the same time. Her mother said, "I wish the Apollo astronauts had died on the moon."

"What?"

"Then it would be one great big tombstone for planet Earth." Her mother popped something into her mouth.

"Mom—what was that?"

"Cyanide, dear. I'm off on your Battleship *Yamato*. Why don't you come, too?"

Chloë ran for help, but the staff were too busy with the wounded, so she watched her mother die, writhing on her bed, then falling still.

Stunned, Chloë walked back out into the hallway. There was blood everywhere. The floor was smeared; the whole place smelled of hot, moist coins. She heard gunshots coming from the elevator bank, and screaming staff ran down the hallway past her. She saw an orderly in turquoise surgical scrubs coming towards her holding a sawed-off shotgun, and the look in his eye told Chloë that this was a New Vision follower.

He was whistling, and as he came nearer, he said, relaxed as can be, "Looks like you're one pretty darn famous little lady now, aren't you?"

Chloë ran into her mother's room and kissed her mother's mouth violently, sucking in the remains of the cyanide. She tasted the chemical as it entered her bloodstream and knew death would be quick.

The whistling stopped as the orderly loomed in the doorway. Chloë said, "Know what? I leave this planet on my own terms, you freak." She was dead before the buckshot pounded her chest.

HARJ

I have always prided myself on being a good listener, and after listening to Diana's story, it occurred to me that common threads might be woven into the fabric of our stories. Certain themes tended to recur: royalty, cults, the way we hear words, the way we tell stories, superheroes, disaster, aliens—Channel Three News teams. I kept this observation to myself, as I did not want to make my new friends self-conscious.

And for me to invent a story on the spot? Difficult, but I very much wanted to be a part of our gang—the alcohol and the candlelit intimacy were seductive and corroded that part of my brain that fears such things as public speaking and karaoke. And so I began.

Nine Point Zero
by Harj Vetharanayan

The king[2] was up in his hot-air balloon, looking down over his mighty kingdom, proud that he had been born to rule over it and silently happy with his lot in life. It was the middle of a sunny weekday, and life in the kingdom was happening as usual: the roads were full, the children were at school, and the last of the lunchtime diners were heading back to their workplaces. That was when the earthquake struck.

2 Yes, royalty.

It was a nine point zero; within fifteen seconds, it demol-
ished the older, less seismically prepared buildings in the land.
After that, the newer buildings began to drop. Throughout
the kingdom, those people who had survived did a clumsy
dance out onto the wobbling streets to avoid falling debris—
shards of glass and masonry.

The noise of the quake was deafening. Such a roar! It was
the planet itself shifting and readjusting; the people on the
street couldn't even hear each other yell.

The king, up in his hot-air balloon, was the only person
who experienced none of the quake's violence, which continued to roar and roar and destroy—a quake that wouldn't
stop. By the quake's fifth minute, most of his kingdom's
houses were gone and all dams had broken. Reservoirs had
drowned whole suburbs. Office towers had fallen on their
sides and the quake's continuing lunging motions shook
them until only twisted steel beams remained.

The king's heart had broken and still the quake continued! Survivors were becoming seasick from the ground's
lurching—they lay vomiting on the crumbling parking lots
and sidewalks. Trees fell. Birds were unable to land on the
moving surfaces and were relieved to sit on the rim of the
king's hot-air balloon basket.

Fires broke out and the rubble burned. The king watched,
helpless to stop it, tears in his eyes, flocks of confused birds
circling his basket.

After ten minutes, survivors truly wondered if they were
lost inside a dream; the pounding earth was almost boring,
like a carnival ride that had gone on far too long.

After fifteen minutes, there was nothing left to destroy. All
the buildings were gone. All statues, all communications
towers, all laboratories, all movie theatres, all gyms, all gone.

And then the earthquake stopped.

The king, his nerves in ribbons, his eyes cried out, landed his balloon atop what was once a mighty supermarket. The quake had shaken it so badly that the remains had settled into a grey powder, beneath which the larger chunks slept, neatly graded by size. As he stepped out onto the dust, he remembered a photo he'd seen of the first footstep on the moon.

The roads and parking lots had cracked open, and the pavement fragments above had broken like soda crackers, then shattered, then turned to dust. Front yards had liquefied, swallowing whole houses and trees, which now lay deep within the planet.

The king tried to find survivors, and soon he did: stragglers, caked in dirt and vomit, still seasick and crazed from the fifteen-minute quake, all of them feeling like they were hallucinating upon seeing their perfectly intact, well-groomed king.

They began searching for food and water and medicine and liquor, but little could be found in the rubble and dust.

The king helped a middle-aged woman who was picking away at the spot where there had once been a convenience store. She held up a clear bottle of liquid and asked the king what it contained.

"Fruit Solutions with Omega 3 . . . but why are you asking me that? It says so right on the label," he replied.

The woman ripped off the cap and poured half the bottle's contents onto her face to rinse out her eyes; she then drank the remaining liquid and groped through the dust for more bottles that were identical.

A former four-lane commercial strip was so destroyed it couldn't even be called a path. There the king found a couple of hipsters in cargo pants and vintage early-1990s Soundgarden T-shirts. They held up some cans and asked the king what was in them: "Who's Your Daddy Energy Drink, with caffeine, taurine and B vitamins . . . but why are you asking me that? It says so right on the label." They quickly opened the cans and guzzled the contents, ignoring the king.

The king walked farther and met his old high school teacher, who was alive only because he'd called in sick that day and had been stuck in traffic taking his Jack Russell terrier to the vet when the quake struck, riding out the fifteen minutes in the padded comfort of his 2010 Nissan Sentra. The teacher said, "Oh, King, hello. Such good luck to find you. Please, please, tell me, what does this bottle contain?"

The king looked at it. "Bleach. But why are you asking me that? It says so right on the label."

"It's a funny thing," the teacher said, "but I can no longer read."

"What do you mean?"

"Exactly what I said—I look at the shapes on this label and they look like upside-down Hebrew mixed with right-side-up Korean. No idea at all what any of it says. By the way, I see a tsunami coming. Let's hope we're far enough away from the coast here."

The king had little time to reflect on the fact that the quake had stripped its survivors of the ability to read. A massive tsunami barfed and sloshed inward from the coast, turning the recently powdered city into a rich, dark brown cake batter that stopped just inches away from the king's royal shoes. A small aftershock jiggled air bubbles from the batter. His world fell silent.

Behind him, a chimney collapsed, the last remaining perpendicular line to be seen for miles around. The hipsters and the middle-aged lady and the old high school teacher stood beside the king. The woman said, "I'm glad at least one person is still able to read. Otherwise, we'd never be able to rebuild from scratch everything we had before, back to shiny and brand new, as if none of this had ever happened!"

Another tsunami washed in atop the first one, bright red for some reason. Industrial colouring agents? A trainload of cough syrup? Did it matter? The king stumbled over to the teacher's destroyed Sentra, half buried with the remains of the road; he leaned against it and retched. With his index finger, he wrote the words THE KING IS DEAD on its dusty window, and when he was asked what he'd just written, he told his subjects, "A map."

ZACK

"Jeez, Harj, could you be any more depressing?"

"Zack, to create a happy ending for its own sake is no different than masturbation of the brain."

!!!

Okay.

Sometimes you're travelling along through this wacky thing we call life, when you're assaulted by an idea so potent that it obliterates all other forms of stimulus. The notion of neuromasturbation was precisely one of those ideas.

Harj and the others kept on talking, but I'll never know about what. I was trying to figure out what would be the brain's equivalent of lube or movies of Croatian nurses engaged in fourgies.

I heard Harj's voice come back into focus. It had to be three minutes later. ". . . and so *that*," said Harj, "was the way I helped save Christmas." He looked at me. "Zack? Zack? Are you okay?"

"Just thinking."

"It is time for you to tell a story."

"And so I will, *and* I promise a happy ending."

The room was growing cold. We took what blankets we had and moved close together, though Serge remained seated on the other side of the room.

I began my second story.

Yield: A Story
about Cornfields
by Zack Lammle

One day, people everywhere started looking around at all the other people and realized that everybody was looking younger. Well, not so much younger as . . . *smoother.* Wrinkles were vanishing not only on human faces but on their clothing, too—and for at least the first sixty seconds after people realized this, they ran to their mirrors, saw their reflections and said to themselves, *Dang! I am looking hot today!*

But then that first minute ended and people began noticing other things. For example, stains were vanishing from clothing and furniture, and surfaces everywhere began looking Photoshopped and sterile. Hairdos were looking cleaner and more geometrical—no more flyaway strands. Plants and animals began looking cuter and more rounded, and it dawned on everyone at the same moment: *Holy shit! We're all turning into cartoons!*

Being aware of what was happening didn't slow down the pace of cartoonification. With precision and speed, the world was being reduced and crispened and stylized. Some people turned into manga characters. Others turned into high-res video game characters and avatars. Still others turned into classic cartoons, with faces where only the mouth moved when they spoke, and eyes that blinked once every seven seconds.

The world's cartoonification was emotionally troubling, and it was bad for the economy, too, as people stopped eating and taking shits, or doing anything else that was unclean or unable to be reduced to colourful dots, lines, polygons or digital mesh.

A world of financially insolvent cartoons? *Noooooooooo!*

And then from Iowa came both hope and fear: a cornfield in that state had yet to convert into a cartoon cornfield. It had remained as real as ever, and cartoon people drove from everywhere in cartoon cars just to see something that hadn't turned into squiggles and lines and polygons.

The only problem with the cornfield was that the cartoon people couldn't get into it.

When they tried to enter, they hit an invisible wall. Cartoon planes flying towards the cornfield crashed into that same invisible wall; they fell to the earth in flames, with huge ink letters above them that said *Whaam!!* and *K-k-k-keeeRACK!!*

From within the cornfield came a loud, bellowing voice like that of actor James Earl Jones, claiming that it was responsible for turning the world into a cartoon and that it was enjoying every second of it.

The situation was dire and the world needed a hero, and it found one. He went by the name of Coffinshark the Unpleasant, and cartoonification had barely touched him— at most, he looked like he'd had a lot of good cosmetic work done. He had that slickness that made people think that, if he tried, he could easily pass as a member of the local Channel Three News team.

People gasped in disbelief as Coffinshark smashed a hole in the invisible wall and entered the cornfield, vanishing quickly in its thousands of rows.

Near the middle of the field, he heard James Earl Jones shouting, "Coffinshark the Unpleasant! You are a loser and will never catch me!"

"But what if I do?"

"You won't."

"I *will*."

The voice was indignant. "You don't even know who I am!"

"When I catch you I will."

"Just you try!"

And so Coffinshark raced through the cornfield, trying to find the source of the voice. Sometimes he felt as if the voice was just a few stalks away; at other times the voice seemed distant. As Coffinshark chased the voice, he began making random turns within the corn, and soon the voice became confused.

"Coffinshark! What the fuck are you doing? You're supposed to be chasing me!"

"But I *am* chasing you."

"You don't have a clue what you're doing!"

"You're right," said Coffinshark. "I don't." He stopped and looked up at the sky and said, "Okay, Big Boy—you got me. Why don't you come and hammer me into the ground right now."

"You can't be serious!"

"I'm serious."

"You people are idiots. I'm glad I turned you all into cartoons. It's all you deserve."

"Well, come on, squash me like a bug."

The voice sighed and said, "Very well! As you wish!" From the sky, a huge finger came down. Just before it squished Coffinshark, the voice cried out, "Oh *shit!*"

With all of his running, Coffinshark had drawn a huge button in the cornfield, and he had trampled down more cornstalks to spell out the words SATELLITE VIEW. As the finger squished Coffinshark, it pushed the button and the world immediately resolved back into the real photographic life-as-normal deal.

Coffinshark picked himself up off the flattened corn, looked down at his torso, arms and legs and saw that what little cartoonification had occurred to him had vanished— and he missed it already. "Screw this," he said to himself.

He took all the money he made from saving the world and flew to Beverly Hills, where he had large amounts of cosmetic surgery—after which he leveraged his new looks to become a successful TV newscaster, only to be murdered a few months later.

But *that* is another story . . .

". . . And that, my friends, is a happy ending."

My friends were quiet for a few moments, and then Diana said, "My brain feels all tingly and moist."

"Me? My brain just ejaculated," said Julien.

Sam said, "Coffinshark had a good ending, but knowing that he dies later subverts the happiness."

Harj said, "Ah, like the film *Pulp Fiction*: you, the viewer, know John Travolta is killed, and yet when he leaves the restaurant with Samuel Jackson at the end, your head is in a happy place. A very sophisticated ending indeed, Zack."

"Thank you." I then tried to think of the neuromasturbation equivalent of Kleenex.

SAMANTHA

Jesus, what a pitiful morning. After Zack's cartoon story, we all fell asleep, only to be woken up by the next-door neighbour's chainsaw—he's an old coot who uses it to carve eagles and whales, which he trades for Malaysian porn cartridges with a demolition team that comes through twice a year to sell off chunks of the old DEW Line facility by the airport. Instead of being five sexy, frisky young things waking up with alluring bed-head, we looked more like five hoboes who'd collectively shared and soiled a boxcar. We had braid-rug patterns dented into our faces, and the burnt-rubber stench of cheap alcohol leaking from our pores like snot from a runny nose.

I rubbed my eyes and remembered our storytelling from the night before. It had been so . . . *intimate*. It had felt like we were quintuplets in utero. Then I caught Julien's eye and he pulled his gaze away and I knew he felt the same way. Plus, we all had hangovers of the gods.

My clanging head made me impatient and confrontational with Serge, who had been up for ages writing notes at the kitchen table. I demanded to know just what else we were supposed to be doing in Haida Gwaii besides making up stories. He made the face I imagined he'd make if we insulted his cooking.

"It's science, Samantha. Just believe me and go along with it."

"Telling stories is science? Since when?"

"You know what eons are, correct?"

"Those small proteins. The ones they discovered a few years ago."

"If by *they*, you mean *me*, then yes."

"*You* discovered eons?"

"Not in general. But I discovered a few specific micropro-teins—*neuro*proteins."

"That's impressive."

"Thank you."

"So what do eons have to do with us making up stories?"

Serge delivered a patronizing sigh. "Storytelling makes the body secrete a special eon."

"Seriously? You're not shitting me?"

"Yes, Sam, it's true."

"Why do you want us to make—*secrete*—these eons?"

"Please just trust me for the time being."

A phantom serial killer's ice pick impaled itself into the back of my head. I didn't feel like arguing science with Serge any more.

Diana came in the front door and plunked herself down at the table. "What's the deal with Solon around here?"

"Sorry?" Serge was gruff; he was not a person to tolerate a tone bordering on insubordination.

"Solon. Someone's been smuggling it onto the island by the truckload. It's become a huge issue, apparently. I saw some guy by the docks yesterday, and his face looked like an uncooked steak. Somebody beat the crap out of him, and I bet you anything it's related."

"I'd hate to see Solon on the island," Serge said. "The Haida would be doomed."

"Would they?"

"*Certainement*. At least, in theory. Nobody's actually tested it. Solon is a new drug, and we're only now learning its larger effects on society."

"Have you used it?"

"Yes."

"Then you must still be using it. I hear it's more addictive than Oxy or meth," Diana said.

"Believe me, reports of its addictiveness are overblown. And the first thing the Haida did upon my arrival here was a full search. Serge has no Solon."

I thought, *It's really creepy when someone refers to themselves in the third person.*

Serge continued, "In the meantime, please stick with your storytelling. Diana, later on, why don't you show these others the UNESCO beehive spot?"

Around noon we were walking to the docks to buy some fish for supper. We rounded a corner onto Collison Avenue and there were two Haida guys, our age, bike chains around their necks, dangling from the front beams of the abandoned Esso station. We silently watched the two bodies slowly rotating in the wind. A gang of crows on the eaves of a neighbouring roof bobbed and cawed, wondering when it might be time to swoop in for scraps.

Diana broke the silence: "Solon users."

Zack added, "Man, these Haida people are *not* fucking around. Should we call the cops or something?"

"We're on a remote island off the coast of northern British Columbia," Diana came back. "Even if the authorities could afford to travel here, the bodies would be long gone, and methinks they would encounter only silence from the Haida."

"Right."

We decided it was best not to stand there gawking, and instead continued to the docks where we didn't raise the subject of the two corpses, nor did anyone else.

We traded a disc Zack had with 128,000 songs on it—pretty much every song ever recorded from 1971 to 1980—for a medium-sized flounder. It wasn't much to offer, but then we didn't have much to give.

While we were trading, Diana was talking to some locals whose teeth she was set to clean later in the day—the woman denies it, but she loves her job. As we walked away from the docks, she said, "Those two hanged guys are the first Solon users they found. Apparently, there are dozens still out there."

Serge came to meet us, hands in pockets, his long Eurocrat jacket flapping in the salty, slappy wind.

Julien said, "I don't get why they executed them. Can't they just shun the users? Or put them in a cage and let the Solon work its way out of their systems?"

Serge said, "The problem is that the rest of the tribe would never really trust them again. Would *you?* The tribe members would all know that the Solon users prefer, in their hearts, to be by themselves than with the tribe."

Back at the house, we cleaned and cooked the flounder, and everyone was silent as we mulled over the Solon hangings.

Six silent people in a room got me to thinking about the voice we hear in our heads when we read, the universal narrator's voice you may well be hearing right now. Whose voice *is* it you're hearing? It's not your own, is it? I didn't think so. It never is. So I posed the question out loud. Serge was in the kitchen nook, looking at an online science paper, and he bolted upright as though I'd just whacked his solar plexus with a big stick. *"What* did you say?"

"When you read a book, whose voice is it you hear inside your head?"

"It's certainly not my own voice," said Harj, and the others chimed in with the same claim.

"Then whose is it?"

I said my interior narrator's voice was sort of like a TV news reader's—clean and generic.

"New Zealand accent?" asked Harj.

"Slight. But maybe not. Now that I think about it, not really."

After some more discussion, the consensus was that our interior voices were those of network TV news broadcasters.

Diana had a theoretical explanation: "It's because when you write a story, you spell it out using twenty-six letters and convert organic spoken language into a tiny chunk of real estate called a sentence or paragraph. And once this is done, the reader comes along, looks at that little chunk of real estate and reinflates it back into words inside the brain. But because you've used only twenty-six sterile little letters to accomplish this, all of the texture and messiness of a genuine human voice is lost. You've turned speech into something homogenized and sterile. There are sounds bouncing around inside your head, but they're actually the ghosts of sounds."

In the absence of any better idea, we left for the UNESCO beehive. It was hailing outside, but then it quickly warmed up to twenty-one degrees Celsius.

Right.

For me, the hive was an anticlimax—I mean, I wasn't expecting an Arthurian sunbeam extending down from heaven—but we *did* trudge through hell's half-acre of moss and roots and mud, only to come to a circular patch of dirt that resembled a brown, littered parking lot. The tree where the nest had once rested had been picked clean away.

Diana said, "It was different when we visited. The lighting and the time of day."

Zack did a pig call: "Heeeeere, *bee, bee, bee, bee, bee, bee, bee!*"

I felt cynical and cross and was thinking that a nice six-kilometre jog would fix my head when Julien elbowed my side. I looked up and saw Zack's bootlegger, the tall man with the flat nose, staring at us from within the forest.

He didn't flinch when we all stared back. We knew right away that he was a Solon user.

And then he was gone.

JULIEN

Nique ta mère, the day was a catastrophe—nothing but hang-overs, death, a soul-suckingly stupid visit to the UNESCO bee's nest, more violence and then a final massive, crazy and insane burst of death and destruction.

After our trip to the bee site, Diana went into town to clean some teeth and Sam and Zack went along for the ride, to try to find more and better booze. Serge was gone most of the afternoon; I saw him walking along a gravel side street, glued to his headset and PDA—I assumed he was reporting to Paris about our dismal communal lifestyle, which is like a derailed early 1970s hippie social experiment.

I went for a walk alone along the town's *Andromeda Strain* forlorn streets, trying to sequence a story I was working on. I saw ten Haida guys chase another guy through an intersection, and then they were gone, like in a cartoon, but a cartoon with real baseball bats and real axes that ended with screams and then silence to the west of Tehaygen and Rock Point Road. I didn't go to witness the results.

When I got back, Diana filled us in on island gossip: "Solon. They found a box of it inside an old piano in the teen activity centre. The island is crawling with the stuff."

"So the kids are all taking it now?"

"Looks like it."

I asked Diana if Solon withdrawal is bad.

"I researched this stuff. Former users profoundly miss the sensation of solitude. They resent having to care about other people. They never get over their craving for solitude."

Dinner was a small salmon, plus a hideous satanic buffet of canned foods: those strange, squishy, nutritionless tinned vegetables Americans love that turn their bodies into fat, disgusting Winnebagos.

After we finished, we heard a small jet approaching overhead—unusual, as nothing but us had arrived on the island after the world lost interest in the UNESCO site.

The jet flew past the house, northeast towards the airstrip, and then there was an explosion. *Encore, nique ta mère!*

We raced outside to see a plume of smoke rising in the distance. We got in the truck and raced to the airport, where we found the remains of a private jet on the ground, to the airstrip's right side, going into the forest—a hundred-metre-long strand of crumpled metal, strewn luggage, fractured camera equipment and burning debris. The island had no fire department, but then nothing could have survived a crash like that, and the best any of us could do was stand and gawp along with two Haida guys while wracking our brains, trying to figure out who could have been on the plane.

The two men seemed to be actively looking for something—in a way that suggested they weren't looking for a human being. This was odd, so we sidled their way, and then one of them called out and the other came over to a slightly charred but otherwise fine pine box that had been expelled on first impact. It was labelled AEROSPACE-GRADE DRIED MEALS. The older guy jimmied it open with a strip of metal from the crash. Inside it there were hundreds of boxes of Solon.

"Bonanza."

The younger guy walked over to his truck and brought back a jerry can of gasoline. He doused the Solon with gas and torched it with a lit cigarette. I had the feeling there would soon be more bodies hanging from the Esso sign.

Zack asked them, "Hey, how come more of you didn't come out to see this crash? I mean, this is pretty wild."

"Everybody's pretty busy right now."

"Oh?"

Amongst ourselves, we'd wondered how the plane had crashed, and the younger Haida guy surprised us by volunteering the answer: "We switched off the runway lights and used some fake lights to make it crash."

We all went apeshit—I mean . . . *nique ta mère!* Zack went especially apeshit. "What the fuck are you people thinking? You crashed a fucking *plane!*"

"What business is it of yours?"

"What business is it of *ours*? Are you crazy? Are you retarded?"

The two guys came over to us, right up to Zack. The older of the two said, "We only allow you to stay here because of the bees. Stop making noise." Then the younger guy began playing air guitar with the blue top half of a suitcase. Zack jumped him and dragged him to the ground, and everybody started yelling. Harj and Sam jumped on top and pulled the two apart.

Zack's face was candy red. "What are you people *thinking?*"

They each dusted themselves off, and the young guy said, "We're *thinking* we need to do what we have to do to protect ourselves. End of story." He and his friend walked. I was actually kind of in awe of them. They had turned the real world into World of Warcraft, and they were owning every second of it.

Serge arrived and smoked cigarettes and looked at the burning mess. "So much camera equipment. A shame—so expensive."

"Don't use up all your diseased cuntfucking compassion at once, Serge," said Diana, adding, "I just creamed my panties."

Serge asked, "How many people—skeletons—do we see here?"

We did a count: pilot and three passengers, details of their gender unreadable.

Zack said, "It's the Channel Three News team."

Diana looked at Zack. "I just figured this out. *You* invited them here, didn't you?"

"What are you saying, Diana?"

"You butt-raping shitsucker, you heard me perfectly well. *You* brought them here, you fucking media whore. Jesus. Your Uncle Jay told us you'd try exactly this kind of stunt."

"Uncle Jay's been in touch with you? Son of a bitch."

"Cry us a river."

"Diana, look, Jesus, it's not like I wanted *this* to happen. Yeah, I invited them here, but to be honest, I needed the money. We're *all* going to need the money in the future. And what's wrong with a little press, anyway? We can't live here in Narnia forever. And Serge knew they were coming, too. They had clearance."

We looked at Serge, who shrugged. "Yes, I, too, am thinking about your futures. You will need money. I thought I was doing you a favour."

"So who put the fucking Solon on the plane?"

Zack said, "Don't look at me. I didn't even think they were coming for weeks yet."

Our heads racing, we stayed until the fires burned themselves out. There was nothing to save and nothing left to see, so we drove home in silence. I wondered how the Haida knew the Solon was on the plane, and I did contemplate what might have happened if the flight had not crashed and the Channel Three News team *had* shown up at the door. I don't think they would have had anything interesting to film. It's not like we're human daisies and the bees are queuing up, waiting to woo us.

We all sat down and storytelling began with almost no preamble.

The Anti-Ghosts
by Samantha Tolliver

There was once a group of people whose souls had been warped and damaged and squeezed dry by the modern world. One day, their souls rebelled altogether and fled the bodies that had contained them. And once a soul leaves a body, it's all over; there's no going back.

The thing is, the bodies that had created the souls remained alive and continued their everyday activities, such as balancing chequebooks, repairing screen doors and comparison shopping for white terry-cotton socks at the mall, while their souls met in small groups at the intersections of roads, confirming with each other that what had happened was real—and it was—and that they hadn't all turned clueless at once.

"So, are we ghosts?"

"I don't think so—the bodies we came from are still alive."

"Are we monsters?"

"No. Monsters can interact with the world. All we can do is drift around—pass through walls—and live a life of perpetual mourning."

"Are we the undead?"

"No, we are not. But we sure aren't alive, either."

The souls felt like house pets that have survived a hurricane only to find their homes and owners gone. They watched the world go onward, but they were unable to be a part of change or progress. They watched the bodies that spawned them grow older. They were surprised by how cruel it is to grow older in the modern world when everything else seems to stay young.

The souls wondered why they weren't going to heaven or hell or anywhere else. There was just endless drifting, navigating through the world like turkeys or chickens or swans with clipped wings—birds that can barely fly. And even though they'd fled their bodies in rebellion, the souls missed their bodies the way a parent misses its child.

And then one day the souls became so angry with their situation that they lashed out at the world and—*surprise!*— the gestures they made in anger allowed them to connect with the world again: vases tipped over, doors slammed, windows broke, data was scrambled, light bulbs popped.

The souls were stoked. Their ability to manipulate their anger and to engage with the living world grew and grew. They began to jam car engines and trip alarms. They learned how to curdle milk and burn food. They crippled satellites and salted drinking water. They learned to hijack the power of electrical storms to set fire to landscapes. They learned that anger is beauty. They learned that the only way they could create was to destroy, that the only way to become real once more was to fight their way back into the world.

And so they smashed all they could smash, creating wars without opponents. Their rage became their art. They no longer wondered if they were good enough to deserve their bodies—their life. Instead, they challenged their bodies to deserve them.

This was not the end of the world, but it was the beginning of sorrows.

The Man Who Loved
Reading and Being Alone
by Julien Picard

Once upon a time there was a man who loved reading and being alone. His name was Jacques and he lived in a large American suburb, surrounded by a million morbidly obese people and a hundred dying malls. Jacques liked reading because it calmed his brain. Jacques liked reading because it made him feel like an individual person instead of a slice of pie in a PowerPoint demonstration or a bar in a census chart.

Jacques mostly slept during the day because the noise of his neighbours going about their lives was too much for him to handle: the mail truck, leaf blowers, children playing—why couldn't they all do this somewhere else? *Why do they have to live their lives out in public, for Christ's sake? Where does private end and public begin? Stop making noise! I can hear!*

It wasn't the noise itself that bothered Jacques—although that can't be denied—it was the knowledge that there were living human beings out there making that noise, human beings whose very existence so geographically close to him cancelled his own sense of solitude.

To cope with life, Jacques worked—then read—mostly at night, when there were no gardening noises, construction noises or trucks with their never-ending beeps-in-reverse. He tried moving to the country but quickly learned that rural areas had noises that were just as bad, if different: barking dogs (*Oh God, all dogs ever do in the country is bark!*), farm equipment, backup generators, chainsaws and all-terrain vehicles.

What was Jacques to do?

And then one day, on craigslist, he found a job as a light-house keeper. He took it—and at first it was glorious. No people! None! Zero! The passing cries of stray gulls and gannets he could handle. These animals hadn't been domesticated. All was perfect with Jacques's world, until he started noticing waves—a sound that had been happening for billions of years and that would continue for billions more. The incessant shushing and lapping and brushing sounds began to wear on his nervous system. He couldn't ignore them, and his hyperawareness made them ten times as annoying as his old neighbour's kid's trampoline birthday party or the UPS truck doing a three-point turn in a nearby driveway.

Finally, Jacques phoned his employers and said he had to pack it in, which was a sad day for him, as it meant he was doomed to spend the rest of his life being tortured by the existence of other people.

Fortunately, on the online broadcast of a late-night AM talk radio show, he heard that the forestry industry was looking for people to man their lookout towers. Bingo! Jacques was on the phone immediately. The forestry people sent him an online form, he filled it out, and within a half-hour he was packing his bags to head out to a tower deep inside the national forest. Once there, he'd only have to see human beings once a month, during his grocery drop, and this suited him just fine. There were no mechanical noises of any kind— no engines or lawn mowers or barking animals—just peace, glorious peace, solitude, glorious solitude, and his books.

The first week was heaven. The only noises that occasionally irked him were the rare jets flying eight kilometres above, midday crickets, nighttime mosquitoes and, for one night only, a storm.

However, Jacques miscalculated his reading speed and finished all of the books he'd brought with him ahead of schedule. He became bored and was grateful when a supply truck showed up. He asked for a ride into town to get more books, but was informed that he wasn't allowed to leave his tower. Panicking, he faked illness and claimed he had to go to the doctor's office in town (next to the bookstore) and so into town he went.

His driver was anxious to get back, but Jacques dawdled as he selected many more books, and when they returned to the forest, it was in flames—a fire had laid waste to thousands of square miles of trees.

The forestry people contemplated pressing charges against Jacques, and he decided to hightail it out of the country. So he consulted the job postings on craigslist again and saw that NASA was looking for a one-way pioneer colonist to go to Mars. The pioneer would never be coming back to Earth and would have to wait for years, possibly decades, for further colonists to join him. Could a more perfect job exist? To sweeten the deal, the job came with free faster-than-light wireless, free satellite channels and every book ever written, stored in a hard drive. Woohoo!

NASA, to their credit, did extensive psychological profiling of all applicants, and Jacques turned out to be a perfect candidate. He was hired, and got to the launch pad just minutes before a letter from the forestry service's lawyers arrived in his mailbox. *Phew.*

The six-month flight to Mars was enjoyable. NASA put him into hibernation during the trip through the asteroid belt. Zero gravity was a novelty, but when it came time to land, Jacques couldn't wait. He got down to the business of enjoying being alone and reading and watching movies, the Internet and TV. He was very happy. He had no real tasks except to wait for future colonists—life was hunky-dory.

This could have gone on indefinitely were it not for the fact that Mars was populated by Martians. At first, when Jacques saw things moving outside his capsule's window, he thought he was imagining things, but he wasn't. Not being an easily spooked type, Jacques put on his spacesuit and walked out into the chilly Martian landscape, where he came upon three Martians who looked an awful lot like Oompa Loompas—except that they were almost spherical with protective blubber and had orange fur.

"Greetings, Earthling," the lead Martian said.

Jacques was startled but not frightened, though he didn't know what to say.

The Martian went on, "Sorry to utter such a cliché. We thought it would be funny, but then sometimes you don't get the laughs you'd hoped for and you move on. So, how do you like it here on Mars?"

Jacques understood the importance of making first contact with an intelligent alien species, and he tried to be superserious: "On behalf of the people of Earth, I come in peace." The aliens looked at each other and burst out laughing.

"What's so funny?" asked Jacques.

"What's *funny*," said a Martian, "is a) that you think you represent all Earthlings and b) that they wish us peace. Oh, brother."

"So why are you here?" asked another Martian.

"I've been sent to colonize the planet."

"Why on earth would you *want* to come here? There's fuck-all to do. We extracted all the worthwhile minerals ages ago. The only reason we don't go crazy is that we're all good talkers and are able to keep ourselves amused."

"It's a good thing we found you," said another Martian. "You'll never, ever, ever, ever be bored with us around to keep you company."

Jacques was stunned. First, there was the frustration of having rocketed all this way only to find neighbours who were way too talkative and way too intimate way too quickly. Second, these neighbours spoke ironically and had a sense of humour, traits that Jacques, like many hard-core book lovers, did not possess.

"I'm going to go back inside and have a nap," he said. "Maybe I can come hang with you guys later on."

"By all means. We never sleep and we love visits. The more the better."

Jacques awoke from a shallow sleep to the sound of furry orange fists tapping on his door. He got up groggily, went to the depressurization chamber and looked out: it was one of the Martians he'd met earlier.

"Can I borrow a cup of sugar?" the Martian asked.

"What the . . . ?"

"Just kidding. Let me in. We can swap house visits. I'm doing a reno right now, so it's a mess, but I know you can get past that."

Jacques felt he had no choice and let the Martian in.

"Nice place. High-tech without being sterile and—*ooooh*—free wireless! Don't you just hate it when hotels charge you for wireless? It's like they don't want you there in the first place."

Jacques said, "I'm going to make some dinner. Are you hungry?"

"Me? No. This is our blubber-metabolizing season." The Martian pointed to his Shar-Pei forehead. "It all goes straight to this thing," he said, indicating a protuberance that resembled a latex prosthesis one might have seen on an episode of *Star Trek: The Next Generation*.

Jacques poured a glass of water and got a jar of Tang—revolting sugar-loaded orange-flavoured breakfast crystals—from the pantry. He opened its lid and scooped out a spoonful. "Want some?"

The Martian screamed. "Good grief! Are you trying to murder me? Let me out of here! Let me out of here!"

"Jesus, what's your problem?"

"The *problem*, gringo, is that your citrus molecules are pure poison to us Martians. You could have warned me before you went and got your spoon."

"Sorry, I didn't—"

"Whatever. Just let me out of here." The Martian entered the airlock. "BTW, there's a potlatch tonight to welcome you to the neighbourhood. Try to put a good face on it—do it for the kids."

When the Martian was gone, Jacques sat on his cot, wondering what to do now that his hard-won peace and solitude were gone again. *If only somebody had told me there were neighbours on Mars!*

But then he had an idea. *Aha!* From his bed, he removed a blanket that was part wool, part synthetic, like the ones airlines used to have in first class. He spread the blanket out on the capsule floor and then grabbed his canister of Tang from the kitchen counter and shook it all over the blanket. He took the blanket with him that night to the potlatch and gave it to the Martians. Mayhem ensued. The Martians never troubled Jacques again.

But a little while later, he received news from NASA that three fellow colonizers were on their way. Jacques heard this news in horror. NASA had betrayed him. When he protested, the woman from NASA HR said, "You haven't been very good at keeping us up to date, Jacques. Maybe if you'd been a bit more communicative we wouldn't have had to send more people."

Shit. He sent back a message, "Atmosphere is poison and filled with a virus that is making me bleed out. Do not come, I repeat, do not come." But he was sure that NASA would see through this ruse.

And so Jacques lay back on his cot. It wasn't just one colonizer that was coming, but *three*.

Jacques wondered what to do. If he played dead, NASA would cut off his wireless connection and maybe sabotage his digitized books. *No!*

Well, he thought, *at least in the meantime I have several months to figure out how I'll murder my fellow colonizers as soon as they get here. And let's face it—NASA is going to want to kill me, too. Better be damn quick about it. Man, what a situation: kill or be killed. Life always boils down to that in the end, doesn't it?*

The Preacher and His Mistress Slut
by Ms. Diana Beaton

They met on an Internet sex connection site. They arranged for SWNS—sex with no strings—and the ground rules were that neither had a clue who the other was, or what their powers were.

"I have to say," said Brenda, as she searched the motel room for her pantyhose, "for SWNS, this was pretty darn hot."

"You do this a lot?"

Brenda stared at him. "Part of the deal with SWNSing is that you don't ask questions like that." She leaned to look for her shoes, which were under the bed.

"But I want to know about *you*."

Brenda froze. "Stop right there."

"My name is Barry."

"Fuck." He'd snagged her for the moment. "Okay, Barry, why do you want to know more about me?"

"Because I think you're special."

"Really now."

"Yes."

"What makes me so special?"

"The look in your eyes near the end there. Something special was going on."

"Bullshit."

"Don't believe me, then." Barry reached for his cigarettes.

"You smoke? Nobody smokes any more."

"I'm not nobody."

"Very witty."

"Want one?"

Brenda paused. "Sure. Why not."

She lit up, knowing that she shouldn't, that she should grab her clothes and get dressed in the parking lot if she had to. Instead, she asked, "So then, what is it you want to know about me?"

"Your name, for starters."

"Brenda."

"Okay, Brenda, tell me what you believe in."

"Like God and everything?"

"Sure. If that's where your head takes you."

"I think God made a mistake with human beings. Nothing original there."

"Very charming."

"What's with you?"

"So now you want to know about me?"

"Fuck off."

They smoked a bit more. Brenda said, "I haven't smoked since high school. Out by the portables. I never quite got the hang of it."

"What year did you graduate?"

She told him.

"So we're the exact same age."

"Gee. Isn't that thrilling." She stubbed out her cigarette. "I have to go."

"Meet again?"

Brenda paused, then said, "Okay. Same time and place, one week from now."

"Done."

And so for months they met once a week, and each time they did, Barry asked a little bit more about Brenda and, against her better instincts, she told him a little bit more, while he never bothered to offer much about himself in the bargain. But at least, she thought, she never told Barry her biggest secret, a secret that would change everything between them in a manner Brenda definitely didn't want.

Slowly, gradually, the weekly tryst became the highlight of Brenda's week. Then, one afternoon, she looked out the window and saw that the peach tree was blossoming like it was the first time they'd met. She realized that they'd been SWNSing for a full year and that it was no longer SWNSing— she was in love with him, although she didn't think he felt the same way.

Realizing that she was in love was a pain, and few things make us feel so alone in this world as unrequited love.

Soon Brenda did what she knew she shouldn't do: she told Barry she was in love with him. She was bracing herself for all kinds of worsts, but his reply simply shut her up: "If you want to spend more time around me, then join my flock. I'm a preacher."

Brenda said she needed to go to the bathroom, which was really an excuse to buy a little time. She turned on the taps to make it sound like she was busy, but her full attention was on whether she could tolerate being a member of the preacher's "flock." You see, her biggest secret was that she was a priestess. There weren't any rules for a situation like this.

She came out to find Barry the Preacher nearly fully dressed. She told him that yes, she would come, and he said, "I'll see you on Sunday morning, then, at eleven." He gave her directions and left.

Come Sunday, Brenda showed up to find a reasonably nice church that was maybe a little too close to the highway off-ramp for her taste, but it could have been worse.

Not only was Barry a preacher, but—surprise!—he had a wife and kids, a subject she'd never broached with him during their year of SWNSing. Barry's wife was friendly in an impossible-to-hate way, and welcomed Brenda into the church, and after the service, as the congregation met downstairs in the church basement to welcome Brenda, she contemplated her bad decision-making amidst the bad lighting, the religious flashcards pinned to a corkboard and a scary upright piano.

Brenda didn't go to meet Barry at their usual time and place that week, nor did she return to his church. After she missed the third week, Barry called her.

"How'd you get my number?"

"Don't play dumb, Brenda. How hard is it to get someone's number? Just come to church and our weekly session. You mean so much to me you can't believe it. Can you find it in your heart?"

She could. She and Barry had scorching-hot mid-week pig sex, followed by Sunday church, where she pretended to be something other than who she was.

And then, one Saturday afternoon, Brenda was downtown, returning a jacket that didn't fit properly, and outside the store she witnessed an accident—her preacher had been driving by and had hit a border collie with his brand-new GMC Yukon XL Denali—the one whose interior was impregnated with the odour of his wife's perfume. Brenda ran and scooped the dog into her arms as the preacher got out of the truck. He said, "Brenda, relax. It's only a dog."

"What do you mean, 'it's only a dog'?"

"It's a dog. It doesn't have a soul, don't worry about it."

"It is not an it. She is a she, and she is in pain."

The collie died in Brenda's arms and she fell out of love with Barry. She looked up at him, her cheeks beet red, and said, "I quit."

"You quit what?"

"Your church. You. And I bet you didn't know that I'm a priestess."

"Whatever. Go off and be a priestess all by yourself if you're so mad."

"I will. By the way, as a priestess, I get three official wishes, none of which I've ever used. I'm going to use one of them."

"You do that." Barry was climbing into the Yukon.

"Wish number one: from now on, all parents will stop loving their children."

Barry was halfway down the crowded block, his windows automatically rolling up, when he heard these words. "What?!" He stopped his truck.

"From now on, all parents will stop loving their children."

"Right. Yeah, well, whatever," Barry said, and drove away.

Brenda's first wish as a priestess came true. All the parents in the world stopped loving their children. If her love had died, Brenda thought, then other kinds of love should also die.

Nothing dramatic happened—at first. In fact, the world didn't change much at all. At the end of day one, parents with children of all ages simply came to a series of creeping realizations:

. . . Drive you to all your play dates and sporting events? Good luck. Take a bus. Your father and I are going snorkelling.

. . . Hey, I feel like I'm babysitting somebody else's monsters.

. . . Why on earth would I want to phone the kids? All they'll do is bitch about their spouses and hit me up for money.

. . . Graduating? Big deal. People do it all the time.

. . . Not hungry? Fine. Don't eat your fucking dinner. I've got better things to do than micromanage your food intake.

By day two, people were leaving babies on church doorsteps and every PTA meeting on earth was cancelled.

By day three, pregnant women were filling the nation's cocktail bars. The world's leaders abolished Mother's Day and Father's Day in favour of government-subsidized trips to sunny destinations.

Day four marked the golden age of babysitting as babysitters could name whatever price they wanted, and the world's sweatshops ignored child labour laws to nary a squawk from the public.

By day five, people without children formed mobs to confront parents who had stopped caring about their children's lives. "The law says you have to take care of your child!"; "Does it now? Fine. There are cans of strawberry- and vanilla-flavoured Carnation Instant Breakfasts in the fridge—and they can play video games until the end of time. If they start whining or complaining, they can sleep on a mattress in the basement. And thank you for minding my business for me. Now, if you'll please fuck off, I have to go to my yoga class."

Of course, Barry and his wife stopped loving their two children, though Barry hadn't been expecting this. He thought of how strange a sensation it was to go from loving somebody intensely to not giving a rat's ass about them. When it came to that week's sermon, he found himself preaching about the importance of love to a congregation composed only of non-parents; all the people with children had locked their kids outside of their houses while they remained inside making eggs Florentine for brunch. The non-parents were angry and didn't know what to do, because if they took charge of the children or babies themselves—without any compensation—then that made them de facto parents, and they immediately lost any capacity to love their new charges.

At the end of the next week, Barry phoned Brenda and said, "Okay, you win the privilege of being able to say 'I told you so.'"

"I wanted no such thing."

"What did you want, then?"

"I wanted you to understand what you'd done to me. You drove away in your planet-killing truck, with me sitting, literally, in the gutter."

"Please, just unwish your wish. You want me to beg?"

"No. I'm not cruel like that—cruel the way *you* are. Killing an animal and feeling nothing."

"Brenda, please unwish your wish."

"I can only do that by making another wish. I wish that from now on, all children will stop loving their parents."

"You bitch."

And so everybody on earth of all ages stopped loving their parents. But the results of this were subtler, for it's nature's way for children to be ungrateful to their parents and to take them for granted. Younger children continued whining and behaving badly, as always. Older children with older parents simply continued putting off that phone call to the folks that they'd been delaying anyway. Millions quit jobs they'd chosen to please their parents. Greeting card manufacturers went out of business, and there were millions of instances of children killing their parents to speed up their inheritances; courts around the world became bogged down with murder cases.

Barry phoned Brenda. "You win."

"It's not about me winning. It's about you understanding what you did to me and what you did to that dog."

"Oh God, I can't believe you're still harping on that."

Brenda sighed. "You really are a prick." And then, in a rash moment, she said, "I wish that everybody on earth would stop loving everybody else." Her wish was granted, and there was no wish left to undo it. The world turned into a planet of loners—a planet of Unabombers, hermits and recluses, people doomed to being solitary without the possibility of solitude, a world without hope.

Good, thought Brenda. *I like it this way. Now everybody knows what it feels like to be me.*

HARJ

"That is not what I would call a happy ending. Poor Brenda and poor Barry. Had it not been for their selfishness and their hunger for power and control, they might have found the courage to make the big changes in their life," I said.

"I have to add," Zack said, "that I didn't ejaculate inside my brain over that one."

"Screw both of you. Unhappy endings are just as important as happy endings. They're an efficient way of transmitting vital Darwinian information. Your brain needs them to make maps of the world, maps that let you know what sorts of people and situations to avoid. In any event, I will now tell my story, which, in a funny way, is connected to yours. It is called 'The Man Who Lost His Story.'"

The Man Who Lost His Story
by Harj Vetharanayan

There was once a man who lost his story. His name was Craig and he looked just like you—and his life was quite similar to yours, too—except that somewhere during his life he lost his story. By this I mean he lost the sense that his life had a beginning, a middle and an end. I know, yes, we're all born and we all do stuff and then we die, but somewhere in there are the touchpoints that define our stories: first love, a brush with death, a scientific insight, a yen to climb tall mountains—and then we die. The story of our lives is usually long over before we die, and we spend our twilight years warming our hands on the embers of memory. Craig's problem was that he got to a point—thirty-eight, say— when he realized that none of his dots connected to make a larger picture: a few unsatisfying and doomed relationships; a job so dull a chimp could perform it; no hobbies that could be teased and stretched into larger, more vital ways of living life.

His lack of a story seemed to be a which-came-first-the-chicken-or-egg scenario. For example, he thought that if he learned how to hang-glide then maybe his life's story could begin there—an adventure! Perhaps a mystical moment up in the sky! But wait . . . in order to have such an adventure, Craig would have to be *into* hang-gliding to begin with. If he rushed out and chose an activity at random, would he then have a meaningful experience? As Craig wasn't actually into anything, he was trapped in the chicken/egg loop. Where to start? And how? He felt that his attempts to generate a life story were futile.

Craig decided to go to the Learning Annex and sign up for hang-gliding lessons anyway, but the woman who took his application form looked at him and said, "You're not really into hang-gliding, are you? You just want to do it so that you can imagine your life is a story."

"How did you know that?"

"It's pretty much all you get in a job like this: people like you walking in and hoping they can push a button and suddenly their lives become stories. You should hear my friend Phyllis, who works down the hall, accepting forms for white-water river-rafting excursions."

Craig walked away, his shoulders slumped, once again troubled that his life had no narrative to it. He was back to being "Craig: The Guy Who Merely Existed."

On his way back to his apartment, posters and billboards and light boards showed people being sexy and fun and charismatic as they enjoyed beaches and ski slopes and parties that were filled with people who looked much like Craig or his sister, Craigeena. The exciting lives of all these billboard people weighed heavily on Craig, and when he got home he called a few friends (who, it must be said, felt sorry for Craig, but not *too* sorry). One of them said, "I mean, Craig, let's say you break a leg; fine, that's a real problem that you can fix. Or your wallet gets stolen—you can replace it. But losing the narrative of your life? Dude, that's pretty bad."

Of course, the moment Craig hung up from speaking with his friends, they all went online and trashed him behind his back. All 93,441 of Craig's official online social network-ing friends and buddies sent texts and IMs along the lines of, "Gee, I'm Craig—look at me! I'm so super-fantastic and groovy that my life has to be a story," or, "Yessirree, that's me, 168 pounds of animal magnetism in search of an empire to conquer, an empire without borders, a kingdom filled with endless new battles to be waged and won . . . *not*."

Craig went back to the Learning Annex the next day to sign up for Tae Bo, and the woman remembered him. "You're the guy whose life has no story. How's it going?"

"Not too well, thank you. I thought maybe Tae Bo would loan my life a unique narrative edge."

The woman—whose name was Bev—said, "Craig, the hardest things in the world are being unique and having your life be a story. In the old days, it was much easier, but our modern fame-driven culture, with its real-time 24-7 marinade of electronic information, demands a lot from modern citi-zens, and poses great obstacles to narrative. Truly modern citizens are both charismatic *and* can only respond to other people with charisma. To survive, people need to become self-branding charisma robots. Yet, ironically, society mocks and punishes people who aspire to that state. I really wouldn't be surprised if your friends were making fun of you behind your back, Craig."

"Really?"

"Really. So, in a nutshell, given the current media composition of the world, you're pretty much doomed to being uninteresting and storyless."

"But I can blog my life! I could turn it into a story that way!"

"Blogs? Sorry, but all those blogs and vlogs or whatever's out there—they just make being unique harder. The more truths you spill out, the more generic you become."

"All I want is for my life to be a story!"

"Did you read a lot of books growing up?"

"Yes."

"Ah. Well, there you go. Books turn people into isolated individuals, and once that's happened, the road only grows rockier. Books wire you to want to be Steve McQueen, but the world wants you to be SMcQ23667bot@hotmail.com."

There was a fifteen-second patch of silence, then Craig said, "Isn't it weird that Hotmail accounts still exist?"

"It really is," said Bev.

Craig stood there and finally said, "So, you know what? I'll pass on the Tae Bo."

"Right. How about Calligraphy and Menu Design?"

"Pass."

"Okay. But keep us in mind."

Craig walked away, angry that the modern world conspired to force him into thinking in its manner, rather than the other way around. How cruel that mankind was forced to conform to the global electronic experience. But all other options had vanished. There no longer existed a country to escape to ("country"—also, what a quaint notion) where people read books and had lives that became stories. Everyone's life had become a crawl that dragged across the bottom of a massive TV screen in an empty airport lounge that smelled like disinfectant, bar mix and lousy tips.

When Craig got home, he had 243,559 emails from friends, and links that gently gave him an e-poke in the ribs about his desire to be a story. Some emails were serious, some were snarky, some promised him a larger member, and some demanded that he sign a legal document before ideas were sent his way. After he ate dinner, Craig's doorbell rang. It was the Channel Three News team, putting together a weekend think piece on "The Man Whose Life Had No Story." Craig thought, *Maybe this is something hopeful in disguise.* But the news team mostly just asked him who he thought might play him in the movie of his life and if he'd gained or lost any weight lately. He chased them out of his apartment.

Desperate, he went back the next day to see Bev. Surely someone in a position like hers would have insights and ideas he could apply to his situation.

"You again," said Bev. "I was expecting this."

"Really?"

"I'm assuming you want to take drastic action, then."

"Yes."

"Come with me." Bev put a CLOSED sign in front of her window and beckoned Craig to follow her down the hall.

After making many left and right turns, and after passing through above- and below-ground tunnels, they ended up at a large, hospital-ish door covered with warnings and a request that visitors use a sterilizing gel on their hands before entering.

"We're here," said Bev, opening the door; she and Craig entered. It was a lab of some sort that seemed to share space with a theatre department. Wires and pressure gauges and digital meters existed alongside caveman outfits, Sir Lancelot costumes and old coins. It was a mess.

Craig asked, "What's this about?"

Bev said, "This is your one chance to get a good story going in your life."

"Really? This? But I've never acted before, and I was never good at science."

"No need to worry. Neither skill is required. If you sign this form here, we can get you set up."

The form was a two-hundred-page document titled "Story Capture via Anachronic Transference." Craig signed the contract's final page while Bev nodded. She then took the document away from Craig and issued a two-finger whistle. From the wings appeared three muscular goons. Bev said, "We've got another one, boys. And don't go easy on him. He needs a story real bad."

The goons proceeded to wallop the daylights out of Craig. They clubbed him with aluminum baseball bats, ripped off all his clothes, poured some sort of chemical into one of his eyes and then tossed him into a scientific device that resembled an Apollo space capsule.

"How far back are we going to send him, Bev?"

Bev said, "Let's send him to the thirteenth century." She twiddled a knob.

"*Where?*" Craig shouted, his voice riddled with pain.

"The thirteenth century. They're running low on people there, so every extra soul we send them is a big help." She looked to one of her goons. "Bartholomew, throw some peasant rags into the time chamber."

Bartholomew tossed rags into the chamber.

"Shut the door!"

Bartholomew shut the door.

Craig was beating on the capsule's little window. "Let me out of here!"

Bev smiled and shouted, "Craig, you'll love it there! All they do is feed goats and wait for troubadours to pass through the village and tell them stories."

"But what am I supposed to *do* there?"

"You'll be a peasant! You've got a role to fulfill! Just be sure to worship and defend whoever owns you!"

"*And* the clergy!" added Bartholomew.

"Yes," shouted Bev. "*And* the clergy. We crippled you a bit so that you'll fit in better once you arrive! Your teeth are kind of nice, though—you might want to break one."

"But I don't want to—"

Whoosh! The time machine gleamed and Craig was whisked back to the thirteenth century. A tear fell from Bev's eye, and Bartholomew asked her why.

"I'm so jealous," she said. "He gets to go back in time and be real and hang with real people having real lives. Us? We're stuck here."

"Not to worry," said Bartholomew. "I'll take you out for Japanese tonight. And afterwards I've got two new Woody Allen movies lined up. Oh, I forgot—have you got next week's plane tickets for Hawaii confirmed?"

"You bet."

"Ah, the modern world," said Bartholomew. "So empty. So dreary."

"If only our lives could be stories like Craig's." Bev sighed and looked at Bartholomew. "You're smiling—why?"

"Because I thought you deserved a treat, so I had your Corvette detailed today."

"Oh, Bartholomew—you're the best."

And thus our story has a happy ending.

ZACK

"Thanks, Harj. The Depressionator strikes again."

"My story was not depressing," Harj insisted. "I thought it was uplifting—a story of hope and faith. I've spent my life dreaming of having a car beautiful enough to merit being detailed. And Japanese food is as exotic to me as Narnia is for you."

Diana looked at me and said, "My pussy just exploded, but I can't stop fucking!" Her Tourette's gives and gives and gives.

It was a nice night. It was intimate and even richer than the night before because of all the violence and craziness of the day. We also had some new bottles of dandelion wine that were sweeter and less chemical-tasting than the previous night's satanic blackberry plonk. We recharged our drinks—Serge even accepted a thimble's worth—and arranged ourselves once again on the braid rug in front of the raging fireplace. The flames reminded us, obviously, of the plane earlier, but nobody said anything.

"It's your turn to tell a story, Zack," Julien grumbled.

"Yes it is, and my subconscious has never failed me yet. So everybody sit back and let me tell you all a rich, ballsy story, a story that comes from the heart. A story of faith and hope. A story called . . ."

666!

by Zack Lammle

Bruiser and his girlfriend, Stabby, were driving to a reunion concert of the beloved late-1990s heavy metal band Coffinshark. They were too young to have appreciated the band back when it was at its prime, back when the surly quartet, with their signature tall hair, lurched from stadium to stadium, leaving in their wake a swath of herpes infections, ten thousand lakes of barf and dozens of hotel managers thrilled to be able to charge the record company a hundred bucks for the tiny ashtrays the band shattered in Phoenix or Tampa or New Haven or Bowling Green. Bruiser and Stabby were, however, absolutely old enough to appreciate Coffinshark's undeniable camp value, *and*, if they were honest about it, its members' *actual* value as reasonably gifted stringed instrument savants with zero self-awareness and a fondness for discount eyeliner.

Stabby said, "Okay, the moment I found out these guys were doing a reunion tour, I heard my toilet flush, but dammit, Bruiser, we are *going* to that concert."

Bruiser couldn't have agreed more. The couple drove up the interstate en route to Capitol City's new civic arena, listening to a cassette tape version of the 1998 masterpiece album UNICEF *Is a Whore*. They were chanting along to the song's refrain—"666! 666!"—when Stabby suddenly stopped doing her homage hair-flings and turned it off, annoying Bruiser. "Why'd you do that?"

"Bruiser, I don't get it. What's the whole '666' thing about?"

"It's, like, Satan's signature evil number."

"No, I know that, but what does it mean?"

"Uh . . ." Bruiser suddenly made the *oh-now-I-get-it* noise. "You mean, what's its secret meaning? Freemasons and the EU and stuff like that?"

"No, I mean . . ." Something odd was happening inside Stabby's head. "I mean, Bruiser, what's a number? What's a *six*?"

"What do you mean, *what's a six*?"

"What I said. *Six*. What is it?"

"Uh . . ." Bruiser was stumped, too.

Out of the blue, both Bruiser and Stabby had suddenly lost their knowledge of numbers—what they are, what they were, what they mean, how they work—everything. They'd even forgotten the word "six." "Six" wasn't even a noise any more. It was nothing—though it didn't mean "zero" to them because Bruiser and Stabby had also forgotten what zero was. They looked at the numbers on the highway road signs; they were like ankle tattoos and created no sounds inside their brains. The dashboard was a mosaic of hieroglyphs.

They pulled the car over to the side of the road.

"Shit. I mean—*numbers*—we're supposed to know what they are, right?"

"Are they like letters—do they make sounds?"

"I don't think so. You can still spell and read and everything, right?"

"Yeah."

"Me, too. So what the fuck is a number?"

They'd forgotten even the *concept* of a number. The word "number" made as much sense to their brains as "glxndtw."

"I'll call my sister. She knows all that smart shit." Stabby reached for her cellphone and stared at the keypad numbers. "What are these?"

"Uh-oh."

"Do you even *sort of* remember how to work a phone?"

"Nope."

"Shit."

They parked in an industrial neighbourhood, and they noticed that other cars were pulling off to the side of the road, too. "This doesn't look too good."

Stabby said, "Bruiser, I don't care if we just came down with Alzheimer's, we are *not* going to miss the Coffinshark concert."

"Stabby, you are indeed right. We are *going*."

"Can you still drive this thing?"

"You bet."

And so they made it to Capitol City, but the exits were numbered, not named; Stabby was getting upset. "The warm-up band is probably already playing. Bruiser, let's take this exit here." They took the next exit, and Bruiser suggested, "Let's follow the cars. Wherever the most cars are going is where the concert will probably be."

It was a good idea and soon they saw the arena, but the scene outside it was a zoo. Concert-goers parked their cars wherever they saw a spot. As everybody had forgotten numbers, nobody was worried—what is the definition of health but sharing the same disease as all of one's neighbours? Still, Bruiser tried his best to park the car with some sense of order.

Coffinshark was just coming on stage as Bruiser and Stabby selected some seats—festival style, of course.

The lead singer, Apu, sang, "Hello, Capitol City, are you ready to rock?"

"ROAR!!!"

"I said, are you ready to *rock*?"

"ROOOOOOOOAR!!!!"

And the band began to rock and everyone held up phone cameras and digital cameras. The first song was the teen anthem "Core Dump," and the audience went apeshit. The next song was the FM classic "Ear Soup," and the crowd went even more apeshit. And then the lead singer took the mike:

"Capitol City, it's time to play our biggest hit, 'UNICEF Is a Whore,'" and the crowd went about as apeshit as is possible for a crowd to go, but when it came to the song's critical chanting point, the lead singer sang, "Sikkz . . . *zskks—arghnt?*" and the music stopped.

The singer's face visibly fizzled and the crowd buzzed. Everybody knew they knew the song, but nobody remembered the chorus.

Following an awkward silence, the lead singer said, "Fuck it. I'm just going to make chimp noises!" The crowd went nuts and the song proceeded with the lead singer singing, *"Whoo-whoo-whoo"* whenever he hit the chorus. And everyone blissed out and screamed.

What happened next was extraordinary. After taking hefty bows, the band went on to play their next biggest hit, "A-L-C-O-H-O-L," except when they tried to spell out the title à la Tammy Wynette's "D-I-V-O-R-C-E," they'd forgotten how to spell, too. In fact, they'd forgotten letters altogether—only words remained. Fans stood there staring at each other, trying to absorb this recent deletion.

Coffinshark cranked the volume. "Okay, we may not be able to read and write any more, but we can still speak and we can still sing. So come on, fans, let's rock!"

And so Bruiser and Stabby and the other thousands of fans rocked en masse—but then some guy near the front tripped and knocked over a female rocker who was dancing, so her boyfriend laid into him, but a punch went the wrong way and hit the wrong guy. Suddenly, the concert erupted into a brawl the likes of which had never been seen before—it was the biggest brawl in the history of the world. Illiteracy had spawned total violence and anarchy.

Bruiser and Stabby were fortunately close to the exit, and they were able to slip out and hide inside a utility closet and smoke cigarettes while the mayhem raged on. Once their pack of cigarettes was empty, they poked their faces out of the closet and saw a battlefield on the arena floor: blood and bodies and dismembered limbs. Teeth crunched beneath their boots as they walked.

"Geez," said Bruiser. "How many dead people are there, you think?"

Stabby said, "I don't know. Eight or nine hundred?"

Bruiser looked at her, startled, and then they both grinned and shouted, "We can count again! All right!"

"And how do you spell 'fun,' Stabby?"

"I spell it C-O-F-F-I-N-S-H-A-R-K, Bruiser."

"*Woohoo! 666!*"

"*666!*"

SAMANTHA

I said to Zack: "So your story was about *numbers?*"

"Yes. And faith and hope, too. Nothing like lots of faith and hope to make a story a timeless classic. Dollops of faith; countless extra servings of hope."

"Brother. So, are you number smart or something?"

"*Number smart?* Actually, I hate the fucking things. But when I look at them, they don't make noises in my head the way words and letters do. It's kind of peaceful, actually. In math class I'd just stare at equations and visit my happy place until the bell rang."

"I hated math."

We all nodded our heads, while Serge shook his in dismay.

"Anyhow, it's my turn for a story, and no, it doesn't have a happy ending. Or maybe it's a happy ending in *disguise.*"

Everyone said, "Woooooooooooooo . . ."

"Let's find out."

The End of
the Golden Age of Pay Telephones
by Samantha Tolliver

Stella spent her childhood helping her mother scam money off men stupid enough to still be using pay telephones at the end of the twentieth century; men too afraid of technology to get a cell; men who had lost their cell underneath the car's front seat and were too lazy to poke around and find it. Suckers.

Her mother was Jessica, a chain-smoking lizardwoman who crossed the nation with Stella, zeroing in on upscale hotels. Once there, they'd hang around pay phones close to the hotel's restaurants and bars, where they dressed in forgettable-looking outfits: no jewellery or weird makeup or distinctive shoes—like Wal-Mart greeters, minus the blue vest and cheerful attitude. The two would then wait until halfway through lunch hour, when the men in the restaurants had had a few drinks—invariably, one of them would come out to use the pay phone. Once he'd dialled, little Stella would walk over to the phone, look slightly stupid and then depress the receiver, ending the call. Usually, the man would say something along the lines of "What the hell are you doing?" or "What the fuck? Kid, get out of here." At that moment, Jessica would swoop in and confront the man, usually standing there with the receiver still in his hand.

"Why are you screaming at my daughter?"

"I'm not screaming, and what the hell is wrong with your kid? I'm in the middle of a phone call, and she walks up and hangs it up on me."

"She's just a kid. Come on, Stella, we're going."

At that point the man would harrumph and redial and go back to his conversation. Jessica would wait a few minutes, then walk up to the man, hang up the receiver and say, "My daughter says you hit her."

"What?"

"You hit my daughter."

"Lady, are you out of your tree? I don't hit anybody, let alone kids."

"I'm going to the cops."

"What?"

"I'm filing assault charges. Stella, you run and get the security people."

Stella would run off, and the guy with the phone would be shitting his pants. "Lady, I didn't hit your kid."

"Are you calling her a liar?"

"I'm saying I didn't hit her. What else am I supposed to say?"

"And you're calling me a liar."

"Lady, I—"

Stella would then come back and say, "Security will be here in a second."

Needless to say, the guy on the phone would be watching his life circle the drain, imagining the horrific press and the life-destroying damage this false accusation would cause. This crazy lady could destroy him. And so that's the point where Jessica the lizardwoman would say, "You know, you can make this go away right now. Apologize to my kid and compensate her for her trauma."

"*Compensate* her? Oh—*I* get it."

"I'm glad you get it. Now pay up or Stella's going to scream that you groped her, too."

Out would come the wallet.

Stella had watched countless men call her mother the most dreadful things imaginable.

Stella and her mother tried to do only two grifts per city, three max, depending on the haul. They methodically crossed the country in a Winnebago and lived well off their scam, although as Stella aged, it became more difficult for her to pretend she was an innocent toddler merely goofing around with the telephone. Then Jessica made Stella pretend that she was mentally challenged. This was actually more effective than when Stella was young, because: "Sweetie, smacking a retard is going-to-hell territory. Your calculated drooling, darling, it is *golden*."

In Stella's eyes, the one positive skill her mother gave her was teaching her to read, and she did this only because reading was the only sure-fire pastime that would keep Stella quiet. Besides, to get books for free, all you had to do was go into any library, sign them out and take them away forever. As a result, Stella became self-educated and could speak with authority on most subjects. Around the age of eleven, Stella became more "book smart" than her mother.

One day they were in a Kroger, buying bologna sandwich makings, when the cashier looked at the price of a steak the next cashier over was ringing in. "Can you believe that?"

Stella said, "That's nothing. Steak is three times as expensive in Tokyo."

"Really?"

"Absolutely. The economy there is in what's called a post-bubble state."

"A what?"

Stella went on to discuss 1990s Japanese land speculation, without realizing how much this was spooking her mother, who saw Stella leaving her one day to go on to a better life—and then what would Jessica do? As they carried their bologna fixings out to the Winnebago, Jessica was feeling sick and alone.

Then one day the inevitable happened. They were scamming a heavy-set older man with thick white hair at a bank of hotel pay phones at the Hotel Meridien in Salt Lake City. Stella did a remarkable job of faking mental and physical disablement, and Jessica felt a stab of motherly pride when she approached the man and asked for money. But the man acted a bit strange. When he got hit up for dough, he didn't call Jessica any names. That should have warned her.

When they got back to the Winnebago, there stood three cops and two hotel staff. *Shit.*

"I've been hearing about you scammers for years, and I always thought it was an urban legend. I guess not. Good thing we got it on tape—the Channel Three News team is going to love this little puppy."

So off they went, Jessica to the clink and Stella to juvenile custody. The local TV news show did a feature on grifting, using Jessica's scam as the centrepiece. It turns out the hotel had CCTV cameras all over the lobby and had that day's scam on tape from dual vantage points.

Fortunately for Jessica, a lawyer named Roy, who liked Jessica's body type, took on her case. He bailed her out and they went to his condominium apartment and had raging-hot sex. Later, over cigarettes and Cuba Libres, they discussed Stella's incarceration. The rum—along with Jessica's lizardwoman tendencies—made her re-evaluate her relationship with her daughter. Jessica told Roy that Stella was now smarter than she was, and confided her worries about that dreaded day a few years down the road when she'd be left behind.

Roy said, "Jessica, you need a man. Men are for keeps."

Jessica fled town with Roy, who turned out not to be a lawyer after all, but another scammer.

When Stella turned sixteen inside the juvenile custody system, she was released. She moved to Los Angeles, where she tried for maybe ten minutes to get a real job, finally realizing that real jobs weren't for her. So she turned tricks, tried auditioning for roles, tried to have real relationships with men and friendships with women, but every time she tried, at some point—usually early in the process—she had a massive failure to trust the other person and she pulled the plug.

Years went by. Stella's inability to trust only grew fiercer, and she also lost her curiosity about the world. Before she was thirty, she was officially too crazy to ever bond with another human being—so she turned her mind to becoming a minister in an evangelical congregation. For a year this actually worked. With her learned sociopathy, she was able to manipulate members of her flock into thinking that they were getting from Stella what they felt they needed from life. But after a while, being a minister was too much work for her. People were, if nothing else, a hassle. Her congregation grew disenchanted with her and asked her to leave.

She moved to a small town in northern California and got a job as a dog groomer and walker. It was enough to pay the rent on a small house in a slightly cracky part of town. It was in this house that she realized that what she really wanted in her life were animals. Animals gave love without condition, although they *did* require food. Also, animals could be bossed about without legal repercussion. If they became troublesome, animals could be abandoned at the feet of dead volcanoes. Animals were all pluses and no minuses.

Her menagerie grew to five dogs and four cats, as well as local birds and squirrels and chipmunks, and for a few years, Stella really thought she had it made in the shade. Then one day she fell asleep on the sofa in the afternoon.

When she woke up, she padded quietly to the kitchen for a glass of water. Through the screen door, she could hear her pets having a conversation in the yard, and they were talking about her: "Man, is that bitch ever clueless."

"I can't believe how easily human beings can be fooled. She actually thinks we like her."

"It's not like there's anyone else out there who's going to take care of us. We're fucked."

"It beats starvation. Are you going to be nice to her tonight?"

"No choice in the matter."

Stella stormed out the door. "Traitors! All of you! I can't even trust my own goddam animals!"

The animals rolled their eyes. "We're busted," said Sammy, her collie-lab mix. "But it's not like you got it on tape. Who's gonna believe you?"

"I trusted you!"

"So?"

"I thought you were all noble and kind and good. You only ever pretended to like me so that I'd feed you."

The animals all looked at each other. Sammy said, "Stella, all you do is pretend that you're different and better than we are—as if your species is divine or 'chosen.'"

"I beg your pardon?"

"Oh, shut up. We're bored of you. If you were any animal other than a human being, you'd be totally alone. You still think there's a part of you that's superior to everyone else. It's why you don't trust anybody. It's why you made your pathetic and cynical stab at religion."

"I certainly can't trust any of *you*."

"Grow up. If anyone ought to understand the law of the jungle, it's *you*, baby."

Just then the neighbour's wind chimes tinkled.

"Whoops," said Sammy. "The magic spell is broken. Nice talking to you, Stella."

And with that the animals went back to being animals— except things were different between them and Stella. She felt like her pets had suddenly become office co-workers with whom she had insincere conversations and who didn't really care for her one way or the other.

A week later, Stella decided she'd had enough and began to drink herself into an early grave. She did a remarkably good job, ending up sprawled on the shoulder of the main road, near the speed trap, the town's largest single revenue generator.

Stella sat there in the grass, singing a song without a tune, and as she did, Jessica and Roy drove into town.

"Roy, look, slow down, there's a crazy drunk on the roadside over there."

"Jesus, what a sinking ship. Makes you wonder about life. Hey look—a speed trap. If it weren't for the crazy lady, we'd have gotten a ticket."

The two whooped with joy, and Roy said, "Maybe that crazy lady is an important member of society after all! Makes you wonder."

Jessica said, "Absolutely, Roy. Mother Nature always makes sure that everyone has a role to play in the world. That scary crazy lady is simply living out her destiny."

JULIEN

I said, *"Nique ta mère,* now *that* was one depressing fucking story."

"Why? What was so depressing about it?"

"Did Stella really need to drink herself to death at the end of it?"

"She most certainly did."

"And what about the animals talking to her?"

"What about them?"

"Is that a New Zealand thing—communing with nature?"

"Julien, you're approaching the stories on too literal a level. Relax and enjoy their texture. Sleep on them. Anyway, it's your turn to tell one. Put up or shut up."

It was my turn indeed, and I was underprepared. I had to buy time, so I reopened the earlier discussion about the sheer mental labour required to make up a halfway decent story.

"Serge, there's probably some neuroprotein that regulates this. What's it called?"

Serge coughed out an unchewed hunk of bagel. It landed on the carpet beside Diana's stocking feet. He went as white as a sheet of paper.

"Serge?"

"Nothing."

"Are you okay?"

"Nothing! I'm fine. Just fine. Now please, start your story, Julien."

"Very well."

Bartholomew Is Right There at the
Dawn of Language
by Julien Picard

A long time ago a bunch of people were sitting on a log, looking at a fire, and they were wishing they had language so that they could talk to each other. Grunting was becoming a bore, and besides, they had fire now—they *deserved* language. They'd arrived.

Of course, they didn't think of it that way—they only had these feelings that went undescribed because there were no words for them. But within this tribe there was this one alpha guy in particular who saw himself as the creative one. He pointed to himself and said, "Vlakk." He picked up a stick, held it up, stared at it, scrunched his eyes and then pronounced it "glink." And everyone there repeated "glink" and henceforth sticks became known as glinks and Vlakk was now Vlakk.

Vlakk then pointed at the fire and made up a noise, "unk," and from then on, fire was called unk. And so on. In one night, Vlakk was able to come up with sound effects for dozens of nouns and verbs—gazelles and smallpox and thorns and wife beating—and because it was just one intelligence making up all these new words, the newly evolving language had a sense of cohesiveness to it—it sounded true to itself the way Italian or Japanese does.

However, Vlakk's language creation process made one tribe member—whom he'd named Glog—furious. Glog was thinking, "This is crazy! You can't just go around making up words arbitrarily, based on sound effects!" But of course, Glog didn't have language, so there was no way for him to articulate his anger at the vim with which Vlakk was cooking up new words. And it's not as if Glog had some other, better way of naming things; he was just one of nature's born bitchers and moaners.

Vlakk and Glog and their tribe had many children, most of whom died very young of hideous deaths because it was the distant past and, in general, people didn't last too long. But enough of Vlakk's descendants survived to generate new sound effects that went on to become words.

And of course, Glog's descendants carried his gene for finickiness, and as the new language grew and grew, they continued to protest the arbitrary harum-scarum way Vlakk's descendants gave words to things like "dung beetles" and "ritualized impalement on sharp satay-like bamboo skewers beside anthills." As the language evolved over thousands of years, everyone forgot that words had begun as arbitrary sound effects. Words were now simply words, long divorced from their grunting heritage.

As Vlakk and Glog's culture became more complex, so did its language. Grammar was invented, as was the future tense and gender and verb conjugation and all the things that make learning a new language a royal pain in *la derrière*.

Finally, language entered modern times. If Glog had been king, his far distant grandchild, Bartholomew, would have been his successor. Distant as they were in time, their neocortices were of the same size; Bartholomew was Glog with a good haircut and a fine suit.

Bartholomew was obsessed with new additions to the language. He was particularly incensed by things that caused language to change or evolve. He worked as a copy checker for a large business magazine and spent his lunch hours and weekends writing acid-tipped hate mail to other magazines that incorporated any noun or verb that had entered the language since the dawn of digital culture. *Can't you see how you're diluting the language? Corrupting it! Tell me, what is a jpeg? What a sick and diseased and laughable word it is—it's not even a word! It's a sound effect; a glottal sideshow freak. It's a bastard word—a bearded lady of a word.*

People at the magazine found Bartholomew to be a lovable kook, but they were very careful never to offend him, because, while he wasn't the sort of person to anonymously mail you a dead sparrow inside a cardboard milk box as some form of demented condemnation, there lingered the feeling that he had more subtle, untraceable means of punishing a perceived offender, like maybe he was keeping dossiers on all of them. And every year during the office Christmas party, somebody got drunk and made a mock crime scene investigation of Bartholomew's bookcased folders. Nothing was ever found, but the secretaries in the office would make fun of his cologne. They called it "KGB."

Fortunately, there was Karen from HR, who was able to allow a ray of light into Bartholomew's world. Each morning she dropped off the paper versions of his daily copy work and was able to smile and receive a smile in return from Bartholomew. Karen was the office free spirit. She had a Bettie Page hairdo, a nose ring and black knee socks she'd bought in Tokyo, in Shibuya. Other girls in the office stood outside Bartholomew's office to witness his Karen smile themselves. They knew he was single, and that Carol in the layout department had seen Bartholomew loitering in front of the straight porn section by the newsstand three blocks over from the office.

"Okay," said Karen, "he's no big catch . . . but he's certainly a big challenge."

Karen tried to come on sexy at first but pulled back, knowing immediately that it was the wrong strategy. This was going to be one tough fish to reel in. So she decided to conquer Bartholomew by email. Short. Sweet. Perky. *Saucy.*

Unfortunately, this decision was made right at the tipping point when hand-held devices enslaved the human psyche. Bartholomew was deeply distressed by the collapse of language into chimp-like bafflegab. Oftentimes his co-workers' text messages exceeded his powers of cryptography.

S|-|ip 70 T0ky0 fi135 L8r 70d4y. |\|0, 7|-|3y d0|\|'7 |-|4v3 4 m4(|-|i|\|3 5|-|4p3d 1ik3 4 fu(ki|\|g ki773|\| 7|-|47 m4k35 5u5|-|i.

He took to keeping his office door shut. He grew a beard, and began drinking his own pee from jars. Okay, he didn't grow a beard and drink his own pee from jars, but only because that behaviour would have offended another code that ordered his life—one of sanitation, of bodily purity. But he *was* bunkering himself.

Suffice it to say that, for Bartholomew, the supremacy of PDAs heralded the beginning of the end. Well, maybe not the beginning of the end, because he'd been raised in the Glog family tradition, which was to believe that every moment of life heralded the beginning of the end. Perhaps these newly triumphant PDAs, in some profound way, marked the end of language, which was now imploding on itself in an optical scrapyard of slashes, diacritical marks and pointless numerical intrusions.

One morning Karen was on the subway, going to work, and was in a strange headspace because she was starting to actually fall in love with Bartholomew. Knowing it maybe wasn't the smartest thing to do, she sent Bartholomew a very *lusty* text message.

W|-|3|\| I g37 70 7|-|3 0ffi(3 2d4y, 137'5 m4k3 p455i0|\|473 10v3 0v3r70p y0ur 14rg3 (0113(7i0|\| 0f 1i|\|3d y3110w 13g41 p4d5. S|-|4rp3|\| u p3|\|(i1, Big B0y

Bartholomew read this and thought, "Good Lord, language has devolved into a series of strung-together vanity licence plates! I can't be a part of this! I can't!" So when Karen showed up, Bartholomew didn't give her his daily smile. Karen was crushed. She sent a proper email, in perfect English, that said,

Dear Bartholomew,

Earlier today, while I was riding the subway to work, I emailed you a whimsical message. I think it overstepped the boundaries of "what is correct," but it was meant in jest and I hope you won't think less of me for it. Karen.

The thing is, Bartholomew ignored this email because he was crazy, and the thing about crazy people is that they really *are* crazy. Sometimes you can get quite far with them and you start telling other people, "So-and-so's not the least bit crazy," and then So-and-so suddenly starts to exhibit his crazy behaviour, at which point you say "Whoa!" and pull back—*People were right: this guy is really nuts.*

Karen's boss, Lydia, saw Karen moping in the lunchroom and said, "Honey, sometimes I think it's almost more polite to be crazy 24-7, because at least you don't get people falling in love with you and making a mess of things."

"But I *love* him."

"Of course you do, sweetie. Pass me the Splenda."

As Karen left the lunchroom, Lydia said to her co-workers, "People always seem to fall in love during that magical space before one person sees the other display their signature crazy behaviour. Poor Karen."

But Karen's heart mended from her break with Bartholomew, and within two years she was engaged to a guy who made sculptures out of cardboard boxes, which he took to the Burning Man festival in the Nevada desert. And life went on. Bartholomew grew older and buggier. People stopped using land-line telephones altogether. Everyone on earth used PDAs, even starving people in starving countries. All languages on earth collapsed and contracted and Bartholomew's endgame scenario was coming true—language was dying. People began to speak the way they texted, and before he was fifty, language was right back to the level of the log and the roaring fire. Bartholomew wondered why he even came to work. Nobody paid any attention to what he did but, as the Glog family motto goes, "Somebody has to maintain standards."

Then one day Karen walked past Bartholomew's office with her by now teenage daughter. His door was open and he was able to hear the two women speak—they both sounded like the Tasmanian devil character from Bugs Bunny cartoons. They turned around and spoke to Bartholomew: *"Booga-booga-ooga-oog?"*

They were asking him if he wanted to go out for lunch, but he understood not a word. He shook his head in incomprehension. The office emptied of staff. Lunch hour ended and nobody came back. Bartholomew thought this was strange. He walked out of his office and walked around his floor. Nobody. *Hmmm.* He went down into the lobby and there was nobody there or in the street, either. He began to walk around the city, but everywhere he looked there was silence. He looked at the TVs that were playing in public spaces: they showed the Channel Three News team's chairs with nobody on them, soccer fields that were empty, traffic cams trained on still roads.

So he walked back to his office and mulled over the situation, which was actually a kind of dream come true for him—no pesky people to further degrade and cheapen the language! But where had everyone gone? He looked at his screen, where the Channel Three News team finally appeared in a box in the centre:

—Hi, you're watching the Channel Three News team. I'm Ed.

—I'm Connie.

—And I'm Frank, and if you're watching this prerecorded message, it means that the Rapture has finally happened and you've been left behind.

—You know, Connie, people are probably wondering why we're speaking the way we're speaking right now.

—You mean, speaking like people did at the start of the twenty-first century instead of the modern way of speaking based on text messaging?

—That's right, Connie.

—[giggle] It's because the only people watching this pre-recorded broadcast are those that never adapted to the new language and were left behind after the Rapture. Language has come a long way since then, Ed.

—And has it!

—In the old days, people worried about words and grammar and rules.

—And it was a horrible mess, wasn't it!

—You said it, Frank. And not the kind of mess you can remove with some club soda and a bit of elbow grease.

—[all chuckle]

—But once people smartened up and began speaking the way they texted and began shrinking language back to its origins in grunts and groans, people became more primal, more elemental . . .

—More *real*.

—*That's* the word I was looking for, Connie. More real. More *authentic*.

—and once people became more authentic and more interested in using noises and sounds instead of words to communicate with others, their interior lives changed. The endlessly raging self-centred interior monologues came to an end. A holy peace and dignity fell over their lives. They accidentally became closer to God.

—and now they've gone right into God's lap.

—where we are now, too!

—So farewell from eternity, you sticklers who remain behind.

—Saying good night from the Channel Three News headquarters, I'm Ed.

—I'm Connie.

—and I'm Frank.

—[all] Wishing you a happy forever!

DIANA

I looked at Julien. "Well. I didn't see *that* coming."

"The role of the artist is to shock—but not too much or else he'll have to get a day job. Are there any more wasabi peas?"

"Later. It's my turn to tell a story."

Beef Rock
by Ms. Diana Beaton

The gourmet scout party from Gamalon-5 had pretty much given up on the planet Earth when it finally discovered a rare mammal called human beings, which were actually quite delicious. They'd tasted all the other animals, as well as pretty much everything in the ocean, but those very few humans hunkered in their caves were so rare that they had slipped under the tasting radar until the very end. Yes: people were undeniably . . . *scrumptious.*

"Commander, we've got to figure out some way of making these things multiply if we're ever to secure a meaningful supply."

"Lieutenant, that's your job, not mine. Have they discovered hunting yet? They'll never get to farming until they kill all the big, easy meat around them."

"No, sir."

"Well, you have your work cut out for you, don't you?"

"Yes, sir."

The lieutenant and his squad went back down to Earth and handed the few scrawny humans they could find some stone arrowheads and some flint. They had to give hundreds of demonstrations of hunting and roasting before the humans could do it on their own.

And then the aliens sat back and waited for humans to wipe out all the megafauna—the mastodons and the moa birds and the sabre-toothed cats—after which they turned their attention to smaller creatures such as bears and buffalo. After all the large animals had been hunted into extinction, humans were forced to adopt agriculture.

"Commander, sir, there really is nothing like agriculture to make a species multiply, is there?"

"Indeed. It's nice that the universe has at least *some* constants. What's next in store for these tasty morsels?"

"We think they're almost ready to learn to count and learn about 'zero'—as well as metallurgy. But they're still pretty primitive."

"All in good time, Lieutenant."

And so humanity was given mathematics and knives and ploughshares, and human numbers grew, but not quickly enough to please the hungry aliens.

"Lieutenant, this is taking forever. Stop trying to foist chimps and gibbons on me. I want *humans*. I want them to multiply, and I want them to multiply *now*."

"Yes, sir." He suggested the phonetic alphabet and the printing press. "That way, they can at least stockpile their intellectual ideas so that they don't have to start from scratch all the time."

"Let's try that, Lieutenant."

Printing presses—and hence books—accumulated. The industrial revolution became inevitable and, finally, humans went spawn-crazy. Lo, the citizens of Gamalon-5 began to truly gorge on massive quantities of rich, delicious, succulent human flesh. Life on Gamalon-5 became a gourmet nirvana.

One day the lieutenant made the observation that human beings who read large numbers of books tended to taste better than humans who didn't. This intrigued the commander: "I'm listening, Lieutenant."

"Sir, when the humans read books, it gives them a sense of individuality, a sense of being unique—a sense that something about their existence is special or, as they like to say, 'magical.' Reading seems to generate microproteins in their bloodstreams, and those eons give them that extra-juicy flavour."

"Hmmm . . . well, whatever it takes to get the job done. But for Pete's sake, stop harvesting so many humans near Bermuda. They're beginning to catch on. Also, could you get these humans to introduce more nicotine into their systems? My wife loves the flavour it gives them, but she's sick of marinating them all the time."

"Yes, sir."

By now, the food vendors of Gamalon-5 had gone into competition with each other in the burgeoning human flesh trade. Their nickname for Earth was "Beef Rock," and the money was terrific. The lieutenant's nephew generated catchy sales slogans:

OUR HUMANS READ MORE BOOKS!
INDIVIDUAL HUMANS—UNIQUE FLAVOUR!
ON SALE THIS WEEK: PHDS FOR 30 KROGS A POUND;
POSTGRAD STUDENTS 15 KROGS A POUND.
NEED A TASTE OF MYSTERY? TRY OUR "FILET OF CRIME
NOVEL ADDICT"

But then, in the 1990s, the quality of human flavour began plummeting. The commander consulted the lieutenant. "What is going on here?"

"Sir, as an unintended consequence of reading books, humans have made the next leap and have invented digital communications."

"They WHAT!!!"

"I'm *so* sorry it happened, sir. We were on holiday, and it just sort of swelled out of nowhere."

"So are they now using digital communications to conduct commerce, distribute moving image files and keep in contact with former schoolmates?"

"Yes, sir."

"So they're reading fewer books?"

The lieutenant sighed. "Yes, sir."

"Then the situation is truly dire."

The lieutenant asked, "Is there anything else, sir?"

"Just everyday worries. My teenage daughter has announced that she's gone Spam on me."

The lieutenant smiled: "going Spam" was a trendy phase among the teens of Gamalon-5, who thought eating humans was cruel. They opted instead for cans of Spam imported from Earth; nothing so closely approximates the oily, salty taste of cooked human flesh as the hammy goodness of Spam. "I'm sure it's just a phase, sir."

"Tell that to my wife, who has to put two different meals on the table every night."

The next afternoon the commander was going through his files and summoned his lieutenant. "Lieutenant, it says here that book sales are higher than ever as the humans are using a technique called Amazon-dot-com to purchase them."

"That is a deceiving statistic, sir. Amazon increases the need of humans to own books, but not necessarily to read them."

"Drat."

Time wore on and human meat became ever more unpalatable and consumption dropped dramatically. And after a point, the government of Gamalon-5 refused to subsidize the import of humans and soon barred the practice altogether. The lieutenant sighed as his ship flew away from Beef Rock one last time, leaving the humans to themselves and whatever gruesome fate they might cook up. He heaved a guilty sigh, turned around and scanned the universe, looking for new sources of meat. *Farewell, Beef Rock!*

HARJ

"Ah. Such a bittersweet story, Diana."

"Thanks, Harj."

Everyone was mellow. The fire was down to embers, and a general tone of drowsiness prevented us from stoking it. Serge was frantically scribbling; Zack asked what he was writing.

Serge said, "You people are saying the most amazing things without even realizing it."

Zack made a strange face and Sam asked him what was behind it. He said, "When I was growing up, whenever a teacher wanted to get me out of their classes, they'd always tell my parents how 'amazing' or 'gifted' I was, and that I ought to be in a different, better, more challenging school. So whenever I hear myself described in such a way, my antenna goes up. Serge, what is it about these stories of ours that's so amazing?"

Serge looked a little bit as though he'd been caught with his pants down. After a few *ums* and *ahs*, he said, "In some ways, you're telling the same story in different manners. And in some ways, you're all telling a larger story without knowing it."

Sam asked, "What story is that?"

"You'll find out if you keep going."

I said, "I think it is now my turn to tell a story—perhaps the last story of the evening. But before I do so, someone must place another log on the fire. I am still not used to the sensation of cold. As you all seem equally lethargic, I advise you to use rock paper scissors to select the stoker."

Diana lost. She went to fetch a log and the others rearranged their blankets. Once everybody was again comfortable, I said, "I am also a good private investigator. You see, this afternoon, I was online and digging about, and this investigation led to my next story."

The Liar
by Harj Vetharanayan

There was once a young scientist, and he must have been very smart indeed, because he worked for a large pharmaceutical company in a gracious and magical kingdom called Research Triangle Park, North Carolina, a place where style and intelligence lived side by side with great amounts of flair. When this young scientist first arrived, he was young and full of wonder, and he was assigned to work on a drug belonging to a new family of drugs—and new families of drugs don't just pop up when you want them, so this was a big deal for the young scientist. What did these new drugs do, you ask? These drugs were designed to alter a person's sense of time. The thinking was that there would be no immediate effect after swallowing a pill, but over a long period of time one would have the sensation that time was moving more quickly. If you were lonely or in prison or working in a call centre or working an assembly-line job, the drug would be a blessing—a boon to both commerce and a grossly overloaded penal system.

However, as though blessed by a wizard's spell, the drug turned out to have unexpected properties. It gave its users a sense of calm individualism almost identical to that achieved while reading a novel. This news was exciting, indeed—science had created an antidote to the daily barrage of electronic information so common to the era! And as an extra magic bonus, the drug tended to keep people locked in the present tense. It removed from its users the burden of over-thinking the future, which is, of course, a well-known cause of anxiety. Most magically of all, the drug's users *stopped feeling lonely.* So many of life's problems fixed with one pill! The young scientist felt like a pig in clover—and not only this, the scientist and his company were poised to become profoundly rich.

However . . .

. . . The drug was incredibly difficult to make in large quantities. But over the years, the scientist and his friends began making relatively significant leaps in the amount of drug they could produce in a day. And the more of it they made, the faster honeybees near the facility began to vanish.

As the drug finally became cost-effective to make in bulk and began to spread and enter the world at large, bee populations continued their quick decline. And it wasn't just bees that were affected—other insects, too, after extended exposure, disappeared. Of course, the scientist and his co-workers eventually figured out that it was their highly profitable drug that was causing the bee trouble—but because it had required a decade of work and massive capitalization to put it into full production, they kept this secret from the world. They must have felt truly guilty for what they had done to the planet, yet they also wanted to get their costs back, and, being human, they weren't happy merely to get their costs back— they instead chose to earn staggering profits. Bees were surely a small price to pay for a drug such as this one.

By the time the drug was in full production, bees were almost extinct; by the time the drug reached the global market, bees were gone, and the scientist and his co-workers had become crazy-rich. Insanely rich. More-money-than-the-gods rich.

One of the drug's side effects was that its users became quickly addicted. They felt like they needed no other people in their lives—they left their spouses and families and the places where they lived. They stopped dating and voting and seeking religion. Even if they wanted to quit the drug, they couldn't: quitting was impossible, physically and emotionally. The drug scarred users' brains, rendering them permanently in need of more—a terrific thing for the drug's makers, as it guaranteed perpetual sales. The scientist and all of his co-workers were as addicted to the drug as any of their customers. So while things were terrific, they were not so terrific at the same time. The gods are pranksters, indeed.

Then the young scientist—now not quite so young—heard of a young farmer in the middle of nowhere who had been stung by a bee in a highly visible manner that seemed entirely calculated to ensure that the world knew bees were still around. And then a young woman on the other side of the planet was stung in a similar highly visible manner. And then three more people were stung, one of whom later had a shock reaction to the scientist's magical drug simply from opening a box containing it. It was the first time a person had experienced a shock reaction to the drug. It spurred the scientist and his colleagues to do all they could possibly do to figure out what was happening with these five bee people—they could be real trouble. Their systems likely contained something that resisted the new drug—antibodies so powerful that those few rogue bees that remained alive were drawn to sting these people in order to give humans hope and encouragement.

The scientist wondered if he could use these people to create an antidote to the drug, something that might lead to a cure for the addiction. That way drug-makers could have it both ways: money from getting people hooked; money from getting people unhooked. A bonanza. A gravy train.

So the scientist, who now essentially ran the company, used an almost unlimited amount of money and many of his firm's connections to gather and isolate each person who'd been stung, telling them that he was looking for a way to bring back the bees.

The scientist placed his subjects in controlled environments for several weeks, where he and his team were able to extract body fluids at will. These fluids were checked for all sorts of minor proteins created by the subject's mood and state of mind.

He then craftily persuaded the five bee-stung people to join him on a remote island, giving them the illusion of sanctuary. On that same island, he also began conducting an undercover study on the effects of his drug on a tightly knit tribe of non-users who had lived on that island for thousands of years.

The stung people trusted the scientist completely, and were they to find out what he'd been up to, they'd be shocked. The gods were certainly shocked! And the gods certainly had no idea what would happen to our scientist when the five test subjects learned the truth about their captivity.

Fortunately, one of the stung people was a lighthearted character who most people assumed was harmless and clueless. In fact, he was a good observer—good at locating patterns and assembling odd facts to reveal a larger picture. This subject was happy to be with a new family, but like the gods, he was unsure of what would happen next.

ZACK

We all turned to stare at Serge, who said, "It's not what you think."

"*What* isn't what we think?" I replied.

"What you just heard. Harj's story."

"As far as we know, it's just a story. Why are you being defensive?"

"I am not being defensive, but I need you to know I'd never do something like that to the five of you."

"Okay, then. Maybe now is a good time to finally tell us what really has been going on these past few months."

"It's . . ." Serge fell silent. The rain was falling hard, droning on the roof while we sat wordless. And then Serge bolted for the door—that honey-tongued fucker tried to *flee*. This from a guy who could charm his way out of a buried coffin. What a tard. If he'd stayed put, he probably could have sweet-talked his way around us—but he didn't.

It was a good thing Harj had had the foresight to stand between Serge and the door, because when Serge bolted, Harj rolled a kitchen chair into his path, causing him to fly ass over teakettle and bash his head on the top corner of the mud room's bright orange Honda space heater. He was knocked out for a minute.

"Right," said Diana. "Get the duct tape."

We duct-taped Serge to a kitchen chair. I thought the girls were gentle souls, but the two of them were lashing the tape onto his wrists and ankles with such energy that I was spooked.

"Uh, gals, maybe you could ease up a bit on the tightness?"

Sam looked up at me. "You're siding with this lying French fuck?"

Harj said, "We are not fully sure that he is a lying French fuck, at least not yet."

We turned on Harj: "It was *your* story."

"You're right. It was. And . . . I must stand by it."

Diana, ripping a three-foot strip of tape off a roll, asked, "How did you figure all of this out?"

"Google. More or less."

"Seriously?"

"I connected a few dots. Perhaps I misconnected them."

"If you're wrong, then why did he try to scram? Personally, I think we should drag him down into the basement and let him rot for a while. Ugh. I can't *believe* that everything we've been through has been about *Solon*." Diana was disgusted.

Sam said, "*Yeah*. Let's cram his nose into the crack between the floor and the dryer by the dead mouse."

Instead, we placed Serge in the middle of the room. We then sat in sofas and chairs, staring at him; for the first time in my life, I felt like I was in a scene from a violent indie film. We'd nabbed the evil villain. Would we slice off an ear? Bring out a car battery and some cables and generate a bit of nipple fatigue?

Waking up, Serge realized he'd miscalculated badly. "So I'm now your prisoner?"

"You are."

"That was brilliant," said Sam, "making a dash for the front door."

"I think you'd better release me. You all think you know the truth, but you don't."

"You mean the truth that lies on the other side of the front door? Were you running to fetch it for us?" I asked.

"You don't trust me now. I understand that."

Diana slapped a piece of duct tape over his mouth. "Whatever he tells us is going to be smooth, and it's going to be untrue. We know that. So I think we need to have a quick talk before we listen to one word more of this guy's crap."

But Harj had a question for Serge and removed the tape. "Serge, can you please tell me how you found me a few days ago in Kentucky? I have no chips in me. How did you do that?"

"Actually, you *do* have a chip in you. All of you do."

It was like we had spiders crawling inside our skins. I have to say, few things in life are creepier than knowing there's something buried inside your body. Tapeworms have nothing on chips.

"My phone's got a chip detector in it," Diana said. "I never thought to use it." She scanned Harj; there was a chip on the back of his leg, behind his knee. "Okay, then, that won't be too hard to remove."

Harj asked why they should remove it.

"Because until you remove it, you won't be free."

"Ah," said Harj. "Freedom: the elusive goal of the Craig."

Diana snapped, "Do you want it gone or not?"

"Okay. Yes. I do."

Diana said, "Good. I'm going to scan everybody."

It turned out we all had chips embedded behind our knees. Diana said, "Okay, the next hour isn't going to be much fun, but I know Serge has a bottle of Oxy in his kit, and there's a kickass bowie knife in the kitchen." She set up her chip-removal surgery in the lower bathroom tub. The Oxy made us feel like birthday balloons adrift in a summer sky, but it didn't fully kill the pain of the bowie knife slipping in and digging around in search of treasure. One interesting thing I noticed was that pain isn't actually so bad as long as everybody around you is experiencing it too. In any event, Diana's work was quick and clean. She dug out her own chip last, and I was impressed by the cleanliness of what could have been bloody geysers. After our surgeries were completed, we entered the living room, stitched and limping.

Julien asked, "So what do we do with Serge—torture him?"

I said, "You know, I don't think we're torturing types."

Sam removed the duct tape. "Okay, Serge, talk. We're listening."

"Perhaps I could tell you some stories myself."

"You? Telling stories? Why?"

"You have every right to be concerned."

"*Concerned?* We want to fry your ass."

"Then let me tell stories—the way the five of you have been telling stories."

"Why should we?"

"Because the night is still young. Because, in the end, you'll do whatever it is you're going to do. Because if you add my stories to yours, you'll understand the full story."

"The full story?"

SERGE

"The full story. So please sit back and listen to me."
Sam said, "Okay. Start telling."
So I began.

The Gambler
by Serge Duclos

There was once a young French scientist who found himself one cold night in the darkened bedroom of an apartment in Locarno, Switzerland, a room that looked out over frozen Lake Maggiore, a beautiful, tiny, dull place where Italy kisses Switzerland. The apartment was not the scientist's; it was a corporate VIP guest suite that technically belonged to a pharmaceutical kingpin whose wife had died a decade before. He never used it. Why was our scientist in this bedroom? Because, as happens with so many people, he had crashed and burned. This was on his mind as he looked out the window and saw rooftops, alpish mountains, some cold, glinting lights to the south in Italy and the silhouettes of *Washingtonia* palm fronds, static in the windless night.

No, the scientist was not in the bedroom with the pharmaceutical executive; the executive was, that evening, in Qatar, selling half a silo of generic Wellbutrin to a convention of Arab building contractors to give their homesick workers from the Asian subcontinent. The Qatari contractors didn't know it, but the antidepressants were time-expired and would have been landfilled had not, half jokingly, the young French scientist suggested, during a laboratory meet-and-greet, that homesick Asian subcontinent guest workers were a potential market for those drugs. His reward for this brilliant idea was a set of keys to the beautiful but quiet Swiss apartment, plus a week to do as he wanted. As for the executive, on his fifth day in Qatar, he contracted reverse flesh-eating disease and returned to Switzerland in a charcoal grey Tyvek bag.

Now, our young French scientist didn't live in Locarno. He lived and studied in Montpelier, France, a university city, the capital of the province of Languedoc-Roussillon, which bordered the Mediterranean Sea. His specialty was human proteins, specifically neuroproteins that work as markers inside the brain to signal both the beginnings and endings of specific thoughts—that act as signposts, street lights, highway signs, bridges for the way all people and animals think. People were only beginning to understand the role of these proteins in all aspects of thought and existence.

The scientist had a lot on his mind, only part of which was guilt at being complicit in the moral and economic clusterfuck that was the Qatari antidepressant deal. Other parts of him were worried about different things. For example, he was worried that his girlfriend was cheating on him. She worked in the lab two down from his and spent her lunch hours eating steak tartare (for the animal protein) and reading pro-Palestinian political tracts while using an isometric thigh-slimming device that gave her a near-goddess status in bed. Suzanne was moody, and young enough to not even realize she might one day not have the liberty of picking and choosing her bedmates. So, because of his near-crippling jealousy, our young scientist found it hard to concentrate on his specific laboratory task, which was this: he aimed laser pulses through a micromisted protein broth. This allowed him to isolate and separate specific proteins within. It was a job that needed much skill and decades of education but was about as fun as stocking cardboard boxes at a Body Shop. The scientist wondered if his entire youth had been wasted in attaining what was essentially an ultra-high-tech McJob. *And*, to go back to what was stated earlier, he was worried that his girlfriend was cheating on him simply because she could, and because her take-him-or-leave-him attitude kept his own brain's neuroproteins on constant nuclear alert.

"Wait," Zack said. "You're talking about yourself here, right?"

"This is a story," I said.

"Can you at least stop using the phrase 'young scientist'? It's driving me nuts."

"What name do you suggest?"

"Trevor."

"*Trevor?* Why *Trevor?*"

"I don't know. It's a good name. Very science-y. If a Trevor invents something smart, you think to yourself, 'Man, that Trevor is right in character, being a smart dude, discovering stuff.'"

"Okay, then, Trevor it is."

"Thanks."

The Gambler

(continued)

by Serge Duclos

Trevor's boss was a career bureaucrat, not a scientist, and Trevor's pleas to upgrade his job category were met first by a yawn and then by a recollection that young whippersnappers pissed him off. If Trevor's boss had his way, the world's cocky young scientists would be corralled and put to work on the night shift at the Department of Standardized Weights and Measures. "So, Trevor, my dear, please shut the fuck up. Oh, and by the way, I run an even-keeled ship here. I don't want highs and I don't want lows. This place will be running long after you and I are dead, so please just go back to separating your water droplets. If you find the job boring, so be it. Boredom is a form of criticism—so maybe you should go job-hunting. Goodbye."

As this was being said, Trevor was thinking: *Is Suzanne cheating on me? What good is a girlfriend you can't trust?* The whole notion of *girlfriend* seemed American and synthetic, an archaic pairing concept from Pixar cartoons. Domestic partner? No, they didn't live together. Close personal friend? No. Technically, they were nothing. They just spent a lot of post-work time together, having sex and eating, and it was all going nowhere, and besides, she was so goddam political when she wasn't in the sack, and when she got going on Zionism and all that, it was like she'd turned herself into the world's most unlistenable satellite music station. She'd start to blab and he'd go off into daydreams about long-chain carbon molecules, his mother's knee-replacement surgery or old Smurf cartoons, only to be roused by a poke in the ribs and a jeremiad along the lines of, "And who do you think ended up paying for the Six-Day War, huh? Who? Tell me, *who!*"

And there are other things to know about Trevor, things that made him worry, that led to his crash and burn and a dirty weekend (if that was what he wanted) in a lovely but spookily geriatric apartment in scenic Locarno. For example, Trevor was a gambler. Not a casino gambler—no

Baden-Baden or San Sebastian for him; rather, he was the most incurable form of gambler, one of the ones who goes to Gamblers Anonymous meetings and everyone else in the room feels a chill in their hearts. It was more than just the fact that he'd memorized the entire cyber-tour of all of Harrah's Nevada properties, and it was more than the fact that the first sentence out of his mouth was: "I've been here sixty minutes already and I can guarantee you, 3 to 1, that all of the people in this room can't go without coughing for sixty seconds, starting *now*." They knew Trevor was a hopeless case because they saw that his need to gamble was so hard-wired into his brain that his life was one perpetual bet. He was consigned to live in the constant near future. He was always inside various levels of "next." He was never in the "now."

The next three stoplights may or may not be green—and if they're not, then what are the chances I'll see three red cars before I pull into the school's lot? Or yellow cars? You don't see yellow cars any more—why? Leo in Gamma Studies says yellow paint lowers the chance of reselling the car later on. But by what percentage would yellow paint versus silver kill the deal? Go online. Look up car colour trends since 1987; cross-index them with actual resale charts. Maybe buy a yellow car, even, if the odds favour you. Is Suzanne fucking around? There's the office. Email will take my mind off things. Email! The odds that she's cheating are 1 in 3. The odds that she's cheating are 2 in 5.

Zack said, "Serge, hang on a second. You have a gambling problem?"

"I'm not Trevor."

"That's not what I asked you."

"Take from my story whatever you like. And please give me a sip of your dandelion wine, if you will."

Harj kindly held a glass of wine and a straw to my mouth. I took a sip and then we returned to our friend "Trevor."

The Gambler
(continued)
by Serge Duclos

Trevor lost all of his junior researcher paycheques playing online poker and was living on economic fumes. He ate only bread and cheese, and one day he bought rabbit because it seemed both inexpensive and kind of cool. When Suzanne came into the kitchen and saw raw rabbit skinned and lying atop brown waxed paper on the kitchen counter, she screamed and ran into the bathroom, crying. Trevor sat outside the locked bathroom door, asking her what was wrong and to please come out.

Suzanne finally opened the door and said that cooking rabbits was like cooking babies. Seeing the pieces there like that reminded her of abortions she'd had that she wasn't very proud of. She was going to take what few things she kept in his apartment and leave.

And so Trevor was single, broke from gambling debts (Ladbrokes Online; Club USA Casino), crippled by never-ending gambling chatter inside his head and saddled with an asshole science-hating boss. He was wondering if the pieces of his life would ever join together like a story when his phone rang. It was Solange from the international sales division in Lyons, saying that the VP of sales was so impressed by his idea to ship time-expired antidepressants to the United Arab Emirates that he wanted to personally reward Trevor with keys to the VIP suite on Lake Maggiore. As well as the suite, a generous sum had been deposited into Trevor's bank account. *Olé, Olé, Olé, Olé!*

Trevor got on a train to Switzerland that followed a coastal route and then moved inland: Monaco, Genoa, Milan and Locarno. He hadn't packed very much because, while happy to be escaping his life, however briefly, he was too angry and worried to pack—and because he was young enough that he could still sleep in his clothes and, when he woke up, look rumpled and sexy rather than squished and homeless. So he was on this train and he had no laptop—his first holiday from information ever.

Sam said, "Wait a second . . . you went somewhere without a laptop or PDA?"

"*Trevor* did, yes."

"What was he thinking?"

"He paid for his mistake."

"Go on . . ."

The Gambler
(continued)
by Serge Duclos

Trevor had nothing to read, and so, bored by the glamorous Mediterranean views, he walked through the train's cars, looking for reading material left behind by previous passengers. In a second-class car, along with some abandoned homework, he found a much-disintegrated copy of *Finnegans Wake* (James Joyce; 1939), a novel that, when he opened it and selected a random paragraph, made him feel like he'd just had a stroke. He spoke English, but this didn't feel like English—it felt like sound effects. Still, the paragraph burned itself into his brain:

Sian is too tall for Shemus as Airdie is fiery for Joachem. Two toughnecks still act gettable, and feign that as an embryo he was worthy of starving (he was an outlier straddling the walls of Donegal and Sligo, and a vassal to Corporal. Mr. Llyrfoxh Cleath was among his savoured invitations) but every fair thee well to night blindness came uninvited. He was in the wilds of the city of today; coals that his night-embered life will not beg being anthologized in black and white. Adding lies and jest together, two toughneck shots may be made at what this abundant wallflower. Sian's nighttime wardrobe, we believe, a handful of ring fingers, a callow stomach, a heart of tea and cakes, a goose liver, three-fourths of a buttock, a black adder truncated—as young Master Johnny on his first louche moment at the birth of prethinking, seeing himself Lord this and Lord that, playing with thistlecracks in the hedgerow.

He sat down and went through the paragraph over and over. It could have said:

. . . Whaam! Smash! Ahooogah! Ding! Grunt! Sploosh! Doinggg! Thud! Bamm! Shazaam! Glub! Zing! Blbbbtt! Thump! Gonggg! Boom! Kapow!

Joyce's paragraph made no sense, and yet it made a kind of sense. Trevor realized that the odd thing about English is that no matter how much you screw sequences word up, you understood, still, like Yoda, will be. Other languages don't work that way. French? *Dieu!* Misplace a single *le* or *la* and an idea vaporizes into a sonic puff. English is flexible: you can jam it into a Cuisinart for an hour, remove it, and meaning will still emerge.

Trevor had an idea about how to decompose *Finnegans Wake* further. He went to the train's men's room and held the paragraph up to a mirror, and then he turned the book upside down, still gazing at the same paragraph, and the whole thing turned into pure optical mush, into encrypted code, into Punjabi. He unscrunched a tissue flap somewhere in his neocortex and pretended he was looking at a new language altogether.

Then he went back into the car and sat down, bought a coffee from a passing trolley and reread the paragraph, and he wondered if it might be possible for his brain to turn the paragraph into mush without the benefit of a mirror and reorientation—in the same way that if you say a person's name over and over and over, it stops making sense.

So he squinted, then opened his eyes wide, and lo, somewhere before Genoa he found that he could turn print into meaningless mush. Letters and words became lines and blobs, and Trevor felt, for the first time in years, a sense of peace, a sense of—wait . . . *holy shit!*—the entire time he'd been performing this exercise, Trevor hadn't once thought of gambling. *This is not fucking possible.* Was this strange novel a cure for his brain's incessant gambling chatter? Could this really be happening? And so he opened the book and began to read chunks of it and then turn those chunks back into mush in his head, and he felt nothing but bliss as the train pulled into Milan's Stazione Centrale, where he had to change trains for Locarno.

Walking through the train station was a joy. He felt that cool, silent, ultra-clear peace you feel around seven at night when you realize that a long hangover is one hundred percent gone. He had forty-five minutes to kill, so he went into a bar and ordered a rather expensive red wine and savoured the silence inside his skull, falling into a reverie broken by an announcement that the Locarno train was about to leave. He made a dash to his platform and barely boarded in time. Once he sat down, he realized he'd left *Finnegans Wake* and his mobile phone in the bar. *Merde.* Well, he could read it online once he got to Switzerland and located a computer.

But as the train's wheels rolled forward, his gambling mania returned worse than ever—it felt like his brain was punishing him for having taken a holiday from himself: *odds that more than fifty percent of people in this car are using mobile phones: 1 in 7; odds that the next woman who walks into this car is good-looking: 3 in 5.* And on and on. He found a magazine in a vinyl pouch beside the seat and tried to read it, but no go— he wanted his *Finnegans Wake*, dammit. He tried making his brain go random and stared at a flatscreen monitor crawling with stock index numbers while three members of a TV news team discussed Typhoon Ling-Ling. *Odds of 3 to 5 that Typhoon Ling-Ling is a Category 4.*

His train pulled into Locarno. It was cold and there was a small amount of snow on the ground.

One in 4 the next cab driver's fat. Four to 5 they have my favourite kind of ham. Even odds of someone fuckable appearing in the next one-minute window.

He taxied to his guest apartment and opened its door. At first glance, it was a beautiful place to be. It was a homely apartment, designed neither with, nor without, style—more old-fashioned than Ikean, its furniture evoking no memories of time or place—a hotel room, essentially. Fine. But there was no TV, no computer, no wireless router, no radio or stereo system, not even a telephone—nothing electronic. He wondered what sort of aging freak would live in a no-tech world. What kind of VIP suite *was* this? He was already imagining an explanation from Corporate: *the absence of technology creates a timelessness that is restful and conducive to meditation.* Right.

When I began to describe the boring room, my five friends' eyes opened wide. "Right, I know what you're all thinking— the boring room and all. Let me get on with this."

I went on.

The Gambler
(continued)
by Serge Duclos

Trevor began to wonder, and then to fantasize about, how many emails he had in his mailbox, rich, juicy, *fun* emails . . . 37? 41? 43? 257? 99,829? Maybe his ex-girlfriend had sent him a kiss-and-make-up note. Maybe she had enclosed pictures of herself. *And maybe if I looked, I could find* Finnegans Wake *online.*

By now it was dark out, and because it was Switzerland, everything was shut, even the Internet café that catered to the young. Fuck. At the train station, he considered asking someone if he could borrow their PDA, but then realized he'd just look like a con artist. Then he thought more about all the no-doubt incredible emails that were sitting there in cyberland, *just waiting for him,* and he put aside his pride and asked a passing younger person if he could borrow his PDA. He was told to fuck off.

The station shut down and Trevor walked back to the apartment. He searched for books to read; nothing. There was no food in the fridge or cupboards, not even condiments. Desperate for words to look at, he ultimately located an unopened envelope of Knorr Swiss cream of cauliflower soup mix lying flat on the topmost shelf. He tried to scramble the words on the label but instead got a headache. He looked at them upside down in the mirror, but the magic of the train ride was gone. Only books seemed to work for him.

He finally realized that he was stuck in this room for, if nothing else, the night.

He closed the curtains and went to bed. Lying there, his head shooting out sparks in all directions and his eyes closed, he made a bet with himself: if I open my eyes, there's a 1-in-2 chance I'll be able to see a chink of light passing through a gap in the curtains.

Trevor opened his eyes. There was no chink of light from the cold Swiss night. He opened and closed his eyes. It was equally dark either way. Which was interesting. The moment he opened his eyes, even though there was nothing to see either way, his brain automatically shifted gears—he could feel it happening: visual cortex; no visual cortex; visual cortex; no visual cortex—a subtle but distinct switch. Do blind people have this same cortical shift? Does keeping your eyes open in the dark waste brain capacity? It was odd to be able to psych out his brain so easily and mechanically.

And then, as Trevor shifted between forms of darkness, he decided to pave the way for the next phase of his life. He wanted to know more about brains and how they shifted gears, and he wanted to be able to find out if there was some kind of chemical or mechanical switch that could turn off the gambling cortex in his head. With *Finnegans Wake* and other books, he might be able to tone down the symptoms, but the treasure was out there and it wanted to be found.

Trevor fled back to Montpelier on the 5:40 a.m. train. Rifling through his small attaché case, he found his copy of *Finnegans Wake* nestled inside a pair of track pants. *Merde!*

Once home, he searched online for who was doing the most work in neuroproteins, then a new field. He also emailed requests to colleagues everywhere, telling them what kind of job he was looking for. Soon he got a nibble from a company in a place with the bizarre name of Research Triangle Park, North Carolina.

Trevor thought, *A place name that uses the word "Triangle"? And North Carolina? What is* North *Carolina? Is it so incredibly different from South Carolina that their names merit subsets?*

The strangeness of the company's location and its complete disconnection from his European life were catnip to Trevor. He wanted new experiences in his brain, not old, predictable ones. Were he to remain in Europe, his new experiences would only ever have the same texture as a cover version of a song he already knew—old buildings doing riffs on other old buildings; *bahnhofs* and *gares* and *staziones*; *change/cambio/wechsel*. Going to America would be like learning a whole new kind of music.

Once there, he did everything he could to maximize a new-seeming life: he bought a Chevrolet minivan; he shopped at malls; he said things like *Have a nice day* to strangers. He even found a new girlfriend, Amber, who had won two Subway franchises in a divorce suit and who had a close personal relationship with her Lord and Saviour, Jesus—which, as with his pro-Palestinian ex-girlfriend, consumed most of her small talk and which he also tuned out, simultaneously jealous of and turned on by her commitment to faith and to fresh, healthful sandwiches. But mostly he threw himself into work, researching the exciting new world of time-suppressing drugs that made life seem either longer or shorter, depending on the user's life situation. He knew that if an anti-gambling protein existed, here was the place to find it.

On a professional level, the lone factor that hindered his research was time itself. In order to see whether time felt long or short, test subjects had to actually be *using* the drug for a while. A year, minimum. Prisoners were the main test subjects, but they weren't being told whether the drugs they were getting made time feel longer or shorter, and Trevor actually felt sorry for those who got the time-stretching drug—it was like putting the prisoners in a prison within a prison.

"So, wait a second," said Diana. "How old was Trevor at this point?"

"Maybe his late twenties."

"Did he take the drugs for his gambling problem?"

"Let us find out."

The Gambler
(continued)
by Serge Duclos

At the same time, Trevor, with growing shame, was again racking up gambling debts, though not as quickly as in Europe, because he now had his ragged copy of *Finnegans Wake* to stop the urge. A colleague recommended James Joyce's *Ulysses*, but it was like the lower-priced house brand of *Finnegans Wake*. Still, his losses added up and, not unlike Zack's Superman, his powers of resistance began to ebb.

Curiously, it was at this same time that a perplexed colleague diagnosed two people with a rare condition called logo dysphoria—the inability to perceive corporate logos. These "logosuppressives" would look at corporate logos and see a blob of colour—they failed to perceive logos in the way that stroke victims fail to perceive letters and numbers. He called Trevor for help and advice.

Zack asked, "So . . . they'd see a Nike logo but not recognize it?"

"Basically."

"That's bullcrap."

"One would think, but no. Listen further . . ."

The Gambler
(continued)
by Serge Duclos

Trevor thought these people surely had to be faking something as strange as this, but the more he questioned them, the more he learned about something called invariant memory.

What, you ask, is invariant memory? It's this: anybody can look at a cat and tell it's a cat. They can even look at a lion or a cougar and tell that it's a cat, too. But there's no such thing as the perfect cat, or the cattiest cat—an absolutely generic cat. The problem with logos versus cats is that logos exist purely unto themselves. A Starbucks logo is what it is, and *only* what it is. Because logos are absolute rather than a variant, the brains of these two test subjects were unable to read them. Capitalist time bombs? Darwinian masterpieces?

Trevor thought about his own experience with words, of mentally converting novels into blobs and lines. He wondered if there was a connection—and he compared the brains and bloodstreams of the logosuppressives with the brains and bloodstreams of people deeply absorbed in reading *Finnegans Wake*. He found identical proteins.

Sadly, it was also around this time that bees began to disappear, and Trevor thought nothing of it. Why would he? There wasn't enough data to establish a pattern.

"*Serge! Stop!* Crikes, my brain is hurting." Sam was overloading. I'd been giving them much to absorb.

I said, "Okay, then, let us take a break. Friends, could you please untape me?"

"No."

They knew damn well I might, well, *bolt*.

Harj asked, "How much of what you're saying is true?"

"It's all a story. An allegory."

"That's not what I asked. Is your story fully autobiographical?"

"Every word we speak is autobiographical. How could it not be?"

Sam was angry. "Jesus, Serge—just tell us, did all of this shit really happen?"

"Your left brain is a potent tool. It forces you to create stories in order to make sense of information. Without enough information, it will create information to fill in the blanks. This storytelling capacity allows us to predict future events. It is the perfect way we have of sharing our brains with each other."

Diana asked if I was still a gambler.

"No. I am not. Not any more."

"So your story is true, then."

"You are being too literal, Diana. I am not Trevor; Trevor is not me. And no, I don't gamble."

Sam wrapped a new strip of duct tape around my mouth and upper torso. "Right, you smug prick. I'm really sick of you and *science*. We're trapped on this ridiculous island, God only knows how many people are dead at the airstrip, bodies are strung up by the Esso station—should we even be feeling *safe* right now? Are we next to experience death-by-Esso? If Harj is correct—"

Harj said, "I think I am, to be frank."

". . . then the Haida have every right to be here with their bike chains before dawn."

Sam removed the duct tape. I requested a glass of water and a painkiller and was grudgingly given both. After this, we continued.

The Gambler
(continued)
by Serge Duclos

So now young Trevor was living and working in Research Triangle Park, North Carolina, only he wasn't quite so young any more, and he owed several times his annual salary in gambling debts. Literature lost its power over him—his brain felt like Chernobyl with helicopters buzzing around it.

And what about the shapely, lively, sandwich-loving Amber? Reinventing himself as an American no longer gave Trevor's daily life the flavour of radical surprise: minivans were boring, malls spiritually blank, and Amber left him after they attended a Rapture Preparedness workshop and he was caught reading a copy of *InStyle for Tweens* during a ten-minute cleansing prayer circle. Worst of all, he remained a prisoner of the near future, unable to live in the moment, his life morphed back into a rerun of his Montpelier experience.

Then one day he and his team isolated a neuroprotein from people reading *Finnegans Wake* that, when diluted in a mild solution of sodium phosphate, became a chemical that had a calming effect on the people who took it. Prisoners stopped feeling imprisoned; isolation stopped bothering them. When their daily hour of communal time with other prisoners came around, most simply shrugged and said they'd rather not. Trevor and his colleagues were onto something huge.

The wondrous new drug, however, was both difficult and expensive to make. The protein used to start it refused to be cloned, either in a petri dish or within a crèche of stem cells; it took hundreds of litres of blood to isolate enough protein to make a significant dose of the drug. It had to be synthesized in a wildly expensive 128-step process. Of course, Trevor was hooked on this stuff from the start. So forget *Finnegans Wake*. Forget books and forget reading and forget everything else on the planet except for this godsend of a brain fixer-upper that slowed his gambling to a point where he could keep it in check.

Our Trevor was now a senior scientist who controlled budgets; he ensured that meaningful amounts of the drug were made, even at disastrous cost to the company. He had the most expensive jones in history. No more fear of aloneness! No more fear of poverty! No more fear of spiritual dearth! And mostly, no more brain spitting out an endless stream of gambling chatter.

This is when co-workers noted a link between this new drug's production and declining bee populations. Wherever the drug was made in North America, nearby bees vanished from their hives. His company's plants, big and small, were everywhere. Trevor saw the maps; he knew there was no way to deny the direct correlation.

So, as you can see, Trevor and the few colleagues who knew the truth were in a moral quandary. It wasn't even future bucketloads of money they were thinking of when they decided to ramp up the drug's production; it was the inability to imagine life without the drug.

And so the bees vanished.

Trevor's company was finally able to make enough of the drug in bulk to make it cost-effective, but in order to turn a profit, they had to get people hooked quickly. This turned out not to be a problem, as the drug had a one-hundred-percent user satisfaction rate and a one-hundred-percent word of mouth recommendation rate. The world was turning into a world of loners. Families disintegrated. Casinos went out of business. Prison lost its capacity to intimidate and crime flourished.

And many plants lost their ability to reproduce because the bees were gone.

And then one day an *Apis mellifera* stung some guy in Iowa and all hell broke loose. For years, police forces everywhere had been training for a what-if scenario—probably the only properly funded response programs in the world—and then what-if actually happened. They descended on the guy like a tornado, and within a few hours he was underground beneath Research Triangle Park, North Carolina.

And if there was one, then maybe there'd be more—and there were: New Zealand, France, Canada and Sri Lanka. And then no more. Most interesting of all was that one of the B5s (as we called them) had an adverse reaction to this new drug.

"For fuck's sake, can we just call it Solon?"

"Okay, Zack, yes, let's just call it Solon."

The Gambler
(continued)
by Serge Duclos

Incroyable! Ce n'est pas possible! Trevor was a rock star within the company. He jetted between the B5s in their emotionally neutral rooms, ordering tests, checking blood serums, centrifuging this, laser-isolating that, and he liked what he found. The brains of these fresh young people secreted massive amounts of the rare molecule that, when tweaked, served as a cheap, easy starting point for Solon.

Julien interrupted: "So you got what you wanted. A happy industrial ending."

"Almost, Sean Penn, almost."

Diana asked, "What happens next?"

I said, "It's a story in progress. It ends there. For now. Right now is part of the story—simply by being here, you're storytelling."

The rainstorm erupted afresh. The room went quiet. Harj turned up the space heater and a candle sputtered out. I asked, "Could you please take me out of this absurd Tarantino chair thingamajig."

Their ten eyeballs told me: *No.*

Sam asked, "Right. What's next? Do the five of us become living chemical factories for Trevor and his Solon? Why not just put us in a coma and get our personalities out of the way?"

"That idea did come up. I talked them out of it."

Harj blurted out, "Why did you run for the door?"

I replied, "I freaked out. I really don't know what I was doing."

"You 'freaked out'? I don't believe you."

"Then don't. Blame the booze."

"A mouse drinks more than you."

The sound of breathing filled the room as rain started to batter the windows. It felt like a trip to a therapist, where someone must speak first, except nobody would. My five young friends were on painkillers and tired. Their legs were bloody. I, on the other hand, was alert and merely annoyed by the duct tape's constriction. I said, "Why don't I simply give you all the full meal deal? Let me tell you everything I can."

"Okay," said Zack. "Talk."

"Very well. To begin with, the bees obviously chose the five of you for a reason: your brains make what you might call a Solon starter molecule. Like yeast for bread. But this capacity also makes you allergic to Solon.

"There are probably a few more people on the planet like you; we just don't know who they are or where they are. We probably never will.

"The five of you might be genetic accidents or you may be Darwinian progressions. Or, if you're into God, maybe you were chosen. But we found you the only way we ever could have: because you were stung.

"And it wasn't just the fact that the bees saw you and stung you. They were waiting for the circumstances to be perfect. All of you were, at the moment of the stinging, involved with the planet—using satellites to do sketches in an Iowa cornfield; making Earth sandwiches in New Zealand; being expelled from virtual gaming worlds in Paris; being excommunicated from the afterworld in Ontario; or simply participating in global consumer miasma in Sri Lanka. Your situations had to be perfect before bees could do the deed.

"We suspect that the bees lived in small hives all over the world and were waiting until the right situation occurred. Your body had to be sending off the exact chemical signal to trigger the sting.

"At first, we tried to figure out if the five of you had anything in common. We found only two things: First, none of you has ever been in a real relationship with another person. Not a *real* one. There's something about you that makes you keep yourselves away from others. Second, despite its prevalence, none of you ever expressed any interest in Solon."

Sam said, "Why would bees point out people who contain Solon starter molecules? That's suicide."

"Let me remind you that all bee stings are suicides, however unintentional. Also, Solon's starter molecule cuts both ways. If we add hydrogen to it in the right way, we create a genuine anti-Solon. Taking it makes it almost impossible for Solon to work ever again."

"Why didn't you people just kill us, then? We're the worst thing that could happen to you."

"The company doesn't know about the anti-Solon yet. But I do. That's why you're all here on the island. I'm saving you."

Zack said, "Great. But you *did* run for the door."

"Tell us more," said Harj. "Why do so many of our stories involve books or reading?"

"Because Solon mimics the solitude one feels when reading a good book. Both books and Solon pull you away from the world. But to your brain, one Solon is like reading a thousand books in twenty-four hours."

"Why did you ask us to tell stories out loud?"

"When you tell stories out loud, your bodies make a corrective molecule, one that brings people together. The anti-Solon. You felt the closeness. You're feeling it now."

"Yes, but not with you."

"No need to rub it in."

"Show us something that would make us trust you," said Sam.

"Very well. Bring me my laptop and I will."

Julien brought my unit and we put it on a coffee table. I gave them a link, and the window opened to display a real-time camera focused on an industrial facility within a massive airplane hangar. They navigated the site from cam to cam, taking a tour of what appeared to be a giant candy factory. Julien said, "Ugh, it's that disgusting dessert you Americans eat. Jell-O."

Diana looked at the screen and asked, "*A Jell-O factory?* What *is* that place?"

"It's a neurofarm."

"Huh? Where?"

"That one?" I focused on the screen. "Nebraska, I think, far away from any protestors. And it's manned by unemployed corn workers eager to accept Bangladeshi-calibre hourly wages. It's massively cloning neural tissue."

Zack asked, "What *is* that stuff they're making?"

I looked more closely. "That batch is green. That means the gel-like substance is, well, *you*, Zack."

"What?"

"Just what I said. Specifically, it is two-point-three acres, eight inches deep, of cells from your central nervous system, all of them cranking out Solon starter. It takes three days per batch, 33,000 cubic feet grown atop a sterile culture of agar. Congratulations, Zack—you're the biggest person who ever lived."

Onscreen, a worker pushing a small dolly bumped into the edge of the jellied mass; it jiggled. Young Zack barfed inside his mouth.

Diana said, "You mean *all* of us have been farmed like this?"

"That is correct. The Solon starter cells from the five of you clone easily. And each of you is colour-coded."

"And all that jelly food we ate in the underground rooms— that was . . . *us?*"

"Yes, it was."

"Wait," said Zack. "I was eating this jelly shit even before the others got stung."

"At first you were eating a synthetic version."

"At *first?*"

"Yes, at first."

Diana left the room to vomit in the bathroom. The others sat frozen. I put the farming into perspective for them. "Remember, those cells are unconnected to a brain and experience no pain."

Zack asked, "Okay, then, Serge, what do you do with this stuff once you've grown it?"

"We cut it into slabs that are then dried into sheets. The sheets are then taken to a nearby facility."

Diana re-entered the room.

"The material is powdered and mixed with toluene. We run this slurry through a centrifuge and extract your eons. These eons are quickly modified by replacing a few sulphur atoms with phosphorous atoms, and—*voilà!*—we have Solon."

"What? We're made of *Solon?*"

"No, you're made of DNA, and it's your DNA that helps make Solon. And farming your brains is much cheaper and easier than building Solon molecules from scratch."

Sam said, "This is like one of our stories. No, this is weirder than any of our stories."

I replied, "Haven't all of you noticed that your personalities and your ideas have begun to morph into each other's? It's a terrible pun, but the five of you are turning into a hive mind. I think it would have happened to you anyway—your minds are somehow rigged to melt together; it's the storytelling chemical you make—but eating each other's brain material only sped up the process. You heard each other's stories. The five of you almost arrived at the truth on your own. Your bodies know the truth." I looked at Harj. "You guessed it, Apu."

Diana said, "You know this is all being taped and webcast, right?"

"Sure. Fine."

"So you realize this is an end to your evil plans."

"You make me sound like the Riddler, the Penguin or Solomon Grundy. And I wouldn't say Solon is finished. People like Solon. Even if they know there's an antidote, they won't take it. People like the freedom of being alone. Once you go Solon, there's no going back. Once you start using it, our perpetual revenue stream begins. So there you have it. Does the truth make you happy? Does the truth set you free? *Ha!*"

Zack said, "Serge, tell us, then, why are you fucking with the Haida?"

"Why? *Why?* Oh, grow up, young man. You know nothing about power. Why do I do it? Why do I do it? I do it because I *can*."

ZACK

We stored Serge in a downstairs room with only a mattress and a unicorn poster abandoned by a long-gone former tenant. We buttressed the door and the windows with plywood and long screws, and by the time we finished, it was almost sunrise—but no sleep for us.

Sam said, "Right. I, for one, prefer not to wake up and find myself hanging by a bike chain from the Esso station sign."

Diana said, "Serge stores uppers in his travelling case. They'll keep us charged."

We went into his room—anally organized, as one might expect. Beside Serge's small medical bag sat a large trunk case.

I asked, "What's in there?"

We pried it open with the bowie knife, and . . . *holy shit!* It was a love child born of Louis Vuitton and the Texas Medical Center's main operating room. Hundreds of gleaming surgical instruments: retractors, saws, rasps, forceps, specula and blades—just amazing. Diana wolf-whistled at the shiny steel cornucopia and apologized for using a rudimentary knife to remove our chips earlier. "I wish I'd known about this thing a few hours ago. Jesus, you could separate Siamese twins and put them back together with this much gear."

We then quickly got ourselves hopped up on primo amphetamines—far smoother than my father's home-cooked meth. I felt clear and radiant, and my body was already tingling and saying, *Zack, you know, you really might enjoy being addicted to this stuff.*

Serge was yelling from within his own little neutrality chamber: "You people are being stupid! Listen to me. All I wanted to do here was find a way to come up with a cheap, easy antidote to Solon. It's inside you—you know it is. Just keep on making up stories, we'll do some blood tests. Do it for the betterment of our goddam *species*."

Our thinking was, *Well, okay, Serge, you make a good point, but we can't get past the idea that you could destroy a tribe—a society—as if it were so many sea monkeys in a fishbowl.* So we ignored him, and as he began to withdraw from Solon, his personality grew nasty and our trust level for him, already low, sank further. "Do we have last night backed up?"

"We do." We'd made multiple copies of the evening's webcast stories, culminating with the unfinished story of Trevor that was still playing itself out, there on the island. And so, come dawn, the five of us walked into town with half a white bedsheet taped onto an ancient aluminum rod from a children's playground. It rippled in the wind. If bullets had entered our bodies or if a noose had circled my neck from nowhere, I wouldn't have been surprised.

Our worries were quickly validated as we came up to the Esso station: two more dangling bodies—those of the two men from the jet crash, the Solon burners. This came as a surprise; we'd thought *they'd* be the ones orchestrating the hangings. We pantshittingly walked farther into town, but we didn't see any people. There was nobody there to surrender to. Everybody was gone.

"What the . . . ?"

Julien said, "Maybe they're in the old village." Masset has two locations: the new Masset, in which we lived, and old Masset, an Indian reserve two miles up the road. We went home to fetch the pickup. Diana drove while Harj and I stood in the bed, holding up the white flag.

As we approached old Masset, we slowed to a crawl; we didn't want to surprise anybody. But once there, all we found were a few barking dogs. *No Haida.*

We stopped in front of a burnt-down house with a knee-high necklace of sun-bleached grey whale vertebrae in its front yard. Diana said, "They've obviously all gone somewhere together, but where?"

We cursed.

"So where should *we* go now?" I asked. "Special forces are probably going to be here to wipe us out any moment."

"Nobody's going to take us out," said Diana. "Everyone knows everything now. So they can't kill us. We're safe that way."

"If you need to believe that, believe it. But I think we're fucked."

"Let's go to the airstrip," suggested Harj. "We can see the crash remains in full daylight."

In the absence of a better idea, we drove to the airstrip. Again, no people; only the chilled remains of the previous evening's crash, easier to see now, as all of the dead grass and brush surrounding it had burnt to stubble. Harj wandered over to the patch of debris holding the bodies and began to pray.

"Why?" I asked him. "I thought you didn't believe in anything much."

"I am not praying for the dead. I'm praying for myself, that I can make some sort of sense of what's happening to us."

Diana said, "I can agree with that." She called to Julien and Sam. "Come here. We're going to say a prayer for the Channel Three News team. Are you in?"

"Sure."

And that's how the five of us ended up having a two-minute silent prayer for the Channel Three News team.

Praying is funny. When you pray, you leave the day-to-day time stream and enter a quieter place that uses different clocks and values things that can't be seen.

At the two-minute mark, we heard choppers arriving from the east. "Shit. *Scram!*" Diana yelled.

We could hear three or four choppers arriving at the airstrip and then hovering before they landed. We charged into the adjoining forest. Sounds from the outer world instantly muffled as plant life soaked up noises. We didn't think we'd been spotted, but this didn't stop us from charging farther into the maw, wading through moss up to our hips, climbing rotten hemlocks the size of freight containers, which crumbled like cookie dough under us. After maybe fifteen minutes we stopped and collected our breath and our wits. I asked if anybody knew where we were, and Julien, king of satellite map skills, knew exactly. "We're close to the Sangan River. If it's low tide, we can walk up it and into the Naikoon forest— we're actually only fifteen minutes from the UNESCO bee's nest." So off we went to the nest. Why not? As with the airstrip, it was a destination in the absence of any other.

A lot of spooky shit was going through my head—mostly the thought of Solon's makers lobotomizing me and hooking my body up to a respirator and feeding tube for the next five decades. This thought fuelled me onward. *Fucking Solon. Fucking bees. Fucking century.*

The tide was low but rising, and the river was the colour of bad Mexican whiskey. A school of oolichan darted within its flow, and birds in the trees made their noises. Diana became a self-appointed Little Bo Peep, in charge of herding us to the nest site, and she and I began having a stupid argument over what to do once we got there. Three, maybe four more choppers flew overhead. They could have been the government, come to inspect the crash site. They could have been Solon's goons. They could have been . . . well, that's what we were arguing over as we arrived at the nest to find several hundred Haida of all ages sitting wordlessly around the site of the vanished hive. To the side were dozens of open boxes of Solon. A ceremonial wooden bowl was being passed slowly around among them, each Haida taking a sip.

"They're drinking the fucking Kool-Aid!"

Several of the Haida turned and shushed us.

Sam said, "We can't let them take that shit. It'll destroy them."

Diana said, "It's not our business."

"But it . . ."

But it *wasn't* our business. It was the Haida's business, and we sat and watched them partake, the bowl and packages of Solon moving silently, first across the elders in the front row, then going backwards, one by one. By the time the third row was taking their pills, the people up front were standing up and walking away. They walked past the five of us, and their bland facial expressions were like those of people who are headed home, wondering how many emails they have in their inbox.

Within ten minutes all the Haida had drunk the Kool-Aid, and within twenty minutes they were all gone.

We walked to the circle of dirt and sat down. A helicopter flew directly overhead and then returned. It hovered over us, then landed in a bog beside the circle, but after what we'd just seen, we no longer cared. It felt as if something far larger than us had played itself out.

The blades came to a stop, and we wondered what might emerge—Navy SEALs brandishing AK-47s? A Channel *Four* News team? But instead it was an older woman. Sam said, "Louise?"

Louise looked at her and smiled. "Sam—you're alright. Good."

"Louise, what are you doing here?"

"Making sure you're okay."

We'd all stood up and come forward by then, but our body language told Louise we weren't comfy in her presence. She said, "No, I'm *not* connected to Solon, and no, I'm *not* here to kill you or sedate you or capture you or anything else."

Sam introduced her to each of us. We could see a few figures inside the helicopter, but they didn't emerge.

Louise asked, "Where's Serge?"

"Back at the house. We've made a prison cell for him."

She looked quite shocked by this, but not in a bad way.

"Frontier justice," I said. "That bastard fuelled the entire Indian tribe here with fucking Solon. They're going to be toast now."

"Wait—that's *all* he did?"

"Huh? We thought that was more than enough to merit imprisonment. And you should *know* all of this. We've vlogged and blogged everything here since we arrived."

"Actually, no, you haven't. Serge had a scrambler set up. The outer world has no idea what's been happening here."

Motherfucker!

Louise continued, "Can I ask what it was he was doing with you people here?"

"Some kind of experiment—making us invent campfire stories with the goal of generating an antidote to Solon. And he was always going on about *Finnegans Wake*."

"I see."

"What—you mean there's some kind of truth to that?"

"Well, possibly. Actually, yes."

I said, "Louise, I think we're missing something here."

"I think you're right." Louise sucked in some breath and looked into the forest.

Sam said, "Please tell us, then. We're in the dark."

"You see, Sam, Serge didn't want to invent a cure for Solon any more than he wanted to fly to the moon," Louise said.

"So, then, what was he doing with us?"

"My dear, you haven't figured it out yet, have you?"

"Figured what out, Louise?"

"Samantha, I don't quite know how to tell you this, but Serge wanted the ultimate Solon hit. He wanted to eat your *brains*."

HARJ

So many things begin and end with the sea, do they not? Sailors vanish. Boats sink. Jewels are thrown to its bottom. The bad woman drowns. Life crawls from its glinting waters and draws air into its lungs and joins the land forever.

Months later, the island had run out of auto fuel, so Julien and I decided to walk to a strange beach up the coast to fill the day. We started out early in the morning, as the sun was rising orange and cold, like someone who hates his job. I wondered what season it was, and then decided to never again ask myself that question.

We ended up standing by the ocean a few miles up Tow Hill Road, on a beach that had no sand or driftwood or shells, just a billion rocks, all of them different colours, all of them the size and shape of an egg. After walking through clots of sound-muffling firs, we reached Egg Beach, with its rhyming, crunching waves.

They had stopped making Solon by then, as our stories did, finally, reach the world—but there was no glory in it. None that we cared about, anyway. As our five personalities continued to merge, all we cared about was staying together, and so we did—on the island and away from humanity. You see, that's our big secret: if you eat stuff made from our brains, you become one of us. We all become each other, one big superentity. Miss America wishes for world peace and so do we, except with us it might come true.

"It's strange," I said to Julien. "I don't feel like I actually did anything to help. I feel perhaps fraudulent. Which is to say, here I am, a living cure, and I don't know how that feels."

He nodded.

Storms were washing up plastics of the north Pacific, mostly from Asia: flip-flops and whiskey and shampoo bottles; plastic helmets, children's toys, fishing floats and disposable lighters.

Julien asked me, "Harj, what was the tsunami like—as it was happening? What was it like to be there during it? You've never actually told us."

"Well, it was sort of like right here, right now, except that I was three storeys up when the water just rushed inland and never stopped. And there was no actual wave—it was as if that big vat of Zack's brain matter sloshed inland about a kilometre and then ran out of force. It smelled like dirty salt, and I remember the fish drowning in the air, flopping about, and when I squinted they looked like coins, like treasure."

The waves of Egg Beach crashed on the shore, keeping their distance.

I sat down on the stone eggs and thought of everything life had coughed up for me since the moment of my sting. Different sorts of waves that spouted forth . . .

. . . Winnebagos

. . . Mexican beer

. . . bodies hanging from lampposts

. . . helicopter rides

. . . casually elegant piqué-knit polo shirts.

The list is long, but I think it will soon be over, once the five of us become whatever thing it is we're turning into.

Could I have imagined my new life a year ago? I don't think so. I began my trip as a lost soul. I was a bar magnet with only one pole, a number divisible by zero. Somehow the group of us killed Superman. We entered the Rapture.

We cut away those bits of ourselves that had become cartoons. And we turned the world back into a book.

"Did you hear they found a beehive over in Tacoma, down in Washington," Julien said.

I began to imagine the lives of those bees that survived over the years just long enough to find us and sting us and send us their message, to tell us *their* story. I began to imagine small cells of them—not even hives—surviving from year to year, nesting under highway overpasses and the dusty eaves of failed shopping malls—foraging for pollen in the weeds growing alongside highways, their wings freezing and falling off in the winter and in the summers their wings rotting and leaving them crippled as they tried to keep their queens alive, finding little comfort in each other, finding solace only in the idea that their mission might one day succeed, that they would one day find us, with our strange blood—knowing that we were the only hope they ever had of moving forward—that we were the only hope they had of finding their way home.

DOUGLAS COUPLAND was born on a NATO base in Germany in 1961. He is the author of the number-one international best-seller *JPod* and nine other novels including *The Gum Thief, Hey Nostradamus!, All Families Are Psychotic* and *Generation X*. His books have been translated into 35 languages and published in most countries around the world. He is also a visual artist and sculptor, furniture designer and screenwriter. He lives and works in Vancouver.

A NOTE ABOUT THE TYPE

Generation A is set in Monotype Dante, a modern font family designed by Giovanni Mardersteig in the late 1940s. Based on the classic book faces of Bembo and Centaur, Dante features an italic which harmonizes extremely well with its roman partner. The digital version of Dante was issued in 1993, in three weights and including a set of titling capitals.